ROOKS AND ROMANTICIDE

J. I. RADKE

DSP PUBLICATIONS

Published by
DSP PUBLICATIONS

5032 Capital Circle SW, Suite 2, PMB# 279, Tallahassee, FL 32305-7886 USA
http://www.dsppublications.com/

Rooks and Romanticide
© 2015 J.I. Radke.

Cover Art
© 2015 Garrett Leigh.
http://blackjazzpress.com/
Cover content is for illustrative purposes only and any person depicted on the cover is a model.

ISBN: 978-1-63476-058-4
Digital ISBN: 978-1-63476-059-1
Library of Congress Control Number: 2014958501
First Edition July 2015

Printed in the United States of America
∞
This paper meets the requirements of
ANSI/NISO Z39.48-1992 (Permanence of Paper).

Special thanks to friends and loved ones for all the support while writing, with a shout-out to Melissa Regan for her excitement and encouragement with any and all spooky, sexy Victorian endeavors.

PRELUDE

They say miracles are past.
William Shakespeare, *All's Well That Ends Well*

THEY CALLED it Lovers' Lane, and he thought that was a mess of something more evil than irony.

The broken ground under his boots was flooded with grimy puddles, which hid the cracks and the gravel and the sharp juts between potholes in the concrete and cobbles. The walls of the narrow alley were no better. Dank and gritty, they dripped with moisture, cracking under the weight of the world. Bandaged water pipes and boarded-over windows offered a bit of aesthetic flair, at least, if one cared for that desolate, grungy look.

Sometimes the water running down the alley was dark with fresh blood. Some stains in the concrete never went away. Corpses and cadavers, the victims of turmoil and violent frays in a world where Her Frail Little Majesty simply could not seem to hold the peace, no matter how many civil agreements and treaties were signed to end the bloodshed, to bring noble families together, to leave revenge in the rich and dusty past with the unforgiving ancestors.

Not too many years ago, Cain had found his parents there, in Lovers' Lane. Shot—execution style. Murdered and dumped on the uneven cobbles, where the dead were left until the undertaker ventured along with his ancient cart and hoisted them away.

They'd been dumped over the tin shingles, strewn bloodied and cocked at frightening angles on the ground.

When first Cain had found the family hound dead and cold in the parlor of Dietrich Manor, puppy-dog eyes never to roll around in greeting again, he'd cried out in grief. Ah, no, not his dog. Not the German shepherd. Not the one that kept him warm at night, the one that looked more like a great wild wolf than a domesticated breed, the one that barked at all the nightmares and monsters hiding under the bed—God, no!

But when, in Lovers' Lane, the toe of his boot had nudged the lifeless side of his father, Cain hadn't managed to do much else but stare.

And the rain fell—a shy and dreary mist the wind tossed to and fro, which felt incredibly cliché even in its monotony—and Cain had stepped over his father's broken neck, petted the matted blonde curls from his mother's blank eyes, and dug into his pockets for coins to close them with. He'd come up empty-handed. He hadn't expected to find much anyway, because the first rule was that you didn't carry money on your person unless you were planning to spend it immediately, or so his father had taught him very early on once he'd hit adolescence. Money matters were pivotal for a noble heir to master. So Cain had tromped through the dirty puddles and the shadows of Lovers' Lane, slipped around the corner, and ducked out of the cursed alley to meander his way home.

Except that was when they found him, and it was a long while until he made it back to his warm bed, because—

"Nostalgia, young one?"

Cain started briefly, a meager flutter of the lashes and twitch of the pale skin between his brows, but he repressed the rest of his surprise. He had his revolvers tucked away safely at the small of his back, under his suit coat. He didn't need them with the undertaker. The undertaker wasn't even worth a bullet shell.

The undertaker had caught him strolling memory's way, of course, and stood slouched over the side of his rickety little cart, straight from the streets of Bombay or Peking, threading his ugly knuckles together. His hands were as gray as the fish in the markets, nails all the color of a bruise. *Dead*-looking. Did one begin to change with one's occupation after working in it for so long? Cain shuddered involuntarily, closed his eyes, and only opened them when he'd turned his face away, because he refused to watch the undertaker hoist the body of a young woman from the cobbles of Lovers' Lane and into the bed of his cart.

Limp. Beautiful. *Dead*.

"Not at all," Cain mumbled, peeking back at the undertaker only after the girl's corpse hit the bottom of the cart with a sickening *thud* and unsympathetic rattle.

The undertaker smiled at him, hair stringy in his eyes and hood pulled down low across the bridge of his nose. "Not at all," he echoed, and Cain's frown pinched tighter at the sharp grating of the man's voice against his ears.

The undertaker was a real freak, if anyone was. Strange and estranging. An ex-resurrectionist, he claimed. Now an honest working man, if anyone actually believed him. His shop was full of horrors. Wondrous horrors. Horrible wonders. All manner of objects from the curious to the funereal—dusty graphoscopes, broken mirrors, bottled specimens, and baby's coffins.

"Then what's someone of your name doing wandering Lovers' Lane?" the undertaker pried.

Someone of your name—

Cain brushed past the undertaker, fingers trailing along the grimy alley wall as he made his way toward the street again. Water and grit squished beneath the soles of his shoes. The rest of Dietrich Security was waiting. Chin held high, Cain said, "Word was that there were bodies—"

"I haven't seen any bodies but this."

"Ah, so I'm to trust everything you say now?"

Those bony gray fingers curled around Cain's arm and tugged him backward, but before the beads of the undertaker's rosary chain had stopped chattering against one another, the rustle of clothing, the slosh of a puddle, and the *click* of a hammer cocking bounced off the opposite wall. Their movement together ground to a standstill with the undertaker smiling that crazed yellow smile of his and Cain regarding him from behind the barrel of a revolver engraved with a crest and the model name Rapier-A227.

"I am, after all, the one you should come to with inquiry about *bodies*," the undertaker chortled, the last word drawn out below his breath.

Cain's nose wrinkled. The man smelled like dogs, dirt, and death. But the body of the girl had nothing to do with the rumors Cain was investigating, probably just another domestic dispute. It wasn't worth his time.

Cain cleared his throat, dismissing the undertaker's interruption. He uttered a dainty scoff and began again. "Word was that there were bodies—bodies found outside Lovers' Lane, below the wall. Bodies of Dietrich patrons. Hanging." Cain shook free of the undertaker's claws, but the gun didn't lower until he'd backed away a number of steps. "Maybe a murder, maybe a double suicide, maybe some kind of cult activity or a petty gang's plot to get a rise out of us." He returned his Rapier to the small of his back. "Yes, go about your business, Undertaker," he husked. "But as a Dietrich, investigating such talk is *my* job."

The undertaker chuckled to himself, drumming his fingers on the side of his ghastly cart. "But what's another citizen to you, the great little lord of the most splendid house in New London?" he simpered, and he accepted Cain's scowl of distaste with a respectful bob of the head. "My lord, because you hold great power, you inevitably fail to understand the importance of those things which we may never ourselves recover."

Cain smirked. It wasn't beyond the greatest little lord of the most splendid house in New London to stand in the mess and mire of Lovers' Lane, caught up in witty remarks with the local undertaker. It was almost fun, really. A flare of humility beneath all the status and the gold. "And what are those things?" he prompted.

"Salvation!" the undertaker gasped. "Repentance! Redemption! The value of one human soul, the same as another human soul after the glamor and name or the lack thereof have all been stripped away, peeled off like the flesh and the bones—"

Cain turned his back, lifting a hand. "Maybe, after the investigation, you can have the bodies," he offered, sloshing through another puddle. His nose wrinkled; it reeked here. "Especially if it's interesting," he added, fingertips grazing the corner of the alley.

He paused before turning out of Lovers' Lane, smiling over his shoulder down the narrow way at the undertaker. "After all, I wouldn't want a goddamned Ruslaniv getting a look at them, now would I?"

The undertaker giggled to himself and grabbed his cart by the handles. Cain disappeared around the corner of the alley, and the front wheels of the cart hit a little bump. A pasty white arm jostled and tumbled over the edge, hand dangling near the undertaker's muddy cloak. Strands of long golden hair hung like satin ribbons between the dirty fingers.

"Oops," the undertaker cooed and pushed the girl farther into the cart so she wouldn't fall out, and the sound of his slightly off-key hums filled Lovers' Lane as he made his way out.

ACT ONE
RAW

I am above the weakness of seeking to establish a sequence of cause and effect,
between the disaster and the atrocity.
Edgar Allan Poe, *The Black Cat*

SCENE ONE

HE COULD see his breath on the air, hanging there like a little cloud. Above the crooked rooftops stretched abandoned laundry lines and rusty pipes. Like drunken eyes, clouded windows looked down on the occasional fallen brick lying in the puddles as the chimney pots belched out their usual smoke and ash. The almost mechanical buzz of the evening coming to life rang in his ears: voices, rattling cabs, shouts, workers, laughter, hawkers. The sky was cold and gray, another dreary winter sunset.

Gravel and glass crunched underfoot. Levi lifted his toe to get a look at the mess on the ground. Trash, debris, the ensigns of a tenement block, the candy trail of the working class. And children played outside in this place—what a nightmare.

"And Levi—"

There was another shuffle of gravel as the rest of them paused, and Levi felt their eyes. He knew that even if the others would let it go without his reply, Eliott would not, and Eliott was nuisance enough without even trying, so why agitate him?

Levi turned slightly. Yes, they all clustered behind him—William, Eliott, the Witch, the Blond One, and the One with Glasses—staring over fur collars and militia jackets, and Eliott pushed those damn obnoxious tinted spectacles of his up out of his face, letting them perch atop his head as he dug around in his pockets for his mask.

"You're not gonna be all moody, right?" Eliott demanded.

The Witch snorted, shifting her weight to her other foot. "He's always moody," she spat, with venom on her tongue. "Brooding about something or another. One shade of hatred here, another one there, and Daddy's never proud of him."

Levi cut her a bitter glance, holding a hand out for Eliott to fork over his mask too. He took it, brushing past the Witch roughly.

"Forgive me," he husked. "I thought you'd have a better insult hiding somewhere in that dark and stinking pit you like to pretend is a heart."

Ha! That was cruel. He was bound to get an earful for that one. Why did they call her the Witch again? Ah, because she was a well-endowed broad with no titles, and a knack for secrets and schemes, and… that's right, she'd been a dancer with Father Kelvin's circus before she'd taken up arms for the Ruslaniv crest—

"*Bastard*!" she growled, kicked up a leg, and snatched her pistol sword from her boot. It was one of her most prized possessions—other than, of course, those more *natural* gifts she hid under her clothes too.

Levi ignored the threat, taking his first look at the mask Eliott had designed for him. Black brocade with metallic thread, rook's feathers, cat's claws beaded into the shape of little skulls. It was gaudy and funereal and absolutely perfect.

"You're one to mock me!" The Witch was ranting and raving despite his obvious lack of interest. "You claim your heart is any less empty than mine? You, sitting there high and mighty, hiding in your father's shadow? The day I lie down and accept such slips of tongue from *you*, you demented little brat, will be a cold day in hell. And if you ever think that it makes you better than us because you inherited BLACK instead of earning its leadership, then I *pity* you, you selfish mongrel. I *pity* you! I pity *your father* for ever thinking you'd make a good leader for BLACK, because all you've ever proved of yourself is never speaking up and simply running off to the library to hide in a book once orders are complete. Ha! Oh, and let's not even touch on that time with poor sweet little Rosalie, when you were so far head over heels, your head was up your ass—"

Levi knew this one. The Witch had played it so often when it had been more relevant to the present. *Your head was so foggy with feelings and romance and love that you forgot your gunslinging side, and because of that unfortunate failure, Rosalie is dead!*

Levi spun with a crunch of gravel beneath his heel, feeling all his hatred narrow itself down into one glance at the Witch.

"Oberon's just as dead," he reminded in a voice almost like ice. To the side, the One with the Glasses smiled slightly, secretly, looking over at the Blond One, who lingered at his arm with those dark eyes.

The Witch lurched forward with her blade ready—but it was all intimidation, the usual fanfare, because as Eliott held her back with one arm around her waist and a rare look of seriousness on his face, she didn't try to break free. Instead she kept her burning gaze on Levi a moment longer, until William pulled her aside and motioned for her to put away her blade.

"That's enough," Eliott demanded. "Good Christ, the two of you and your tension! Can't we go one day without you at each other's throats? You'd think you were related or once… *involved.*" He said the word with a little wrinkle in the nose, like it tasted bad. "Come *on*, now. This is supposed to be fun! There'll be lots of delicious things to eat, and free liquor, and at least a few good-looking guests. This isn't an assignment, it's *leisure!*"

Eliott threw his hands out, and it was quite dramatic, and quite comical, with the hand-painted sign on the building behind him proclaiming *Fierce and Fearless Ladies at Foxe's*, surrounded by stuttering gaslights. Beyond Cleveland Street, storefronts and clubs and hotels crumbled together as night fell. Innocent civilians retreated and the shadier faces emerged—a whole new catalogue of virtues and vices, launching the commotion and mishaps of the nightlife in neglected corners of the city. Ladybirds, cash carriers, toolers and palmers, and the flashy mobsmen organizing fights, this their haven on the cobbled streets. Drinks and drugs and duels and the flames of streetlamps slithering within their glass.

Eliott dug in his jacket again, distributing the rest of the masks. Black lace, silver chains, fake spiders, and velvet and leather.

"The scheme might be too obvious," William insisted, frowning thinly. Behind him, along with the One with the Glasses, the Blond One pranced about, utterly pleased with his mask, peeking into dirty windows and trying to scare anyone who might be around.

Levi took a deep breath. The smoldering rage had died down into a nasty but more tolerable aftertaste, like the burn in the chest after a particularly rich meal. He tucked his mask into his jacket, patted William on the shoulder in reassurance, and sought out Eliott's eyes behind the black velvet and fur that framed them.

The scheme. They were sneaking into a Dietrich ball, after all.

"It's a night of leisure," Levi vowed, for Eliott's sake.

Eliott took him by the shoulders and shook gently. Buckles and holsters echoed the motion.

"That's the spirit!" Eliott cried, hooking an arm on Levi's shoulders and glancing around the group.

At his gaze, the Blond One snapped to attention and saluted, grinning. The One with the Glasses placed a hand on the Blond One's head and led him back into their midst. William ran his hands along his sides, his back, checking and rechecking the access of his weapons. The Witch glanced up at Levi from where she lounged on her haunches against the wall of Foxe's.

"Hey," she mumbled, voice low and sulky.

She looked away with a frown like a stubborn child afraid to admit their fault, and Levi knew it was because of the outrageous way she'd just spoken to the Ruslaniv heir and how bold and stupid it had been. She tucked a few loose dark curls behind her ear, meeting his eyes again.

"We're going to eat, drink, and be merry, all right?" she said, echoing Eliott's sentiments. "And we're going to give those filthy Dietrichs a proper scare. Sounds like leisure to me! Wouldn't you agree... *Rook*?"

Levi didn't say anything. *The Rook.* The Witch, the Lion, the Spider, the Snake, the Wolf. All of them and their guns, the most feared and enigmatic of all the Ruslaniv gangs, like a bunch of ghosts whose reputations preceded them until they whipped out their guns and the other gangs bowed down to kiss their feet—*BLACK.*

And what would the world say if they knew the leader of the most notorious Ruslaniv gang in New London was actually the son of Lord Ruslaniv himself? What would they say after years of the Ruslaniv sons being removed from public view for their own safety, of Lord Ruslaniv's indignant protests: "I won't have my children involved in this petty blood thirst, this ridiculous feud between two equally great families, I won't have them see it or think of it or be caught in the middle of it!"

What would they say if they knew the hypocrisy and the lies, and the secrets that had been kept, so very carefully, swept under elegant eighth-century Persian rugs?

Levi sighed. His breath was a little cloud on the brisk night air. As the leader of BLACK, he had to brush off subordinates' attitudes in a responsible way. "That's the plan," he agreed, looking out across the city, beyond the dirty rooftops and broken windows and sagging bell towers, out at the gated manor on the hill that was their destination.

"But I think first...." Levi turned into the racket of the street as night descended and a new world awoke. Some ladybird had emerged from Foxe's, swaying her hips and waving at possible clients with her sable scarf. Levi sighed again, crossing his arms and refocusing his attention on the matters at hand.

"I think," he said again, a small smirk trying desperately to break free, "we need to find some more fitting attire for the occasion, hmm?"

"Party!" the Blond One cried.

The One with the Glasses tried to reach him, but he slithered past Eliott and William and threw his hands in the air, joining Levi under the eerie lights. "Listen, I want something purple, with a fur collar and proper little cameo buttons down the front—"

Dietrich Manor awaited them, overlooking New London with its gates open for the annual invite-only All Hallows' masquerade. And for the first time in ages, since perhaps even before the long and relentless feud between their families had begun, after paying a rampsman to pick pockets for invitations, BLACK had decided to attend. Unobtrusively, of course. Anonymously. Covertly. For some simple fun, a little spying, nothing more.

And why not be stylish about sneaking around?

SCENE TWO

SHE HUMMED, and even in the preparty rush, it seemed too loud. She tapped her toe on the polished floor, her ankles crossed, and ran her fingertips to and fro along the baluster overlooking the vestibule. Innocence. Sweet, blissful innocence.

But it was driving Cain mad, plucking at his nerves somehow, because it was the sweet blissful innocence of a girl about to brave the distance between lady and lord of the Dietrich manor again in tentative conversation.

"Cain…." Emily murmured.

Past the footsteps of busy servants and the echo of voices from below, Cain picked up on the nervousness in the back of her voice. It was almost swallowed by the rustle of silk and lace as she shifted, a soft lilt to her words as she tried her best to sound cool and collected and proper. She rolled her eyes around to meet his, waiting patiently for his sign to continue.

Cain just frowned at her and cocked a brow. Informality was the great luxury of being promised to a cousin.

"How is business?" Emily asked, finally making the leap.

Cain could tell by her rigid, serious tone that she dreaded talk of *business*. The question felt far too forced. She hated talk of *business*, maybe because she didn't believe in it, because she didn't feel it was her place, or maybe because she knew how important it was to Cain. The shyness around her great fiancé would break her like fine china thrown to the floor, surely, her with the pearls in her hair and the blonde curls swept up off her lily-white neck.

Ah, yes, thus was the luxury of being promised to a cousin, but room to be casual and conversational was no remedy for still feeling like an absolute stranger.

"As uneventful as always," Cain replied flatly, squinting down into the vestibule as hired hands hurried to finish setting up tables and the footman adjusted his clothes at the door. Emily fidgeted. Cain dragged a thumbnail along the baluster, adding, "But that isn't exactly something a lady should worry herself over."

He hoped it would save him from a bottomless pit of sugarcoated business talk, business talk watered down for a cousin trying so hard to mean something to the infamous and controversially young earl. She was trying so hard to mean as much to him as she had when they'd been small and she'd visited from the country, and they'd taken tea with their toys in the garden with the nurses and governesses fluttering around them like the butterflies.

When he'd still been innocent, just like her.

"Well...." Emily's cupid-bow mouth tightened in concern. She was determined.

Cain propped his chin in hand and watched the thought darken her face. God, he wanted to be annoyed, but she was trying *so hard*.

"How was your scouting today? I heard there was a... *hanging* at Lovers' Lane." Emily paused, frown dimpling deeper. She turned to face him directly. "Why do they call it Lovers' Lane, Cain? Oh, you know what, never mind that. I probably won't like the answer. What happened, though? Was it a murder? Were the Ruslanivs involved?"

Cain couldn't help but smile, even bitterly, as he closed his eyes and searched for the proper words. Miss Emily Kelley just was not familiar with the Dietrich world of parties and bloodshed and hide-and-go-seek vigilante politics. Talk of bodies petrified her. The twisted normalcy of it to the heads of households who dealt with uprisings and gunfights on a weekly basis was beyond her. She hadn't grown up seeing the way bodies littered the alleyways and cobblestones, or hung with cockeyed heads from fraying rope as their wounds began to rot in the setting sun. Emily was a bystander, practically. An unfortunate witness from the countryside where everything was roasted duck and boating and reading by the fire.

And still Aunt Ophelia insisted she stay at Dietrich Manor through to the next season, that it might help as the wedding slipped ever closer, hanging on the horizon like a smoky gray storm cloud. Cain wanted to believe it wasn't a scheme or some sort of stunt for public reputations, but that was just how Aunt Ophelia worked. The inner machinery of a great family, masked by social functions.

God, but everything in life was a chess game of sorts, wasn't it? It wasn't that Cain didn't like Emily. Really, that wasn't it at all. It was just that the courtships that really got his heart thumping weren't girls like her—or girls at all, actually.

"I ran into the undertaker in Lovers' Lane. The police had already taken the bodies. We went to speak with them. We don't think it was the Ruslaniv family, directly."

Cain cast Emily a glance through his lashes. She was struggling to maintain her solemnity, absolutely angelic in all the folds and layers of her party gown. She was a woman; her big coming-of-age had been last summer. But when she pouted like that, it was difficult to imagine she'd grown up at all. She was just a soft, beautiful girl playing dress-up.

Cain cleared his throat. "More than likely it was a gang of Ruslaniv supporters, trying to get a rise out of us. They're the worst, really. Not blood related, just blind dogs, so driven by distorted passion that they become animals, violent and irrational animals."

"Oh, so you crossed out cult activity, then, and have already pinned all the blame on *that family*?"

Both Emily and Cain turned sharply, leveling equally disgruntled stares on the source of the voice. With a red-lipped scowl and a flutter of lace fans, Aunt Ophelia approached from across the upper hallway. Behind her, among the curtains and portraits, her servants waited tentatively as if unsure whether or not to intrude, despite the rush before the ball.

Cain returned the scowl—he was pretty certain he'd inherited it from Aunt Ophelia, anyway—and glanced at Emily quickly, hoping he wouldn't find another desperate question biding its time there.

"Yes, I did," he edged out tartly. "And so did Uncle Bradley and Mr. Renton. We discussed it. We spoke with the police. And I would appreciate it if you stopped butting into my business, Auntie. I was *just* telling Miss Emily here that these aren't matters ladies should worry themselves over...."

Aunt Ophelia clucked her tongue, a sound of disapproval. She finished the gesture with a roll of her eyes, leveling them finally on Cain in a stern and unyielding way. "I'm not butting into your business," she countered, and really, convincing Aunt Ophelia of anything she wouldn't be convinced of was like setting fire to a downpour. "Your papers were still lying out on your desk, dear nephew, and I just *happened* to see the ones regarding that particular scouting mission."

Cain understood then. Aunt Ophelia was hurt he hadn't invited her to Lovers' Lane with the rest of the security party. And the worst part was that he could have. The worst part was that Aunt Ophelia was as capable as Uncle Bradley or any of the others at the head of the house—perhaps even more so. She had a mind-boggling way of straddling the line of the boundaries between the sexes, navigating both the duties of a lady and the duties of a man like she belonged to neither. She knew how to work dinner parties just as well as street missions, and Cain hated that. She'd protected him long enough, but he was, for the most part, a full-grown man. He would be twenty in February. He wanted to protect her now. She didn't prefer protection.

"You're my aunt, not my business partner, and as the head of the family I'm asking you to stop forcing yourself into my tasks," Cain hissed, but then he remembered that Emily was still beside him and the brunt of responsibility pried an impatient sigh out of him. His expression softened into a frown and added, "I'm sorry, Auntie, I only mean to say that I have it under control, so please don't burden yourself with it."

Aunt Ophelia peered at him darkly for a moment. Her eyes moved with her thoughts, like the sky before a storm. Perhaps she evaluated him, or the situation, or perhaps she just saw right through him as she always had and always did, playing all the right cards to get him riled up and then kissing him on the head with those bright red lips of hers.

"I swear, my nephew has got to be the most heartless creature I've ever met." Aunt Ophelia turned her nose up, a cream-colored cameo bouncing at the nape of her neck. Her complaints echoed; Cain blushed. Her voice was like burnt velvet after years of business and cigarettes. His skin crawled beneath the weight of her stare. Taking anything Aunt Ophelia said at face value was foolish; there was always a secret message. And Cain heard it—the love in her remarks, hidden behind the words. She had to give the proper impression to Emily, didn't she? Emily didn't have many other role models at Dietrich Manor.

"And I've met many a heartless and foul man in my lifetime, Miss Emily, you just take my word on that," Aunt Ophelia went on. "Really, this boy's got such a gorgeous young lady staying here in his home until New Year's—"

"I'm not a boy, Auntie," Cain protested, but it came out in a grumble, and so his frown deepened in dismay because the point was already moot. *I'm not a boy. I'm a man.*

Aunt Ophelia was still making quite the scene, jabbing her closed fan like an accusatory finger. "And he can't even crawl up and out from under his massive *ego* long enough to relax and have fun and appreciate her for what she is—a smart and capable lady, worthy of his respect. Really, I ought to throttle you, Cain. I really should."

"Coming from a woman in pants!" Cain sputtered, but it was a truce.

Aunt Ophelia's raucous laughter filled the upper hall. Cain surrendered to a smile. His aunt hugged Emily to her side again as she whipped open her fan. She shifted her weight to the other foot and cocked out a hip to show off her trousers. Her belt clinked against the end of the red corset she wore, but there was nothing Cain could do about her rebellion against femininity or her ability to somehow wriggle her way into every aspect of his life. What else was she to do with his father, her brother, dead and in the grave, worms making beds in his skin?

"Really, though," Aunt Ophelia added, "I wish you'd be more appreciative of this arrangement, nephew of mine. I doubt any other family would allow their daughter to stay in a man's home unless they were *already* wed. You're lucky, do you know that? Don't take it for granted, and don't abuse it with your sour moods."

Lucky, sure. Except that with Emily around it was much harder to keep up appearances utterly opposite to his actual inclinations. But maybe that was exactly what his aunt intended with Emily's presence—to *keep up appearances*. She didn't really expect him to love her, did she?

"I'm not sour," he grumbled, slouching over the banister and watching the bodies mill about in the vestibule. There wasn't much else he could think to say.

"Have you given in and decided to wear the costume I had made up for you?" Aunt Ophelia clucked her tongue. Really, she was like a bothersome older sister sometimes. But thank God she'd changed the subject, quite aware of Cain's discomfort. This banter he could handle. This kind of back-and-forth he cherished.

"It's ridiculous," he replied.

"It's a proper political statement," she shot back.

"I don't need a costume to make a political statement."

"Please wear it! When you tried it on last week, it just looked too perfect. It's a masquerade, for Christ's sake."

"Fine. I'll wear it. I'll change into it later. I promise. But I won't play into it."

"As long as the crowd whispers about it, its mark is made and I'll be satisfied."

"Auntie, have you been drinking already today?"

Guests were beginning to arrive, all dolled up and flashing masks. Cain watched from the overhanging balcony. And there, that was an interesting one—black, all sleek black, with feathers and a sharp nose. Like a bird. The guest wearing it wasn't in much more than a simple black suit, but the mask and his glinting brocade waistcoat redeemed much. Behind him, Aunt Ophelia cooed over Emily for a moment, until Emily laughed shyly in turn, and then Aunt Ophelia reached over and brushed a few loose strands of hair out of Cain's eyes like he was still a child to be fussed over. She leaned in to whisper, breath hot on his ear and sharp with the scent of mint:

"My nephew, seek happy days to happy nights…. You never know when they might come to an end."

How prophetic. Cain closed his eyes, mouth bitten into a thin line. Aunt Ophelia's words brought forth a rotten knot in his stomach, of impatience and subdued thoughts. He gripped the baluster as he tried to maintain control of it all, especially in front of Emily. Aunt Ophelia was gone already, back across the hall with her servants, who tailed her back to her apartments where they'd make her up into some Greek goddess or other in Empire silhouette and rings of gold. Damn it all to hell, why did his aunt do that, throwing her words all around and leaving him lost in the wake? She knew she did it too. She got him thinking too hard, and it always made him doubt himself. He didn't like doubting himself. There was no reason for it.

Cain reached behind, pulling his mask out from under his cropped jacket. He glanced at Emily. She'd already donned hers—soft white and deep reds, big blue eyes peeking out. The low collar of her striped polonaise left little to imagine about the silky skin below her throat.

Cain sighed, trying to keep his smile level as he adjusted the mask on his nose.

"Should we go greet guests, then?" he asked, offering his hand to his cousin, this girl the daughter of his mother's country brother. She looked startled at first by his return to proper etiquette, then smiled brightly in turn. She gave a curt nod and linked their arms at the elbows.

"We should, my lord."

SCENE THREE

LIGHT FROM the crystal lusters blazed from every window, spilling out into the night.

Colors and sounds swirled like a tide—music, voices, the rustle of carefully calculated costumes as people danced.

The decorations were ghastly. Papier-mâché lanterns in the shapes of skulls had been strung between scarlet ribbons. Other lanterns projected grisly cutout imagery on the walls, spinning round and round. Black drapes hung above the marble floor. Headless skeletons danced near the windows. Painted roses were affixed on the tables and the Persian dancers would be snake charming soon. Masterfully stacked towers of wineglasses stood before carved ice, and candles sat in the gaping mouths of jack-o'-lanterns. Fans fluttered. The tintinnabulation of bells blended with the voices, the rain, the musicians. There was a trick mirror set up in the corner of the room near the Persians' divination table, where guests took their turns scaring each other. The gypsy hag reading tarot cards for delighted guests read to Cain from the hand he drew. The Seven of Coins, the Hanged Man, and the Fool.

"Tch!" Cain spat, and wandered off to find his aunt again.

If Emily's mother had been there, she would have ranted and raved about the contemptibility of it all, as on the narrow little stage in the corner rowdy half-dressed dancers made a burlesque out of Faust, and on the old, painted keyboard, a man in a powdered white wig punched out a slow but upbeat tune. A witch's doll sat atop the painted harpsichord case, a grisly little thing that looked made of real human bones strung together by wire, with a mane of horrid black hair and Xs for eyes.

There were fruits and jellies and gray-grained caviar of the finest sort. A scene from *The Tempest* was painted on the wall across from the windows, tiny white figures and lush forest scenes. The french doors opened onto a stone courtyard, and upstairs important rooms were closed off. Paintings and granite sculptures smiled down at guests—and those who belonged to the respective court wore the family crest as a silver brooch over their heart.

Such was a masquerade ball thrown by the Dietrich family.

Cain knew it all back and forth, in and out. It was as familiar in detail as the back of his hand—and equally unmoving.

He made his welcome speech to a hall full of vivacious supporters. He danced thrice with Emily and sipped idly at a glass of Mariani wine as he suffered through attempted conversations left and right. Aunt Ophelia snatched him aside and waited while he reluctantly changed into costume, bemoaning the entire way. It was definitely a *political statement*, to put it kindly—a fine slate-gray suit with the bones of a skeleton painted down the front of it so that he looked like some sort of macabre clown playing Death. There was a sloppy stitching of the Ruslaniv crest upside down on the right lapel, and a scarlet fur-lined cloak with a nice little hood. It was quite blatant mockery, a jab at the hated family, and the crowd would love it, surely.

"Sit still, now!" Aunt Ophelia cooed as her dress man, Ulrich, painted Cain's face like a skull to match the costume, and Cain felt a little knot of tired pride.

He was only dressing up for Aunt Ophelia. She was far more excited about it than he was. She called it, theatrically, "the Death of the Ruslanivs." Ridicule or not, Cain couldn't have cared less. Full costume had never appealed to him. He was the Earl, for Christ's sake. But he found comfort in the hope that maybe the costume would keep him hidden in the crowd, even in its shining political glory.

To an extent it worked, and he was immensely relieved.

The unveiling of the costume came with Aunt Ophelia's hollering and wild laughter, and after the initial shock of the disrespectful costume, it dawned on the crowd like a ripple in water that it was him, their earl, wandering around and mocking those damn Ruslanivs in the lovely defamatory getup.

"Everyone, please welcome the Death of the Ruslanivs!"

"Look at that!"

"How delicious!"

"Only our earl would extend himself so far—"

"Take that, Ruslaniv dogs!"

But their whispering and laughter and wonderment from afar became enough for them, and Cain was so grateful to avoid conversation, with a wry little smile under his mask and hood.

Once the concerto started up, he sent Emily off to mingle with other young ladies jealous of her high standing, and the moment she left his side, the colors and voices and racket swarmed unapologetically around him. The commotion threatened to swallow him.

There was no escape from this sea of colorful garments and masked faces, cresting and crashing through the yawning ballroom to the moans of the cello and the prancing of other strings. Dancing, dancing, like the creatures of the fairy world painted on the wall over there. Glorious fashion, velvet and silk, delicate lace, masks, and jewels. The liveried waitstaff glided through with silver trays of wine and bubbly, biscuits and ices and other tasty things, their powdered hair like their sails as they drifted through, ships on tumultuous waves.

Cain just wanted to get this over with and retreat to his room, scrub off the greasepaint, fall into bed, and sleep.

But even that would not be easy, because the moment his head hit the pillow, his mind would probably refuse to rest and consume him with business concerns and vital items of contemplation—

There, shifting through the crowd, subtle, but not quite subtle enough—an obvious glance in his direction from behind the black mask he'd noticed earlier.

The eerie black mask, which stood out to him in this mass of eerie masks and clowns and monsters, painted faces, tributes to the spooky. The black mask that was simple but effective and looked like a raven.

Cain met the eyes behind the mask and startled to find them staring right back—in fact holding his for a distinct moment—before the mask disappeared into the crowd and was lost again in the sea of faces.

"My lord—"

Cain looked over. Butler's uniform clean and crisp, Dietrich crest flashing in the light, Weston stepped closer and leaned to speak into Cain's ear, confidential as always.

"Those on guard tonight have sent me with an update of security," he said, voice like the last dry leaf rattling on a tree in winter. "They've located a rather rambunctious group. They send their promises to keep a close watch on these persons and will send periodic updates should anything urgent or significant arise."

Cain scoffed wearily. He crossed his arms. "There's always *something*, no matter what the hell's going on. That's just the way it is. Tell Security 'Very well, then, but don't slack on the rest of your duties for some simple delinquency.' Thank you, Weston."

He left Weston and followed the wall to the other side of the ballroom, where all the multipaned doors stood open upon the courtyard. The night air beckoned him, refreshing and cool, and he dropped his hood and pulled his half mask off as he stepped out onto the stone. He closed his eyes and took a deep breath.

It was much better out here, under the moon and the lights strung up along the balconies and eaves of the manor. People out here were not really dancing, but talking, lingering, getting fresh air and sipping their drinks, and Cain didn't mind that. The overwhelming bustle, the socializing—that was inside. Outside, it was not as constricting. Nobody would bother him. Nobody would care apart from the comments from a distance on his costume—

There, again.

The black mask with the feathers and the chains, the sharp nose, and little skulls at the temple.

Before he really deemed the idea fit or not, Cain dipped into the thin crowd outside, skirting guests and waitstaff. His eyes cut over someone's shoulder and met those behind the black mask directly. Again he was shocked to find them looking right back. He blushed, embarrassed by such brazen eye contact. He averted his glance immediately, continuing on his way to the other side of the patio as if that had been his intention in the first place.

But there was heat on the back of his neck, obvious and heavy, and he glanced over his shoulder as he strolled to a stop below some overhanging shrubbery.

Yes, once more.

The man in the black mask met his eyes briefly and then vanished into the crowd again.

A smile twitched at Cain's mouth, amused. So the fellow wanted to play that game, did he?

He brushed past a woman in purple silk, slipped between her and a man in a gray suit, and his smile broadened as he used his admittedly smaller stature to his advantage. He slithered through the crowd between the shoulders of others, scanning faces and glancing to and fro, and—

Yes, the black mask.

This close, he saw just how young the man wearing it was. Why, maybe not even that much older than Cain himself. And then he was gone again, and Cain came to a stumbling halt as a woman who smelled a little too strongly of brandy touched his arm and cried out, "O Death, where is your sting? O Grave, where is your victory?" Her laughter was drunken and shrill, and over her shoulder was the sprawling shadow of the manor, above it the star-studded sky.

Who was the man in the black mask? More importantly, who did he *think* he was, playing games with Cain? Even *more* importantly, why did it make Cain's heart thump so to play right back?

Cain could see his breath as he realized the stumbling woman was still talking to him, going on and on about his getup, but he didn't know what to say, so he just shook loose and brushed past her. He escaped by turning past one of the hired hands with a silver tray of turkish delight. As he sidestepped back-to-back with the waiter, he looked up and met the eyes of the young man in the black mask, and his heart gave a thrilled jump.

Everyone was dancing—and obviously so were they, in their own way, Cain and this stranger. The stranger hovered just a few inches away, standing at the back of some burly man in red, and beneath the chained bottom of his mask, the young man's mouth turned up in a most curious smile.

"The Death of the Ruslanivs, is it?" he whispered, just loud enough for Cain to hear, referencing Aunt Ophelia's introduction in a strange manner. It wasn't overexcited like everyone else, tickled by the satire. It was soft and thoughtful, with narrowed eyes. "It's an honor...."

Cain straightened with a little glimmer of pride, a gentle smirk tugging at his mouth as he waited for the guest to bow—but he didn't, and Cain's smirk faltered. Disrespectful bastard. Oh, right, perhaps the man still didn't realize it was him. Or perhaps he meant it was an honor to be meeting "the Death of the Ruslanivs."

"It's an honor more than you'll ever know again in your lifetime," Cain retorted coldly, and strode back into the crowd.

He didn't make it far. The young man in the mask slipped into his periphery again. Somewhere to Cain's left, a lady gasped, and before he could take another step, the man in the black mask waltzed right past him with the gasping woman in his arms.

He found Cain's eyes and smiled as if to say, *Your move.*

As the young man circled by, he purred, with a voice like burnt silk, "Oh, I think I understand the importance of this moment in my life. Very much so."

"What—?" Incensed, but in a good way, Cain followed as the man in the black mask waltzed away. The young woman taken as dancing hostage glanced between them, lost, and as a waiter came through, the young masked man twirled the lady out of his arms and released her into the crowd again, offering a slight bow as Cain stumbled to a sharp stop before him.

Cain didn't even notice his own smile as the young man looked up at him through the mask without lifting his head, which was something Cain found unbearably attractive. So casual, so indifferent, so cool and confident—

But Cain wasn't satisfied yet. "The import in meeting me face-to-face?" he spat, hoping to clarify in this game of quick words and wit.

Another waiter passed and Cain followed him around at the coattails until he stood behind the man in the mask, still bowing as he was. Ah, didn't the man know never to leave his back unguarded?

"Why…. Yes." The young masked man stood, casting Cain a heavy glance over his shoulder.

Cain's gaze roamed him head to toe, appraising: the modest black broadcloth with the blue lily-of-the-Nile stuck in the pocket—Dietrich blue—the brocade waistcoat of perfect gold, the chain of a pocket watch and the loose linen shirt with the top few buttons unfastened. The man was handsome, dangerously handsome, like men were before life destroyed them, and he showed the sideways glances of a clever mind and a slight shadow to his dimpled, saintly smiles. He finger combed his fine, dirty-blond hair out of his face, and it broke into almost curls just behind the ears.

"Oh, did you want to dance?" Cain smirked, pleased by his own scathing humor. "Let me guess, your favorite author is Oscar Wilde."

The man in the black mask laughed. It was a confident laugh, a charming laugh, a dry, rustling laugh that was totally unaffected by Cain's curt jab. A laugh that said, *Ah, you've caught me, but two can play at that game.*

Cain took the opportunity to move back into the crowd, gaze lingering on the laughing stranger, shoulders tense. Who was this fellow anyway? A Dietrich supporter, obviously, or the son of a Dietrich patron. God, but why did the laughter catch him up so? Why was he wasting his time with this fool in the first place? Briefly he considered having the young man thrown out, just out of giddy spite, but the ball would be unbearable again if he did that. The rest of the masquerade threatened to destroy his sanity tonight, and sometimes it was nice just to bicker and banter with strangers who could hold their own—

Cain snatched a glass of port from a passing waiter and threw it back in one hasty swallow. And as his vision leveled again, of course, *there he was*, quick and efficient as a ghost. That cocky stranger, smiling at him from behind the elegant black mask as he danced by with yet another unsuspecting lady.

Cain scoffed. He was not about to be trumped. He turned, shoving his empty glass into the hands of some gentleman behind him and taking the hand of the woman at his side. The man sputtered at first, angry, but he seemed to get over it quickly, smoking a fat cigar and cradling a large tumbler of brandy.

Cain led the lady with far from a patient step, scanning the faces around them intently until finally catching sight of the feathered mask and curious smile once more over the woman's bare shoulder, near the bushes. Cain turned, drifting closer to the young man's side until their elbows brushed.

"Is playing this game of cat and mouse really more entertaining than the offered festivities?" Cain demanded under his breath. The nighttime air fell to voices and commotion as the music from the vestibule came to an end and the dancing stopped until the next piece was struck up. The woman Cain had stolen smiled and gave a warm glance before moving off to find her date again, and the young man in the black mask motioned his own dance partner off elsewhere. She gave a little curtsey before hurrying off toward a group of girls, waiting on the other side of the patio with faces just as pink as hers.

Cain cast the masked man a cold and calculating eye. The masked man peered back, still smirking in that sly and disarming way.

"Forgive me," the masked man confessed below the buzz of the crowd, "I'm just honored to have the Death of the Ruslanivs playing with me."

Cain looked away with a little huff, stunned by the shy jump of his own heart. He'd had probably a little too much to drink already, enough to loosen his usually oh-so-tight nerves. "Don't flatter yourself," he scoffed, but the truth was, if he really didn't want to waste his time on this fellow, he would have moved away already.

"It's someone else's satire, isn't it?" the young man observed.

Cain bristled. "It's my costume, isn't it?" he fired back.

"But you're not wearing it," the masked man murmured. "It's wearing you."

Cain shrugged and shook his head, slowly, and limply, clamming up at how easily the man could see through him. "I'm not really one for lampooning and parodying. Poking fun, sure. But this kind of mockery is a waste of hatred *and* I have to wear the ugly Ruslaniv crest too. No, I'm more prone to direct and rather undiluted hostility."

The masked man smirked faintly, regarding Cain with hooded eyes. He didn't say anything, but something seemed to pass between them then, unspoken and intimate, in the vicinity of sweet nothings.

Cain ducked away under a lamp-strung tree, letting the shadows of the parterre swallow him. A maze of rose bushes and carefully trimmed trees, a hallway of leaves and petals, which through delicate branches filtered in the lights and sounds of the courtyard. There was a safety there, among the walls of the garden, a safety for secrets, and when Cain peeked over his shoulder and saw the blond man in the black mask was indeed tailing him yet, he couldn't repress a guilty grin.

"Either you're an assassin sent to *take care* of me...." Cain whispered, stopping with his back to a large and full corner of shrubbery, which hung over the stone path like a roof woven of vines and twigs. He offered the masked man an admittedly daring stare. "Or you and I share a similar idea of fun."

A shadow seemed to pass through the masked man's eyes then, some fast and sudden thought like he'd been hoping for the very words Cain had spoken or he hadn't expected them at all. It distracted him for a moment, though it did not take the smile from his face.

"But what if I'm both?" the masked man suggested gently.

"Then I suppose I'd just have to hope the fun you have with me convinces you to give up arms," Cain countered, meaning to sound quite more threatening than he did as the young masked man caged him in against the bushes and caught his mouth in a masterfully stolen kiss.

It really was a wonder how many gentlemen one could find who leaned *that way* on a regular basis.

There was no way the stranger was a hit man, but as surely as always there was the constant possibility, a dance with the devil that Cain danced quite eagerly. He couldn't help it. Something about living in the womb of danger and thrill was just an intrinsic part of him—not to mention that in moments such as the present, it was an absolute turn-on.

Sparks of lust clustered at the base of Cain's spine. In the dark of the garden, they kissed—in a soft and passionate way at first—and Cain shuddered when the blond man's tongue darted out across his lower lip. He could feel himself giving way to the cupid's dart. He wanted the blond man, *badly*. And he didn't even know his first name yet. Whatever, it didn't matter, this was how boys kissed. Boys and men. Rough and raw and aggressive, and the blond man's hands tore at his clothes as their kisses deepened, not to rip them off, but to feel every angle and curve beneath the velvet and brocade. It was a bracing sort of anxiety, colliding in the dark like this, a stimulating sense of the illicit. The greedy graze of teeth left Cain's mouth feeling bruised. There was something liberating about it too, like screaming at somebody or throwing something across the room.

Imagine, if the night just went *well* for once! Uneventful, free of care… No one to stop him from having a little fun the way he wanted it, not even the newly invasive presence of his cousin and fiancée. Oh, but it wasn't Emily's fault. He was an awful, awful man to be doing this behind her back. But no, it wasn't behind her back. It was not like he did this with her, anyway.

The young blond man's eyes gave him the chills. With half his face hidden by that mask, his gaze was more intense. All right, so maybe the man wasn't a complete nuisance. His kisses sure as hell weren't. Maybe he was just as unmoved as Cain—by the ball, by the world, by responsibility, and paperwork, and the stars overhead. Maybe it was something to be said that he'd managed to keep Cain entertained for the last quarter of an hour or so. Not that Cain could afford friends or really even wanted to, but perhaps tonight was one of the nights he would let his guard down low enough to enjoy himself. He'd toss back another drink or two and show the masked man around the upper wings of the manor. And after some more witty back-and-forth, flirty as it was, the sexual tension would just snap and Cain could snatch off that black mask and let curious hands crawl into his trousers—look, the man had perfect hands, wide but slim in an elegant way. Tragic how difficult it was to get the head of the Dietrich household alone in a world where two families warred one against the other and no one was safe.

Cain felt himself bending to that heated stare, to the arm snaking around his waist, and his heart leapt—goose bumps chased his fingertips—the blond man's hand slid shamelessly to brush along his upper leg, so dangerously and deliciously close to finding the nearby sign of reckless desire. Ah, this could be the start of something, Cain decided with a guilty chuckle against the blond man's hungry mouth. Something that endured in secrecy—every nobleman had a *lover*—

Gunshots ripped through the night and everything but instinct came screeching to a halt.

In an instant the tryst was abandoned. Indeed instinct kicked in, consuming all rational thought and focus.

Footsteps scraping on the flagstone, Cain dodged out of the garden. He dove beneath the stone of the courtyard arcades, pressing into the shadows of a mossy pillar and flipping up the end of his cloak. He dropped his mask as he drew his gun. The click of the hammer cocking gave him an excited shiver.

This was the life of a Dietrich, after all.

Guests scattered. Cain watched from the shadows of the arcades. Some ran for cover, flocking in his direction or stumbling for the ballroom doors, while yet others panicked on the courtyard stone. The waitstaff slammed shut the doors to the ballroom and screams echoed, demanding they be opened again. And *where the hell was Security*? Hazel, Percy, Mr. Collins—those damned servants were hardly good at anything else. *So where were they*?

More bullets flew, this time shattering abandoned glasses of port and brandy, tearing through bushes and trees, spraying water, and marring the stone of the fountain, popping the fronts of lanterns strung along the courtyard. And good, it sounded like the shooter was outside, probably up on the balconies somehow. Cain craned out of the shadows, trying to see the closest terrace.

There, almost directly overhead, in a black mask—there was a blond boy aiming what looked like a semiautomatic pistol. Cain shot twice in his direction, then ducked back into the shadows as bullets rained down on the cobbles in response, chipping the pillar he hid behind and scarring the stone walkway. Cain's fingers were ice-cold.

Guests cried out at the sounds of open fire. It seemed there was more than one shooter aiming at him. It was a group attack on the house. And a pathetic one at that, Cain decided. It was clearly not an ambush with intentions of bloodshed. The attackers wouldn't have been relying on handguns, reckless aim, and disorderly fire if they were on a mission like that.

No, this was something worse than that—this was another brazen act of provocation, a scare tactic, a show of skill and defiance, and it was meant to do nothing else but piss Cain off.

He didn't quite register the screams around him beyond the sharp urgency of the moment as he shoved through the throbbing, panicked crowd, packed against the side of the manor like a bunch of animals. He ran along the flagstone walk. The moonlight passed in streaks through the vines over the arcades. He followed around to the opposite side of the courtyard, where he could plainly see the balcony on which the blond man had been.

But the blond man was gone, and as Cain skidded to a stop behind another column, he found Hazel, pulling revolvers from under her maid's layers and already aiming for the redhead on the roof who had taken the blond man's place.

"*Fuck*," Cain hissed, crouching down behind Hazel with a hand on her shoulder to keep his balance.

Hazel pulled the trigger.

Cain braced against the kick, watching over her shoulder. The redhead danced around a few shots, then returned fire with wild abandon, hollering something utterly inaudible above the panic of the guests. Bullets shredded through the trees of the courtyard, ricocheted off the wrought iron garden chairs and tables. Cain moved behind the stone column again. There was Weston, herding everyone inside through the northwest servants' doors.

Lead scattered from above the courtyard, hitting the column a few feet over Cain's head. Shards of granite and Portland stone tumbled down in clouds of dust. Cain ducked around the other side of the pillar and listened to the fight for a moment or two. The shots from the roof weren't constant now, just defiant replies to the shots Dietrich Security fired from below. From somewhere overhead came the sound of a shout, a few dull thuds, and a clatter. It sounded like Mr. Collins and Percy had split up from Hazel and hurried upstairs to surprise the attackers there. A small pepperbox rifle clattered down from the balcony above, and Cain made a mental note to snag it afterward. If he knew the model and distributor, he could determine possible suspects—

Hazel threw an empty gun down in exchange for her second, but then there were footsteps, crunching on shattered granite. Cain stiffened. Had the attackers sent someone down below or was that Hazel moving closer?

The movement stopped on the opposite side of the pillar. Cain sank down into a crouch, searching for a shadow to judge by. But whatever shadow might have been cast slanted into the swarm of shadows of the arcades, far from helpful. Hazel was over there somewhere, after all.

"Don't worry," someone said in a cool whisper from behind—and Cain recognized the voice instantly. It was the young blond man in the black mask from earlier.

Cain's heart gave a little flutter, and he felt the pinpricks of a shameful blush. God, but why was he so excited? How had his interest for the night been so irreparably ensnared? He pressed back against the granite again, narrowing his eyes at the other side of the courtyard and watching for movement on the roof and balconies. He readjusted his clammy grip on his revolver and hissed, "You really decided to stay out here when all the guests were ushered in?"

"I have no intention of dying tonight," the masked man vowed. Cain uttered a gentle scoff. The young man chuckled, and Cain heard the click of a hammer from the other side of the stone column. This was as dark and impure as the confessional booth felt to him, full of lovely secrets and sins and the chill of not looking each other in the eye.

"I have no intention of accepting responsibility for your death, you know—" Cain spat, borrowing the blond man's overzealous words.

"I would never expect it from you, my friend. Being prepared does not make it your responsibility to accept."

"Prepared, ha! I'm always prepared. Well, whatever, perhaps you can just repay your host with good aim—"

There was a short silence. And then, from the other side of the column:

"O Death, what do you mean?"

"Get your head out of your ass!" Cain hissed. "I'm the Earl under all this ugly garb!"

There was a brief spray of bullets between those on the ground and the last of those on the upper eaves of the manor, until finally the redheaded one yelled something—something Cain couldn't hear from below the arcades.

And then, as quickly as it had begun, the shooting stopped.

The whole foray had lasted maybe only ninety seconds, but it was another long minute or two before Cain stood again, legs cramping and hands quivering like they always did at the end of such events. He pressed his face to the cool granite column, trying to reclaim a bit of composure. He wasn't sure if he was more shaken up or just infuriated by the situation, and for a moment, breathing was difficult and he panicked at the possible advent of an anxiety attack.

"Hazel!" he called cautiously. He heard the *clatta-clack* of her gun as she lowered it. He glanced over, meeting her eyes.

And the young man in the black mask was gone.

Damn it all to hell.

He hadn't even gotten his name—

Cain moved out from under the arcades, kicking some chipped granite and stone as he trudged into the courtyard. The pepperbox rifle was gone. An eerie silence had fallen, the terror of the guests a muted roar from inside the house.

"My lord!" Hazel beckoned from the shadows, deeply and professionally concerned. "My lord, it's not yet safe—"

"No." Cain scowled. "It's safe. I know it. They've retreated. They weren't here to kill, just to crash the party." He shook his head, hands still shaking. "Hazel, meet the rest of Security upstairs and search the house. If you find anyone, hold them in the kitchen. It was probably some petty gang or something."

Hazel hesitated, then nodded curtly and took off toward the servants' doors, her little plaited braids coming loose at the nape of her neck. Bushes rustled as a lone waiter climbed from his hiding spot among them. Cain slid his gun back into its holster and surveyed the damage.

The courtyard was a mess of broken dishes, tattered foliage, holes in the cobbles, and dropped food and drinks. Cain's fingers twitched into fists, and he kicked a shard of fine china, watched it shatter into smaller pieces a few feet away.

Yes, a petty gang, he was more than certain of it. A gunslinging street gang who thought it fell on their shoulders to pose riots and stage rebellions in the name of the family who hated the Dietrichs as much as the Dietrichs hated them.

"Fucking Ruslaniv *bastards*!" Cain howled, kicking a few more broken dishes. He felt like a child throwing a fit, but there was no one there to hear except for a few scattered servants and Weston.

Jaw tight, Cain propped one hand on his hip and cradled his temple in the other. How ridiculous he probably looked, how comical, all painted and done up and screaming and stomping.

"Weston," he mumbled, "were there any injuries?"

"Scrapes and bruises, sir. One young lady was grazed on the shoulder. She collapsed from fright soon after, I'm afraid, and another man in the initial frenzy twisted his ankle. As it stands, those are the only grave injuries."

"Lovely," Cain whispered, dropping both hands and taking a deep breath. "At least there's no need to fill out another civilian casualty report for the queen—just mass hysteria left for *me* to deal with. And, I suppose, this mess out here to clean up. I've sent Security in to search the house, but I'm sure they've all fled already."

Cain kicked a dirty fork, watching it skitter forward along the stone. The rush of the fight was starting to fade, leaving not much else but cold, distilled hatred for the Ruslanivs and their unruly gangs. Not much else, sure, except for the bruising frustration of the night being ruined right when he'd decided to have a good time for once. He'd been on the right course for a little bit of ass tonight too!

"Just start cleaning up out here, all of you," he grumbled. "I'll go calm the crowd...."

"Yes, my lord," Weston murmured, dropping low in a bow.

"*Damn those Ruslaniv dogs and all their supporters!*" Cain stormed around a lawn chair someone had knocked down in their panic. He left Weston and the other servants to clean, and by the time he slipped back inside to a sobbing Emily and a fuming Aunt Ophelia, he had a splitting headache to go with the subsequent tremble of such a demanding affair.

And quite a few guests to placate.

Damn those Ruslaniv *dogs*.

SCENE FOUR

Levi thought of everything he'd ever heard about the young Earl Dietrich, and the cool night air felt good on his flushed skin.

Maybe it was the last of the thrill from the gunfight, a rusty exhilaration that he hadn't felt so fresh and hot in a long time. Or maybe it was the liquor he'd snatched before hopping the outer wall of the manor, throwing back one gulp after another like a man on the streets flirting with death. Or maybe it really was just the rush of having been so close to the Dietrich head, close enough to shove his tongue in the Earl's mouth, to wrap his fingers around that pretty little neck and—

Damn!

There were a few things commonly known about the young Earl Dietrich, the first being that of his general peculiarity. It wasn't exactly every other day a powerful and infamous household was run by a lord of nineteen, let alone one as ruthless and methodical as the one in question.

Then there was the matter of the Earl's disappearance a few years back, when his parents had been murdered… and the matter of his random return.

Although Levi knew the circumstances of the Earl's kidnapping, those of his homecoming were still unexplained.

Lastly there was the fact that his eyes were a color somewhere between winter-sky gray and pale blue, a failure of pigmentation from birth that had just never gone away. That had been one of the favorite topics a few years ago, back when the Earl Dietrich had just been *the heir.* Over bonbons and vodka, they'd laughed in Ruslaniv parlors and salons about how weak the Dietrich genetics seemed to be, spitting out an heir with colorless eyes. Probably the result of incest. Or perhaps it was God's curse on them for their sins—whatever sins those were. The sins his family loathed the Dietrichs for.

Levi had seen them for himself, those pale colorless eyes, while he'd sat above Lovers' Lane one unfortunate, sludgy afternoon. God damn it all, he should have *known* when he'd seen the "Death of the Ruslanivs" and felt that those haunting eyes beyond all the paint were familiar!

Levi squinted into the empty liquor bottle, wondering if there was even a sip left. Drinking so much so fast had rendered him a little dizzy.

He thought about the Earl and the way the lights had danced in that colorless stare. He'd been so guarded and mysterious in that mocking costume of his, which he himself had admitted was not his style. What a terribly bewitching creature, so dark and beautiful—like a stormy sky—and his kisses had been so hot and inviting—

Damn, damn, *damn*!

Levi doubled over, wondering if he might be sick.

It seemed utterly melodramatic to him, more like vicious butterflies ripping him apart from the inside.

He'd been so close to the Earl Dietrich, this heir of the house his own family hated, this notorious lord he'd only ever seen from a careful distance. He'd been so close he could have killed him with his own two hands.

And he hadn't.

He didn't loathe himself for tangling with the Earl when he'd been unaware, but—under those mossy arcades, when his heart had fallen and he'd realized that the little cloaked figure of Death was the earl it was in his blood to despise, *he could have killed him*, and he hadn't!

In betrayal of some sick sense of loyalty or twisted justice that really didn't move him one way or the other at all, he'd felt a strange, inchoate shiver deep inside, like the first whispers of an inner renaissance. He'd fled as if fleeing would really stop an inner awakening of something numb and deadened. *He'd fled.*

Levi sat with his back against the wall of the Dietrich grounds, glaring into the empty bottle where it reflected light from the windows on the other side of the Lincolnshire wall, and he was in awe. It was a cold, wondrous emptiness like the feeling of rage without any of the resentment.

Odd.

There was a rustle in the foliage outside the wall, a muffled hiss of "There! Found him!" before Eliott tumbled out of the bushes with quite a few leaves stuck in his hair and his suit coat falling off one shoulder, glasses on and mask casually stuck atop his head. His tinted spectacles were in his breast pocket. The Blond One followed, in his purple brocade, and behind him, the One with Glasses, tailed by the Witch and William, all looking a bit disheveled and reckless but satisfied all the same.

Eliott came to a stop in front of Levi, perhaps not as steady on his feet as he should have been, and Levi threw him a proud smirk.

"You know," he said decidedly, "I have a pretty capable team if the lot of you managed to pull that off *drunk*."

"I'm not drunk, I'm tipsy," Eliott insisted, tossing bothersome hair out of his face. He grinned down at Levi with a suspicious gleam in his eye, and Levi's smile faded.

"What's that look for?" he asked, but the Witch interrupted.

"They didn't even search the damn place!" she cried triumphantly. Surely she was freezing with what little she wore below the fur-collared coat so kindly offered by William. "Well, I mean, Will, that one guard almost caught you, but you weren't being careful. Really, it's like they didn't even care!"

"It's because they *don't* care," the One with Glasses replied, so cold and calculating, per usual. "It was a taunt and nothing more, and they knew that. Why would they search for tricksters when they can just strike back later?"

"Good point," Levi agreed, jabbing a finger in his direction.

It should have been sickening, how right he was. How these things were so normal, such commonplace events all throughout New London. Gunfights and threats, games of back-and-forth with bullets. *Tag, you're it. What's your move, white?* What a world to live in, where it was just the natural way of things to continually shoot at one's neighbor until finally someone really got hurt, and then everyone was outraged like they had no idea how someone could do such a thing.

Eliott waved his hands, frantic with a sudden thought. Levi suffered a gnawing feeling of dread it had something to do with the dark gleam in his eyes. "Listen, be quiet for a second—Levi, we've got an idea, and I think you're going to like it...."

All at once, the other members of BLACK circled closer, like ravens over the dead on street corners, excitement quickening their faces. And, in their shadows, Levi felt his stomach drop.

"Do you, now?" he whispered.

SCENE FIVE

"IT WAS the Earl in that disgusting costume—"

"Can you believe his audacity?"

"Ooh, I just wanna make him *bleed*—"

"Levi, you *held a conversation* with the Earl!"

And kissed him too, and surely the Ruslanivs' enemy shouldn't have tasted so sweet and ready for action.

"Disrespectful—atrocious—mocking us like that, so flagrantly—"

"Did he know it was you, Levi?"

"No, he didn't know it was me. Nobody ever knows it's me. My father's made sure of that much, you know that."

"But Levi, here's my idea…."

If Levi was getting as close to the Earl as the Blond One said he was, he should get closer to him—or so was Eliott's logic. Yes, Levi should get *really* close. Pretend to be arbitrary, get the Earl to trust him. It would be a connection straight inside the Dietrich house, direct access to all the most pertinent Dietrich secrets. Maybe even a glimpse inside the mad little earl's head too. Imagine *that* advantage.

"It's too dangerous," Will snapped. "I don't think your father would approve of it at all, Levi."

Levi shrugged. "I don't either, anyway."

It was just preposterous. It was asinine. It was laughable. The proposition left a bad taste in Levi's mouth. Or maybe it was the fruity Dietrich liquor. But drunken schemes were the best and the worst. Weren't they…?

With a scatter of rocks and dead leaves, a scuff of his heel against stacked stone, Levi slipped down the inside of the gothic wall that ran around the grounds of the Dietrich estate. Palms raw and knees sore from uneven Lincolnshire stone, his feet hit the grass, and he dropped to a crouch, waiting for any sign of guards nearby. Putting his mask back on compromised his peripheral vision. He didn't like it.

Even from the back, the Dietrich house was altogether the essence of grandeur. The house was monstrous. Parapets and chimneys soared.

The windows were tall. Dark gnarled and knotted trees, which had lost most all their leaves already, lined the courtyard. The ornate fountains bore roaring stone lions. A wooden swing swayed idly from the branch of a deadened tree, but it was broken and hung cockeyed, mossy and seemingly untouched for years.

A juvenile little exhilaration pumped through Levi's veins like a current, and as he caught his breath, he shook his head at his companions' words again and thought, *They jest at scars that have yet to feel a real wound.*

Levi followed the wall to the manor, passing the vast courtyard and slinking toward the shadows of the house, barely breathing just to keep a keen ear for the sound of anyone tailing him. He'd heard stories that Dietrich guards were brutal, and while that was a thrilling challenge, he didn't really feel like facing it tonight. He inched along the southern wing of the manor, lingering under the vines and little poplars that grew along the stone.

The house was unlit save for a few upper windows and one room with its balcony doors open, spilling warm light down on the dark lawn. Levi froze in the shadows at the slight rustle of movement. He fell still, wondering if he'd been seen. The night was silent for a breath or two, just the rush of the cool wind through the trees, the sounds of activity inside the big house muffled and faraway, leaking out from the balcony threshold. And God, what had he gotten himself into now, letting BLACK talk him into this? Stop, wait, don't breathe, where had the sound come from in the first place? And then, brisk and unsympathetic from above:

"You're lucky I've kept the hounds in tonight. Haven't you heard? They're beasts. They'll tear you limb from limb."

Crouched in the shadow of the Dietrich wall, Levi almost choked on his tongue. But he recognized the voice. If anything, the cocky tone gave it away in an instant.

Levi stood with a creak of leather holsters beneath his fine shirt as he noticed a familiar-looking revolver poking out over the edge of the balcony, around the side of a stone gargoyle perched on the corner. Reflected light bounced off the muzzle. How opportune that he had been passing by this balcony of all the ones on the house—

"Show yourself." It was the same demanding voice, but this time Levi realized that the hidden speaker already knew who it was lurking below his balcony.

The Earl Dietrich's face appeared then, peeking around the balcony gargoyle. When Levi shifted forward into the pale slant of light, the Earl seemed to falter a little, uncertainty darting behind the mask of importance on his face. God, but what a face. He was an eerie little prince, sage-like and cruel, perfect youth and the bleakness of tragedy. There was still some paint left on his throat and face from that gaudy insult of a costume—the *"Death of the Ruslanivs,"* really, now?

The bitter night chill kicked the hair off the Earl's temple and lent Levi a clearer look at the soft white skin of his face, the haunting eyes written through with confusion—and just as he'd seen earlier in the grand hall and the courtyard, just as they all gossiped, his eyes were a pale, washed-out gray. *Weak genetics.* Or fragilely stunning, like ice in the sun.

"You—" was what the Earl said next, spitting it out like the word was the worst tasting one he'd ever spoken. Cain was his first name, if Levi remembered correctly. *Cain,* like the Biblical story, or *fair* in Welsh?

Cain scowled, pulling his revolver back but not abandoning it just yet. He leaned forward. "How the hell did you—? Have you been hiding out here all this time? The ball is over, and most everyone's gone. What are you still doing here? I'll have you arrested for trespassing!"

"Many apologies, my lord…." Levi jumped in before the Earl could finish his tirade, and he dipped down into a wide bow. That empty cold was still there, filling him up to the point of breathlessness. Like rage, but no anger. It was the strangest, most restless feeling he'd had in a long while. "'The Death of the Ruslanivs,' hmm?" he mused aloud, smirking bitterly.

"I will be. I am." The Earl issued an indifferent shrug and a cold scoff from the balcony above.

"I was just concerned about your well-being after…." Levi trailed off on purpose, shaking his head.

"Well," the Earl said, and the nighttime wind carried his voice perfectly, "thank you for your worries, but really, do you have any idea who I am at all? Are you foreign or something? New to New London? I don't need anybody's *concern* for my well-being, especially not from a mere civilian."

Levi moved closer to the wall beneath the balcony. The liquor had made his skin warm and itchy; he needed to stay sharp. The Earl scowled down at him with murderous intent, and Levi couldn't help but grin now, attempting humility but really inexorably pleased. By the Earl's lack of sympathy, or by his obvious relief at seeing Levi again. There was no denying the Earl had hoped to see him again. He would have called Security by now if it had been any other way. Looked like BLACK's plans were right on spot, after all.

"Pardon me," Levi called again, knowing exactly what to say, "but I thought the intrigue in the air was mutual, in the garden when we…."

"Tch!" the Earl spat down at him, lip curling gently.

But Levi caught the flare of color in his face, the spark of something in his eyes. He was thinking of their assignation in the garden, just like Levi, yes. The kiss. The tongue, the teeth, the wandering hands.

The Earl was in his bedclothes already. The lingering face paint made him look ghostly. Levi wondered if he was cold. Again he thought about the taste of his mouth and he had to stop himself from touching his own lips in sweet memory. This was *the Earl Dietrich—*

"Well," the Earl said again, curtly, "you were horribly mistaken. I was bored and you weren't annoying me—*at the time*. Now, if you'll escort yourself out, it'll save me the trouble of alerting my officers."

"Oh, I wish you wouldn't lie." Levi offered his best smile. *That* was a bold move, and if it worked like he thought it would….

The Earl studied him coldly. Clearly he was startled, disgruntled, but in a very guilty way. Finally, after a few long, torturous moments, he set his revolver down and gestured with one hand for Levi to close in on the balcony. The Earl leaned forward against the stone, hooked one ankle behind the other, and called down coolly, "What do you want?"

Success. Levi's neck ached from looking up. He wished there had been some vines or lattice to climb to get even closer, out of any light.

"Remove your mask," the Earl demanded suddenly, and Levi bristled as he realized the revolver was back and pointed his way once more. When had he…?

Levi thought about it a moment, gnawing his lower lip.

He was certain there would be no recognition past the black mask on the Earl's side of their acquaintance. His anonymity as Ruslaniv heir, thanks to his father's protectiveness, had never failed him before. However, this was the enemy. This was like laughing in the face of the devil.

Well, the alcohol made it an easy choice. With fleeting hesitation, Levi pulled his mask off and let it dangle idly from his fingertips as he met the Earl's gaze again, steadily.

"I've been dying to meet the head of the Dietrich family," Levi declared, and there was a moment of silence in which his heart pounded below his throat and he wondered if the clouds slipping through the Earl's eyes were those of recognition. He needed a sign, a code word, some sort of impending meaning.

But the Earl just shifted, drew his gun back, and smiled thinly along the barrel before it went out of sight. "If it's death you want, I can arrange it," he retorted, low, below his breath, a joke and a promise all in one. The relief washed through Levi, cold and refreshing, and he wondered if it was too soon to accept it.

"So you admit that the intrigue is mutual?" he tried a second time.

"I admit that you entertained me, and that's hard to do." The Earl propped his chin in one palm, raising his brows. "So, congratulations. And now that I finally see your face, sir, what do you want?"

"To talk to you." Levi shifted, passing his mask from hand to hand. He tried to soften his smile, to make it more pleasant. It seemed the Earl really had no idea who he was, he who stood below him, but the Earl was known to be a scrupulous businessman, so Levi couldn't be certain yet. He had to keep on his toes.

"And what makes you think I want to talk to *you*?" The Earl sniffed daintily, drumming an idle finger on his cheek. Scrupulous businessman or not, he was flirting. This was the notorious Earl Dietrich *flirting*.

"Even the most capable of men need a confidant," Levi insisted. "Especially those as young and encumbered as you."

"Oh, hell. You'll rot me like sugar on the teeth," the Earl mumbled dryly, the words barely audible on their descent from the balcony. "Why the devil should I trust a complete stranger beseeching me from below my *window*? Which, by the way, you're the first to ever do as much. Congratulations are in order again, I'm afraid."

Levi shifted, smile fading. With his mouth bitten into a thin line, he peered up at the Earl somberly. "Because even as a complete stranger," he husked, and—he had no idea where the words came from, or if they might work for BLACK's scheme, but they felt right—"I think you might find me reliable. And... *talented*. I was sure someone of your standing could use that, someone to *rely* on, someone *skilled*. A man who you might find useful in conducting your business as a Dietrich, to whom you might go for opinion or information—"

"I have someone like that. He's called my secretary. But, stop, let me guess." The Earl held up a hand, eyes hooded. "You're a gunslinger who no longer has a regular payment coming your way—I won't assume any circumstances—and you thought that maybe I was in need of someone with your *abilities*."

Levi floundered for just a moment, gawking. He considered arguing, considered trying to sweet talk a little more, but then he just swallowed and smiled humbly, because the Earl had so flawlessly set up the *perfect* opening for him.

Levi called up, in true gunslinger spirit, "If that's what you want me to be, that's what I am."

The Earl squinted down at him, and his expression was something that caught Levi momentarily rapt—soft, childlike eyes at half-mast and no longer sharp and deliberate but distant with thought. His hair danced along his temple like his collar danced along his slim shoulders, and in that moment, Levi wanted nothing more than to climb up the side of the house and join him on the balcony, to sit and talk about everything in the world and stare into an expression like that all night long. He couldn't say why. There was just something mesmeric about the Earl, something indomitable and powerful that drew him in, a primal kind of force that Levi had no right to deny. It was a pull as subtle and dangerous and undeniable as the moon's. The kind of thing a man didn't speak of in the daylight for fear of destroying its sanctity.

"What do you think of what happened tonight?" the Earl hissed, and Levi realized he was being tested. "What do you think it was all about, the attackers?"

"Why, it was obviously a show." Levi didn't miss a beat. "Party-crashers, reckless Ruslaniv supporters, ruining your good time in the name of their crest. Pathetic, right?"

"Very pathetic. So pathetic, I didn't even apprehend them." The Earl chewed over Levi's answer for what felt like eternities, glaring down at him. His unwavering stare was slightly unnerving, but Levi reveled in it. He basked in it, really.

The Earl sighed, shifting to his other foot. "You make me nervous," he conceded after a long pause. The impatience had faded from his voice. "However, don't think that means I like you just yet," he added hastily. "I confess, all right? That intrigue you mentioned… it was mutual, yes. And maybe it was intuition or something. I don't have an answer for you just yet, but I'll consider your proposition—"

"Will you meet me tomorrow night?"

Levi hadn't a clue where that question had come from. He shook his head, but he didn't say anything more.

The Earl reared back. "What?" he called down, brow knotting.

But Levi caught sight of the ghost of a smile that flickered across his face.

"Will you meet me tomorrow night, to discuss business matters further?" Levi said again. "We can meet at St. Vincent's Church, in Romanov Square—after night's fallen if that makes you feel more comfortable."

"Right, meeting a stranger somewhere in the dark just makes me feel cozy and safe." The Earl draped his arms over the side of the balcony and leaned down again. His eyes flashed with the passing of quick thoughts, but that soft smirk had finally come to life on his pale lips. "St. Vincent's in Romanov Square is fine. As long as it's not St. Mikael's."

"Never," Levi husked, feeling a tight pinch in his chest. "That's Ruslaniv territory."

"When?"

"How does nine o'clock sound? In the safety of night?"

"I don't see why not." The Earl shrugged. "Well, then. Now that that's settled. Is there anything more, or should I call Security to escort you out? Perhaps you could give me your name? Maybe an oath of loyalty? You don't find it a little odd that a gunslinger looking for a position *just so happened* to be on the scene when a shooting occurred, do you?"

Levi laughed, because what a smart little man this Earl was. But then he bit his lip, eyes flickering up to meet the Earl's. He lifted a hand, straightening up solemnly.

"A name, what is a name?" Levi sighed. There was no catch to this. He'd always gone by his middle name, anyway, and surely the Earl would never make the connection to his formal first name.

He said, "A rose would smell the same if called anything else, wouldn't it? Names are as dangerous as the guns we wave. With a man's name you hold so much power over him—but if you should need a name for me, you can call me Levi—and I swear by the moon above in the sky—"

"Oh God, who are you? Romeo?" The Earl's voice was thick with disgust, but his eyes danced.

Levi was slightly offended. He'd thought that had been a grand play of words.

"The moon is powerful," he insisted, offering the Earl a frank frown. The Earl's expression didn't waver. He returned the stare, stubborn and smug in his austerity. Levi sighed. "What do you suggest I swear by, then?"

"Your life." The Earl motioned down to him, that awful emotionless mask passing over his face again. Levi much preferred the paint-stained and tortured smile. "Because, *Levi*, if I find reason to suspect you of betrayal, I'll have you executed in front of everyone you love and hold dear. And then I might kill them too, if I feel the need. And you'll all be tossed in Lovers' Lane to be picked up by the undertaker and taken away to his shop to be used as guinea pigs for his medical experiments. Does that sound good to you?"

Levi gawked. His heart leapt up beneath his throat, hammering there excitedly. Because the more the Earl spoke, the harsher he was, the more that cold little flame in Levi throbbed up, filling him with an exhilaration he hadn't expected. He smirked, turning honest eyes up at the Earl, silhouetted as he was against the light spilling from his room. And in the back of his mind, he heard Eliott again, laying out the new scheme with that suspicious gleam in his eyes.

If you were getting as close to the Earl as Petyr says you were, here's an idea, Levi: get closer to him. We're talking really close— pretend to be arbitrary, get him to trust you. And through that, we'll have a connection straight inside! An express ticket straight to the top! You will *do it—right, Levi? I know you can. You can't fool me with that apathetic act of yours. I know that proud Ruslaniv blood still runs through you. You can't deny it.... So, you're gonna do it. Right, Levi?*

Levi's smile widened, and he straightened up, letting the Earl's critical, pale eyes flicker over him.

"I swear by my life," he murmured. "I hereby do give you the power to do all you said you would, should you ever feel the need."

The Earl turned his nose up, and Levi watched, wishing he wouldn't stifle the smile so obviously waiting at the corners of his mouth. His smiles were like the sun shining on a grave. The Earl took a step away from the balcony with a curt nod, retrieved his gun, and backed away toward the open doors. There was a clatter, a sound of voices from within the house, and finally the Earl conceded to the smile, offering it in the last of the light as a servant appeared next to him carrying a rather large and out-of-place smoking jacket.

"Weston," the Earl murmured, motioning over the edge of the balcony with his free hand. "Please have Security escort Mr. Levi here off the grounds. He was with me earlier, in the courtyard, but he got a little lost in all the commotion."

Levi chuckled beneath his breath as he watched the butler pull the balcony doors shut, heard his faint answer and the latch of the locks, and through the glass of the doors, the Earl Dietrich was still smiling as he turned away and slipped into the smoking jacket held out for him.

The well-trained part of Levi wanted to believe it wasn't that easy, but the part of him that had downed half a bottle of drink in ten minutes rejoiced in the victory. How easily the Earl had been fooled!

Five minutes later, Security shut the gates at the front of the manor behind him, and Levi threw his mask in the air with an accomplished laugh before hurrying off to find the rest of BLACK.

ACT TWO
REVENGE

SCENE ONE

ON THE night of All Saints', the rest of New London drank and danced to the bank holiday. Hallowmas was such a mockery to the saints in the modern age, but empty and at night, St. Vincent's in Romanov Square seemed a monument to all things dark and daunting. The November air was wet and deadly, and the railing around the cemetery was a sharp row of shadowy wrought iron teeth. The trees reached up into the black sky for salvation like gnarled hands.

Cain should have been at home, organizing mail and business files. Instead he was checking his guns. He'd managed to keep a straight face out on the street—but once he'd slipped through the heavy doors and into the orthodox and the cliché, chills had rattled through him, because it was like slipping through a rip in reality and into another world altogether.

A sinister world, a demented world, a place where bad men's faces danced in eternal mockery in the back of his mind, where morals and values were branded into the soul, broken and bruised, like litany after litany.

He was well aware of the state of his own spiritual being, but when his footsteps echoed on the smooth marble floor of the sanctuary, he couldn't help feeling small and helpless again. Vulnerable, at the mercy of some greater power—God, or something like it, he was never quite sure.

Cain stopped as the sanctuary doors shut behind him, and he stood in the candlelit dark, gawking down the aisle at the tall painted glass window over the pulpit. The crucifix beneath it, the sacred font, and the altar were all draped in the shadow of the night. A shabbily dressed stranger hunched quietly near a wealth of prayer candles. Cain considered shooing him out. Sharper instinct prevented it. It was good security to have witnesses. Moonlight filtered in through the skylights in the vaulted ceiling. His heart fluttered in a sick way.

There was movement off to the right, a little creak of leather, and just as he had done three or four times on his way to St. Vincent's, Cain whipped out his gun and waited, hiding behind the lifted barrel.

There was silence as his eyes adjusted to the darkness. Silence, and maybe the sound of the night outside, the rustle of the wind, and for the umpteenth time, Cain thought about his plan should the evening be a trap. Aunt Ophelia and Mr. Renton were waiting outside on the street, patiently biding their time in the gloom for the signal from him, should he signal at all, and if he did…. Oh, St. Vincent's would be bloody tonight.

A body moved forth from the gulf of shadows near the confessional booths, and as it slipped into the meager swell of candlelight, Cain recognized the soft face of the young man who had hidden behind the black mask the night before.

"Good evening, Levi," Cain greeted, evaluating him from behind his revolver.

"It's a pleasure, my lord," Levi returned, and his smile was almost eerie in the dim light.

Cain's frown tightened. He shifted to the other foot. Levi held his hands up, innocent, as he moved forward a bit more, and Cain instantly retracted a step or two in turn.

"Please, Earl Dietrich, believe me," Levi said, "I am not armed."

"Bullshit!" Cain uttered a cynical laugh. "You're a gunslinger for hire and even civilians are armed these days, especially on the streets of New London. I think the first thing you should keep in mind if you want to work for me, Levi, is not to lie."

"Duly noted."

Levi's voice was clear in the hush of the church, the hush that was so timeless and alive. His words were almost frivolous, but not quite. He dropped his hands, discarding the act of mystery as he moved over to seat himself casually in the last row of pews. Cain followed him with the point of his gun, frowning. Levi raked stray blond hair out of his face and turned, draping an arm over the back of the pew as he met Cain's eyes in the dark sanctuary. His voice cut through the silence again, this time far more serious.

"Do you trust I've come alone?"

"I trust no one," Cain replied with well-mannered contempt. "Did you really think *I'm* alone?"

"Will you join me?" Levi invited, smiling innocently and drumming his fingers on the back of the pew like a trouble-making schoolboy.

Cain narrowed his eyes in scrutiny. He didn't drop his guard entirely yet, but in the silence, the sounds of metal and movement were cold and sharp, footsteps echoing as he lowered his gun and moved to the pew across the aisle from Levi. He sat down, leaned forward on his knees, and cradled his revolver between them, watching the young man with lashes lowered on a critical glare. Ah, he was still as good-looking and cool as the night before, unfortunately. Cain had been hoping for a reason to detest him, but even in the tense dark of the sanctuary, he wanted to be near him. *Fuck.* The hymnals and scripture were yellowed and dog-eared, tucked neatly in shelves on the pews before him, and the smell and the chill of the vast room rank with bad memories.

Cain shrugged idly. He glanced at the man across the sanctuary, still praying alone. What if he was no stranger? What if he was undercover backup? No. A gunslinger needed a contractor more than backup. Cain was overthinking things. He would die before letting the Ruslanivs turn him to paranoia. Without looking back to Levi yet, Cain murmured, "It's an unconventional setting, but it's still a meeting you requested. Speak."

"Yes, sir," Levi complied gaily, and Cain grunted, unable to determine if it was mockery.

Again Levi became suddenly and drastically serious. The shadows danced from the candles in the prayer corner as the stranger wandered out of the church, tucking a small cross necklace back into his pocket. He nodded to Cain and to Levi on his way out. Judging by his faded and dreary appearance, he was a working-class man. It was uncomfortably obvious he'd been crying over the prayer candles.

"To be honest," Levi said in a low and ragged way, his stony eyes hooded, "I wish the feud between houses didn't place such a margin on who is trustworthy and who is not. It makes for a rather difficult living as an arbitrary citizen."

There was a pause. Whether he was thinking carefully over what he said or building the courage to say it, Cain couldn't tell. Then Levi drew a breath and went on, eyes flashing as they met Cain's bitterly.

"I'm no more a follower of you than I am of the Ruslaniv family. In truth, I'm not sure I have a purpose on this earth beyond my guns and who pays me to shoot them. I was trained, you see, from a young age, and I don't really know any other kind of life. But recently, I've decided to follow *my* whims and see where they take me. I've been praying again, you see—"

"Ah. Thus, we meet in a church." Cain's heart gave a greedy little jump. A nonpartisan, huh? Trained from a young age? *Praying, you see....* God, Levi was lovely in the worst way.

"I'm a poor excuse for a man, I know." Levi offered a tiny chuckle of chagrin, face darkening. "I suppose I'm a little *different*, for a gunman. Look, the other day a man dropped his invitation to the Dietrich ball out on the street, and.... Well, I wasn't going to just give it up. And I'm glad I went, because you and I became acquainted...."

Acquainted, yes, through tongue and teeth and gently groping fingers. The ghost of Levi's kisses still flitted across Cain's mouth.

"I confess now there is just this constant nibbling at my mind and soul," Levi continued. "It won't let me move on. So I thought, perhaps it's the strings of fate I feel moving? *Following my whims* and all. And there you have it. That's my pathetic deposition, my reasoning as to why I should like to work for you. I just *want* to."

When he spoke, it was careful and calm. Maybe too collected, too composed—but there was something in the shadows of the young man's face, a muted kind of honesty, the look of someone who had lived a life full of suppressed opinions and subdued thoughts and was finally speaking his mind, as uncomfortable as it was. Cain felt himself giving way to that subtle pinch to Levi's brow, and whether he believed Levi more out of pity or sympathy or something more shameless, it didn't matter.

That wasn't to say he could trust him completely yet. Oh no, not at all. In a world such as theirs, nobody was innocent. He shrugged, face twisting in a tart frown. "Well, Levi," Cain countered, "as endearing as you are, I already have a capable team working under me, and plenty of private hit men, and I'm afraid I'm not in need of anyone new."

The words hung in the air like poison. It seemed fate had already decided things for itself.

Cain sighed.

"But perhaps I *could* use someone with different experiences, or if I need counsel from someone of your, ah... status. If you understand what I mean," he added hastily. "Maybe you could be a street runner. If you're as unsided as you claim to be, your anonymity could be highly beneficial. You could dance the border between Ruslaniv and Dietrich. I could send you into places that are too risky for even my armed agents—Ruslaniv territory, the seediest pits of the city. You'll be my spy, my double-hander. My connection to the dregs of society that just skitter away into hiding when we scout the streets. Levi, how does that sound to you? Would you be willing to be that, my ace in the sleeve?"

The echo of his offering was cold. The silence that followed was thick and daunting. It seemed Cain could hear the crackling of all the wicks on all the candles, the world was so quiet in the wake of his admittedly brilliant plan. Well, it was brilliant to him, at least. Was Levi offended? Was he unconvinced?

"I'll pay you, of course," Cain offered, and he wasn't sure why he was so desperate, "but don't expect a sum of money as large as you might have gotten when contracted by certain others—well, never mind, I suppose we can *discuss* it."

Levi leaned back on his arms and kicked a foot up to rest his heel atop the pew in front of him—and then he laughed. It was a dry, rustling chuckle under the breath, but it was laughter, and Cain was a little perplexed by the way Levi shifted from embittered to cocky again, all in the blink of an eye. Clearly he was the type of man who did what he wanted, how he wanted, and when he wanted. It was almost sly, like a fox. Cain shifted, tapping an impatient finger on the butt of his revolver. Levi didn't exactly *look* like a whimsical killer either, in his sable-collared jacket, loose shirt and leather weapons belt. God, that blond hair, that dimpled smirk, and the silvery sound of belt buckles and buttons hidden along his body. His eyes sparked with the worst kind of intelligence, and Cain wanted to kiss him again already. Ah, this was bad. He couldn't mix business and pleasure, but damn it, he really wanted the pleasure.

"Oh, I don't need money," Levi insisted, almost cavalierly. His kind smile seemed patronizing in the throb of candlelight. "Rather... I won't accept it for an odd job such as this."

"Are those your *whims* talking?" Cain cut across the aisle, hatefully. Really he was just angry at himself, because he couldn't not like this Levi fellow. He despised it, and yet he was relieved by it, and he kept seeing the way Levi had moved through the crowd the night before, black mask and gold brocade waistcoat.

"Maybe." Levi grinned, and his fingers twitched in the air, his elbows propped on the back of the pew.

Cain wondered if he was a smoker or simply fidgeting.

"You could always… pay me with your company, my lord."

A chill zipped through Cain, sharp and fast. He blushed. He didn't know why he blushed. There had to be a catch here. He scoffed but had no words right away, so he just glowered at Levi and wished hard that he could feel more insulted. He could not. He was bewitched and ready to be selfish.

"I admit that I'm a little suspicious now, Levi," he spat. "That maybe you harbor clandestine intentions here, that you're trying to trick me. You're too charming, my friend. Too good-looking, too collected, too clever. Christ, even 'following whims,' who in their bloody right mind would refuse recompense from one of the wealthiest old families in New London?"

Levi laughed again. This time it infuriated Cain—for a moment, a brief moment, because then he was just too distracted by the way the candlelight pooled in Levi's face to really care about being offended. With an air of ready apology, like he'd expected to be so direly misunderstood, Levi husked, "Oh, no. Please, Earl Dietrich, if you don't trust me on my word, *shoot me right now*. Right here. End your doubt, and be troubled by the empty threat nevermore."

Cain was rendered speechless again. Damn the man and his unwavering charm, straight to hell. It was just too much. But really, he had to consider it in a realistic way. If Levi was a man with no personal loyalty in New London, who became who he was required to become upon assignment, contracting himself out to stay alive on these streets… wouldn't he be a master charmer too? That was dangerous— dangerous, and a little alluring.

Levi stood. Cain bristled and tightened his grip on his gun. But Levi just dropped into a low, respectful bow in the aisle outside Cain's pew. Cain scowled at him. He hated feeling transparent, especially before strangers, and that was exactly what Levi made him feel. Transparent, and childish, and utterly torn up inside.

The light from the vaulted windows hit Levi just right. It struck Cain motionless. Levi's dark eyes pierced into him as if they could see every filthy secret of his damned soul. His stare was sensual and flustering, but Cain didn't really mind, and he couldn't say why. It was thrilling, like a game. Again he felt the nascent suspicion that this lure was bound to stay for a while. It was like witchcraft, Levi's stare, because Cain could feel himself bending to it, willfully, ready to lay the rocky depths of his soul bare before Levi barged his way in.

"My lord," Levi whispered, smoothly cutting the silence, "judging by the eyes you give me, you like me a little too much. You like me more than you expected to, and you hate yourself for it. And that's why you'll agree to many more meetings with *the ace in your sleeve.*"

Cain choked on a laugh two notes shy of a scoff, but gathered composure again quickly. The nerve! He lifted his chin, narrowed his eyes, and spat, "As long as my hidden ace remembers his place. Any amount of *intrigue* will never change that, I promise."

"Oh, trust me," Levi murmured. "I will always remember my place so long as I am graced by your presence."

"You confuse me," Cain hissed, motioning for Levi to go away. "This meeting is over. Where are you from, Levi? How will I get in touch with you to meet again? This is stupid, you know, setting up a deal like this and lacking such basic information about you. You're not a *whore* or anything! You're employed by me now. But maybe anonymity is the smart way to do it. I don't know. I don't care."

Levi stood, smiling down at him. But his eyes were distant. He said nothing. He turned and began walking away, footsteps bouncing off the stone and woodwork of the nave. And Cain was left reeling, again. He frowned darkly, watching him go, foolishly turning his back on an armed stranger. *What a bastard.*

But lo and behold, Cain's fingers relaxed on his revolver, and Levi stopped near the sanctuary doors to say over his shoulder, "I'll send a packet with all the information you'll need to contact me. That way you can have it on file, as verification of our understanding here, which I presume is important to you. Therefore should you ever suspect me of betrayal, you'll have documented proof of our deal, evidence of my injustice. Is that satisfactory, my lord?"

"Why not?" Cain huffed, standing in turn among the pews. Levi eyed him in silence a moment longer, then pushed through the heavy doors and disappeared into the night outside.

Cain lingered, his thoughts torturing him.

He didn't like the way Levi had already wormed under his skin and made a home there, flustering him, managing to garner a bead of Cain's trust even amid strict and deeply structured misgivings.

But then the discomfort of being alone in the church began to creep in on him, and he hurried out to the mausoleum near the cemetery, where Aunt Ophelia and Mr. Renton loitered in waiting. Although Aunt Ophelia asked many questions, Cain couldn't get himself to even lie in reply as they made their way back to the Dietrich manor in the fog that pooled beneath the streetlamps.

SCENE TWO

THE MESSENGER navigated the flood of holiday festivities out on the streets and delivered the package to the Dietrich footman the next day, as promised. It was a string-tied package, including an apartment number at some lodgings on the Rue and a number of written references from previous contractors that Cain didn't care about at all. It seemed silly, references for a gunslinger. It seemed foolish for anyone to admit they'd hired a hit man at all. He didn't dwell on it.

The package contained books too, which was what caught his interest and held it the strongest.

There were two books—three of Poe's works bound in one leather volume: "The Masque of the Red Death," "The Spectacles," "The Fall of the House of Usher," and one individually published poem, "The Raven."

Cain scoffed, throwing the little paperback down on the package torn open on his desk.

"Whatever," he said, pushing the items to the side, where Weston waited patiently for directions. "Put the information into a file and throw the books on the shelf in my room. Now, to discuss more important matters...."

Uncles and agents were waiting. The package had interrupted a Dietrich meeting. Cain turned his attention back to the men smoking on the couch in his office as Weston hurried out with the papers and books. Uncle Bradley, and Mr. Renton, and Rodney, and Graham. And Aunt Ophelia, sifting through the shelved books in the other corner of the room, humming to herself and pretending not to be involved.

Cain sighed, cradling his head in his fingertips. He had to struggle not to get caught up in the memory of Levi in the church, candlelight and moonlight marrying so flawlessly in his mysterious eyes.

"So," Cain said, "Uncle Bradley, tell that railway we'll gladly help fund their new plans as long as we get at least twenty percent of their biggest profit. Mr. Graham, you still owe me that check from the last shipment of your *goods* from the Orient, and Rodney, Mr.

Renton—what's the word with the robberies on D'Laim? Are the Ruslanivs involved? Hey, are you still planning on screwing that Ruslaniv order from Bohemia? I mean, it's just a bunch of worthless junk for their wives and daughters. It doesn't really matter, does it? Even in silk and pearls, they'll always look cheap."

THE RUSLANIV library housed thousands of books.

The black walnut shelves followed the walls nearly to the vaulted ceiling, lamps casting light over the second floor and its banisters, stepstools, and ladders. Globes and an army of collected figurines sat among divans and leather sofas and the custom-carved oak desks. The room was a vast chamber, gothic and elaborate, dim even with its regal stone fireplaces continually ablaze. It might have been spooky to those who didn't find it either oppressive or elegant.

Near the servants' entry sat a candelabra on a smooth-surfaced marble table, and when this candelabra was twisted sharply to the left, there was a creak as muffled and ominous as if the large house were groaning, the snap of a hidden latch, and the screeching moan beneath the floorboards of a secret doorway opening onto a private lounge.

That was where Levi liked to hide away with a stack of books, the company of which never failed him, as the company of others almost always did.

And the secret room was exactly where Eliott found him on All Souls', the day after All Saints', when all the faithful were burning candles for the departed and crossing themselves before paintings of holy figures. It was just as Eliott had suspected, because this had been Levi's preferred haunt since he was ten years old, closing himself in with all the leather and velvet furniture and the iron-faced hearth.

Eliott jerked on the candelabra and as it was revealed, greeted the secret room with a sunny grin and one hand propped on a hip, the other waving idly.

"Hello," he singsonged. He waltzed in even though Levi refused to acknowledge his arrival. No, Levi kept his nose in the book he was reading, legs drawn up and crossed beneath him on the sofa, and Eliott lingered in the doorway, false shelves hanging open. His smile faltered. For a moment he was struck by a nostalgia drenched in something heavy and forlorn, and he couldn't place a rhyme or reason to it. There had been many a rainy, boring afternoon during which he'd searched the house over for Levi, only to find him holed up here and reading away—lore, history, theology, science, make-believe. And he'd always looked just like he did now, quiet and gone. Like there was no possible reason he could kill someone in cold blood, like there was no physical way he could manipulate someone as flawlessly as the devil himself, seductive and sweet and carefully calculated, painfully detailed in his motions and never satisfied until he was triumphant.

In the secret room, Levi seemed harmless, and sometimes Eliott wondered if, perhaps, that was what destiny had wanted of him in the first place.

Eliott heaved a dramatic sigh, skirting the back of the couch. He leaned down over Levi's shoulder, purposefully getting in the way. Levi was absorbed in one of Machiavelli's works, this one another long-winded and dreary piece that Eliott could have cared less about. *La Mandragola*, the page said at the top, and Eliott sighed another heavy sigh, in need of attention.

Eliott had been introduced as a cousin and joined the Ruslaniv family in their manor when his mother married Lord Ruslaniv's half brother nine years ago, he'd been little and pretty-eyed with thick auburn locks already past his ears, ready for nobility. And Levi had always found it so easy to ignore him. He ignored him again then, in the secret room. Surely he'd turned it into a talent.

Eliott reached for the book in Levi's hand—which Levi effortlessly held too far away for him to snatch from behind the sofa. So instead Eliott grabbed a handful of blond and moved it out of Levi's eyes. It was the normal pestering act until Levi finally gave in. Which he did eventually, as always, but over the years it had gone from well-mannered scowls and polite fists to obligated sighs and cold glances. Just such a chilly glance finally landed on Eliott, and Eliott smiled.

"Your father's looking for you," he announced, even before Levi opened his mouth. "Dinner's to start, and then prayers for the Faithful Departed, and after that, BLACK's meeting in the billiards room to clean guns. You coming?"

Levi's silence was curt. But maybe he was just traveling back from the places the books took him, wherever they were and however great they were to him. Far away, where brothers weren't dead traitors and families didn't kill out of vengeance like angry children smashing each other's toys out of spite. Levi closed his book and tossed it at the pile next to him.

"Of course," he grumbled.

"You've got a lot on your mind," Eliott guessed. He was focused on the crease between Levi's brows that had formed a permanent home there recently. "You only get that look when you're really eaten up by something. The last time you had it was before Quinton and the others left BLACK."

Levi left his books where they were, which was fine because nobody would touch them. He climbed off the sofa as if it were a great task to do so, motioning for Eliott to follow him as he slipped a hand into his hip pocket, just below that oversized sweater of his. It was old. It needed to be thrown out. The buttons had all come off at least once, and Eliott's mother had sewn them back on for him. Some of them weren't even the same buttons anymore.

Eliott was pretty sure the sweater had been Quinton's at one point.

DINNER IN the Ruslaniv manor was four-star, per usual, at the long polished oak table in the main dining hall. An ancient-looking iron chandelier hung, studded with fat red candles. The soft light set a rather castle-like feel, of being closed up and closed in, and the private All Souls' feast and prayers seemed almost ritualistic as they did every year—honor for the dead.

Eliott sat near his mother, bejeweled and equally as talkative as Eliott, and next to them were William and his parents. The Witch was present, and Petyr, the Blond One, and the men and women in between that connected each one of them to the Ruslaniv name.

At a corner to his father's left, Levi sat opposite his mother and ate his dinner in silence. And, probably, his mother was taking mental notes on how he was too withdrawn, too steely, giving off an air of melancholy not proper for his social stature.

Lord Ruslaniv didn't notice, of course. He was always talking, his boisterous voice and quixotic gestures booming down to the opposite end of the hall as servants hurried back and forth like animated pieces of furniture, just a handful of tiny cogs in the clockwork of the house.

In the billiards room afterward, BLACK wasn't just cleaning their guns and shooting the breeze.

There was talk of recent activities and current events, and as Levi polished the lever on one of his pump actions, a cigarette balanced on his lower lip and the smoke curling up, silky and smooth, into his hair, he felt all eyes fall on him as the talk turned to the latest scheme: infiltrating the Dietrich house.

"What's the news on that?" William prompted.

"How did St. Vincent's go?" the One with Glasses spoke up.

"Swell," Levi grumbled, flicking cigarette ash into an ornate crystal dish and refusing to meet any of his teammates' stares. He still felt rather detached and disoriented—he always felt that way when his intentional solitude in the library was interrupted. He just couldn't bring his mind back around, for eternities, it seemed. Or maybe he was just exhausted today.

"Just swell?" the Witch pressed.

Levi sighed. He shrugged and leaned back in the brown leather armchair and crossed one leg over the other, finally reviewing them all as if he were a man considering his possessions. He shrugged, offering a half-cocked smirk.

He wasn't sure why he dreaded saying it to them. In all honesty, he just wanted it to be his little secret. But the words simply pried their way out, and he felt guilty for confessing, like it was something meant to be private.

It wasn't, though. That was the problem.

"Well," he said, and he knew they were all on the edge of their seats. "Anonymity is a man's best friend, you see. And in my anonymity, I've been contracted by the Earl Dietrich as a freelance gunslinger."

Their laughter and sneers at the Earl's stupidity only made him feel worse for admitting it. He was protective over his own half of the scheme, for whatever reason. And before bed, when he said his last holiday prayers for the dead, he kissed his fingertips, made the sign of the cross, and pinched out the candles in his room feeling strangely dissatisfied with the world.

SCENE THREE

FINALLY, BY the end of Hallowmas—which was more an excuse to drink and be merry lately than anything to respect beyond tradition—Cain sent a message in code to the apartment on the Rue. He decided that if Levi was sharp enough to decode the hidden missive, he was a worthy enough candidate for hidden ace. Surely he'd be able to pick up on the nuances in the note—the missing letters in misspelled words stringing together to form their own message, and that message was that if Levi were still interested in the position, they should meet again at the place of Levi's most recent favorite activity. Praying.

So in truth it was a message in a message in a message, because Cain referred to Levi's self-confessed reinterest in the divine, and St. Vincent's at night it was again, with Security outside and the candles dancing among the velvet and painted-plaster faces and the fraying lattice on the doors of the confessionals.

With all the casual air of some fallen angel, in through the heavy church doors came Levi again, like a sprite of the candles and moonlight as Cain waited patiently under the altar, sitting with one leg hooked over the other. Guiltily, thoughts of an unfortunate betrothed were far from his mind, because he just could not get over the way Levi's collar danced on his sun-kissed throat and the perfect way his trousers fit at his narrow waist, weapons belt chattering away along another brocade waistcoat whose metallic threads glittered richly in the dark.

"You must be accustomed to wealthy employers," Cain remarked, eyes roaming Levi's gentlemanly dress.

"I prefer to be fashionable," Levi explained merrily.

Ah, those dark and devilish glances, that dimpled smirk, that loose blond hair darker at the crown. He was clean-shaven and he smelled like proper cologne, and Cain appreciated that. Too many freelance gunslingers were sloppy and lush.

It was the same wary and rigid back-and-forth as their first unorthodox meeting in the dim light of the sanctuary, with the holy figure on the crucifix grimacing down at them.

"I assume you have an extensive knowledge of bullets and barrels," Cain said, cocking a brow at Levi where he'd joined the invisible congregation in the second pew back from the altar. He listened patiently as Levi rattled off about this and that, a detailed introduction to his indeed extensive knowledge on guns and their use and care.

"And what do you think about bullet wounds?" Cain asked next.

"I think they're rather unfortunate," Levi conceded with a chuckle, to which Cain offered a light scoff and a roll of the eyes. Levi shrugged limply. "I've had a few," he confessed, meaning bullet wounds. "I've *seen* many more, however. Fatal, survivable. I know removal methods and tourniqueting methods, though given the choice, I would rather be at the hands of a doctor than depend on the rudimentary tactics I was taught."

"And what defenses are you trained in?"

"Militant style, my lord. The Persian, the Southend, the Muscovian, and the Albertonian, God bless Her Majesty."

"So you're well rounded, then, from traditional to vigilante."

"Afraid so, my lord."

"What's your favorite?" Cain asked, pinning Levi with a critical smirk. "What's your favorite method of fighting, friend?"

Levi was quiet for a long moment, like an animal in the wood sensing danger. Then he blushed—he truly blushed, and Cain thought, *Ah, so there is some weakness to this man's perfect pretense yet!*

"The Muscovian, sir," Levi murmured, and Cain laughed, because the Muscovian was perhaps the most cruel and rebellious style on the streets.

"The oath of the gunslinger?" Cain prompted next.

Levi smiled, recovering quickly from his little moment of sheepishness. He made the sign of the cross and blew a kiss to the plaster statue of the Virgin. "*Ad meliora, ad honorem, aut vincere aut mori.*"

Ah, he was a fine, flawless thing, wasn't he? Cain smiled and hoped he didn't look as dreamy as he felt, sitting on the steps of the altar with chin propped in hand, watching Levi as he uttered the militant oath of the gunslinger.

They were little tests, after all, and Levi was passing thus far. And what a lovely interview it was, with that underlying sexual tension still holding fast, left over from the very first night in the Dietrich courtyard. It seemed nothing could derail them from the course that night should have taken had they not been interrupted, and Levi's capabilities and insistence on working for Cain were just a few more small, attractive details.

Equally as important, however, was that Levi's character was becoming more and more real and more trustworthy to Cain.

Levi was like a thief in the night, a shadow, a nameless face in the crowd, the unfortunate type of man born to be nothing else but an ace in someone's sleeve. That much was quite clear to Cain. And he decided he was very lucky, actually, because he appreciated the Dietrich agents, and the Dietrich Security, and all his consultants—really, he did—but the dark thrill and cunning of having a street man was something he couldn't resist. He wanted all his openings covered, anyway. He didn't care if it was a dirty trick. He wanted the Ruslanivs terrified. And a street man would never try to give him unwanted advice either. A contracted hit man was both intimate and distant at the same time. What could be better?

"And what do you think of physical oddities?" Cain asked on the second night in a row that he met Levi at St. Vincent's to talk. He paced under the altar, his arms folded across his chest and revolvers tucked safely in against his sides.

Levi squinted at him in the dance of candlelight, otherwise staying utterly still. "Physical oddities?"

"Dismemberment. Blood. Deformities. Mutilations. Women with beards, pygmy folks, twins joined at the side. You know, general grotesquerie. Like they exploit at carnivals."

Levi seemed to chew on that one for a very long time, like he knew there was a particular answer Cain searched for. "I hope you are not asking to determine," he said deliberately, and in that lovely gravelly tone of his that was really starting to grow on Cain, "whether or not I judge you for your eyes."

Cain bristled. He hadn't expected that to be brought up. It was something he forgot about until someone looked at him funny, like he had a crooked collar or a stain on the sleeve. He blushed, fixing Levi with a cold and vulnerable stare. He had no words. Did he feel offended? Or did he feel embarrassed? Or, better yet, did he not really care at all? Eyes with almost no color… It wasn't that monstrous. Was it?

God, *was* that why he'd asked, without even knowing it?

"That's not why I'm asking," Cain spat, jaw tight. "I want to know if you can stomach more than just the regular blood and gore of street fights."

Levi's footsteps echoed as he moved out of the pews and over to the altar, strolling to a stop directly in front of Cain. Cain gave no rebuttal. He was still reeling, actually, face on fire and words stuck under a sore knot in his throat. He was so choked up, and he was not prepared for that.

Standing elevated on the altar steps, he was taller than Levi. The night's rain had left Levi's hair damp. Aunt Ophelia, Rodney, and Uncle Bradley were out there in the rain, which misted still beyond the safety of the church. Droplets had stuck to Levi's lashes too, like dew on a garden of roses. And, oh God, Cain wanted to kiss him.

There was that lust, a shuddering bass chord of dissolution, and it shot through him like all the worst nerves, hot and cold and merciless. He wanted those damp lashes to tickle him as their mouths met. He wanted to feel the graze of Levi's nice teeth. He wanted that handsome heat right up against him, dominating, crushing, stimulating, real and strong. It was torture, revisiting their masquerade rendezvous in the back of his head each time they met—the sweet taste of those lips, the manly pulse of that body.

Levi's eyes didn't reflect the candlelight; they held their own flame, and there was no denying Levi felt the same. That thrill of secrets and sin was like a tightly wound string on a violin, and quite suddenly then and there in the silence of the church, a brittle hush, that taut tension snapped, and Cain yielded to Levi's arm almost immediately as it snaked around his waist, fitting snugly at the base of his spine.

He swayed forward, Levi's arm winding him closer. Their mouths didn't crash together—no, the impulse was held in check. Instead Levi craned in and Cain accepted the kiss with parted lips, and it was not slow or shy, but just seemed to flow into being like a sigh or a subtle glance.

Ah, yes, he'd been waiting for this. Teeth and tongue and little breaths shivering from Levi's silky lower lip, and the rattle of buckles and whisper of brocade as they molded together under the damning shadows of the Virgin and Christ.

With both arms now, Levi hoisted Cain off the steps. Cain wasn't much smaller than him. He was pleased with how easily Levi lifted him and deposited him on the front pew as their mouths worked together. Levi sank down to his haunches before Cain and Cain let his knees twitch apart as he welcomed Levi forward with greedy fingers.

They kissed. Cain's heart was in his throat. He was hot and nervous and full of reckless lust, and the thrill tasted like metal on the back of his tongue. Levi nipped at his lower lip. He ripped open his waistcoat and unfastened Cain's shirt down the front, raining kisses on the pale skin there and driving Cain wild in the pew before him, like a wayward churchgoer moved to tears by the Mass. It felt so invigoratingly dirty, to be colliding like this under the watchful eyes of the angels and other holy figures. Felt utterly wrong and oh so good. Cain was a defiant thing by nature. Perhaps it came with the name.

Levi's lips were almost like silk, and he smelled like rain and gunpowder and something else exotic. He lit a Turkish cigarette, staying on his knees before Cain, and peered up at him through his lashes, without lifting his head, in that tender and carnal way that had ensnared Cain from the start. Cain curled his fingers in that soft, damp blond hair, the last of the heated shivers running through him as he convinced his more impulsive parts that this was as far as they were going tonight.

"What do you know about me?" Cain whispered.

"I'm sorry?" Levi whispered right back, lashes lowered on those deep eyes as he flicked cigarette ash over the edge of the pew and filled the sanctuary with smoke. It was like sinful incense.

"The feud between the Dietrichs and Ruslanivs," Cain reminded him, and when Levi stared back stupidly, Cain narrowed his eyes. "The feud itself runs deep. You know that, surely, even claiming neutrality as you do. But with *my* standing as the Dietrich heir, my focus is not on ancient bloodlust. My focus lies in the present." He paused. He shook his head, throwing his gaze elsewhere. He could feel the hatred coming down over his face, washing away all the good feelings. "You know what happened to me, don't you? It wasn't that long ago, and it was the talk of New London for months."

Levi stared at him, eyes heated and alive with that raw dark passion of his.

"My parents were murdered," Cain filled him in, coldly. "And I *know* the culprits are Ruslanivs in some way or another, because no petty street gang could manage something so calculated—killing my parents and making *my life* a living hell for as long as they did. I'm going to make them pay. I'm going to make them bow down and kiss my feet. That, Levi, is the Dietrich focus while I am head of the family. You get it now, I assume?"

Cain knew the weight of such a revelation was crushing. He understood the gravity of his place, and his motives, and his history, and his impetus. He was aware of the demands it made of others. But if Levi did not get it, then there was no point in using him for anything— scouting, patrolling, fighting, *nothing*.

"You will not rest until you've exacted your revenge," Levi surmised in a husky voice, Turkish cigarette smoldering between his knuckles and a new curious light sparking in his aloof eyes. "I understand."

He put out his cigarette against the front of the pew, a blatant desecration that pleased Cain for some reason.

"Do you?" Cain drilled. "Do you understand, Levi? I know you want me."

"Like you want me."

"I won't deny it. But I haven't contracted you as my paramour. I've contracted you as a fighter."

"Ah, my lord," Levi said quietly, "I told you before, I am whatever you want me to be."

Cain's face pinched. He felt the stab of a tiny and guilty fear, the dreadful idea that perhaps the primal throb of lust was unreciprocated. *I am whatever you want....* Did Levi mean to imply he was simply going along with all this for money—killing and sex for money? Could one really hold it past a man to do something so depraved? Did Levi pity him? Did he think he was lonely or something? A wave of cold, black, insulted rage crested in Cain quickly, to feel so pathetic and manipulated—or at least, to suspect as much.

"I want you to be honest with me," he whispered urgently through his teeth, before he realized the depth of the ache at such a suggestion.

Levi's eyes moved across his face, almost frantically. It was odd. It was like a man with a secret, looking a complication right in the eyes. Maybe it was just that he had been trying to convince himself he would be whatever Cain wanted, because it was too much for him to admit inside that the feelings were real. If freelance gunmen hadn't buried all their own feelings early in life. Maybe Cain was just lucky enough to have found the last gunslinger on the streets of New London who possessed a functioning moral compass—and whether it might one day spin wildly out of control like Cain's own, didn't matter.

"Honest...." Levi echoed, and Cain couldn't bully him any longer.

He could see the emotional struggle blazing in Levi's eyes. And he looked so little and defeated, on his knees before him, wide dark eyes and loose blond hair. It was like he was trying to piece together normal feelings inside, his own version of bruised and broken trust after the world had stomped on his soul too many times. Or so Cain guessed.

"Honest," he repeated. "Be honest with me. I told you I wouldn't accommodate lies, not even lies to yourself. You're not on your knees before me just for me, Levi. Admit it. There's something between us, and it has a mind of its own. There's no fighting it. So be my lover, and be my soldier, but don't ever let one influence the other—"

Levi kissed him again. Cain yielded to it. He'd said his piece. He'd meant every bit of it. He was satisfied with it.

And that was it, then.

That was the inevitable *click* of destiny's hammer, fate sealed by hungry kisses.

Bloodstained fate for two children with bloodstained hands, and they were helpless to change it.

SCENE FOUR

LEVI KNEW it was a secret and that he had to keep it. And keep it he did, because he was greedy.

Imagine, the notoriously young and unforgiving Earl Dietrich, a bloody queer!

That is, he didn't want BLACK to know what he knew about the Earl, because this twisted victory over the Earl's private moments was something he wanted to savor on his own for a while. He couldn't explain why, but he didn't try either. It was just that simple.

Be honest with me, the Earl had said, and God, that hurt so sweet and twisted.

It was much easier to take on the role of the Earl's hidden ace than he'd expected—slipping into character wholeheartedly was nothing—but at the same time, it was also quite taxing.

He'd passed the Earl's series of tests, and by Guy Fawkes Day—when all the nonpartisan folks of New London were burning little handmade popes and filling the streets with their silly hymns, a sea of candles lighting their crooked alleys and children prancing around in those awful white masks—the demands of his and BLACK's tentative little scheme became fully clear to Levi.

"You're not allowed on the manor grounds without an escort," the Earl outlined, standing on the front steps of St. Vincent's as the autumn rain fell in dismal slants through the fog and spill of light from the gas lamps along the street. A fierce wind had kicked up, and leaves danced along the slick cobblestones. *An escort.* It was a smart move. The Earl was no fool, not even after desperate kisses. Levi could see the Earl's security, shadows like ghosts slinking about the churchyard. Ah, what fun this was, to literally have the enemy in his grasp and make the conscious decision not to strike yet. After all, what *was* the rest of the plan? He'd have to speak with BLACK later…. If he felt like it, anyway.

"Understood, my lord," Levi whispered.

"We will meet every night here to discuss missions I have for you, and if we don't, I'll forward a message to you explaining why. I'll also send assignments."

We will meet every night here. Would they? Levi couldn't suppress a devious smile, a little ironic chuckle. Of course they would. Because there was a mutual *intrigue* between them, or however the Earl wanted to put it. Clever little imp.

Be honest with me.

As it turned out, by the very next day, the courier Levi had stationed on the Rue at the fake address came to him delivering a wax-sealed packet. It seemed the Earl already had assignments for his new ace in the sleeve.

There was no real fighting involved, and some part of Levi was thankful for that. Those on the streets knew him better than the Earl did, after all, and he would have hated to stumble upon some familiar face here or there and have to explain what he was doing and why he was doing it alone.

No, the Earl just wanted to use Levi like another set of eyes, peeking into the worst parts of New London that he himself was loath to enter.

First it was that Levi had to patrol a certain neighborhood where rather insignificant Ruslaniv gangs were terrorizing Dietrich working class, like packs of angry dogs chasing rabbits in and out of their burrows.

Then there was a minor dispute on the bankers' block down by Alderstower, and masked thieves outside Leroy Square, and a scouting mission that required Levi spend some time in the East Streets—strictly Ruslaniv territory, and slummy territory at that. It was already familiar to Levi. Cleveland Street and Dalley's Street and Old Yew Bailey Court where gamblers organized boxing matches and swordfights, Foxe's and Fleet's Inn, hotels and cafés and all other sorts of haunts the parties of nightlife loved. But still he was always on edge, waiting to be caught as this Other Levi, this spying spy—caught by those who knew him, or those who thought they knew him.

Not long after that the Earl asked him to infiltrate a notorious Ruslaniv dance hall where opium and cocaine barons spoke of their sales and deals, and he was to report back to the Dietrich house with overheard plans so the Dietrich men could hijack the barons' shipments and hold them over their heads.

It wasn't hard to roam the streets unchallenged by Lord Ruslaniv.

His father was confident in Levi's anonymity. He'd helped to fortify it, anyway, and after all that had happened over the years, he had stopped asking about anything. Now and then it was just a weary glance over breakfast or luncheon, when Levi was frequently hungover, or distracted, or sporting badges from a night of carousing—tousled hair, darkened eyes, yesterday's clothes, bloodied knuckles, broken blood vessels.

It was the same now, sneaking around for Earl Dietrich. The servants noticed Levi was gone, as did his father's dutiful agents. They whispered and exchanged looks when he came trudging through the marble halls at daybreak, exhausted and accepting guilt for their simplest suspicions. They'd go whispering to his father by midday about his antics, but they were clueless of just what *antics* he was up to lately. They judged him as a rowdy and ruthless young man, taking advantage of his good looks and fat wallet with the rest of the gang he'd inherited from his older brother, the older brother who actually *had* taken advantage of his good looks and fat wallet.

But that was the thing. Levi was not out gallivanting with the crew he'd inherited. And to avoid BLACK's questions as to why he didn't join them at all their favorite clubs and casinos, raising hell through New London as the Ruslanivs' most elusive and ominous gang….

That balancing act was the part that really grated on Levi's nerves.

"How's it going?" they'd ask carefully, with critical glances—Elliot, the Witch, William—when what they really meant was *What the devil are you doing with the Earl that makes him get you more than we do now?*

Their resentful glances made him giddy.

Be honest with me.

"Listen," Levi said, and he looked at Eliott because he knew Eliott would understand the urgency even if it went unexplained. "BLACK needs to lay low while I'm involved with the Earl. Let us become shadows in the night again, because we can't afford to draw attention to ourselves with as much as he's watching the streets."

He was twenty-four years old, the Honourable Lawrence Levi Ruslaniv, elusive heir of the Ruslaniv fortune and infamy, and until he'd been seven, his world had been one of governesses, the nursery, the high walls around the manor, the screams he sometimes heard outside those walls. Screams cursing his family, sometimes punctuated by gunshots.

He'd learned about his family's history and burdens for the first time when he was eight. He'd whispered to himself the reasons he couldn't go outside the Ruslaniv walls like he whispered his prayers. *Too dangerous, too dangerous, not safe for an heir.*

He'd pulled his first trigger when he was nine, entered into BLACK's training when he was twelve, killed for the first time when he was fifteen.

And now, almost ten years later, he was tangled up with an earl— *the* Earl, the son of the enemy, the new enemy *now*, apparently.

Wasn't it absolutely wild?

"THE SECURITY on the western wing of the manor might be a bit lax tonight," the Earl whispered, a sly hint in the dancing dark of St. Vincent's. He turned his eyes up so seductively, so serenely as they lingered close together in the shadows near the doors after another business meeting, which had quickly gone from talk of guns and politics to talk with tongue and teeth. It was curious how the hot golden glow of candles in the dark could seem like something hellish even in the dusty peace of the sanctuary. That light rendered the Earl utterly dark and dangerous-looking, a little devil, mastermind of these rendezvous, a vagrant agent of Cupid or Venus or some less well-intentioned deity sent to test the convictions and willpower of men. Such assignations were clearly nothing new to him. He knew what he was doing, what it meant, and how illicit it was. The utter lack of shyness in his eyes was mesmerizing, like staring into a flame as it changed colors. And God, but he was so hot and slim and perfect, and the way that knowing smirk passed across his face as he bid Levi good night and disappeared from the church, out into the dark…. Oh, it was just too good.

Levi turned and scowled up at the Virgin Mary, who peered down at him in such mournful disappointment.

"Shut up," he hissed, and pinched out one of her prayer candles before leaving.

Levi played along, because it was his duty to play along. The name of the game was to get on the Earl's good side, wasn't it?

He was surprised, of course. Who else in all of New London knew the young Earl's shameful inclinations? Who else in New London had the Earl romped with? Had Levi really expected anything else from someone who had seen the belly of Father Kelvin's brothel and lived to tell the tale, like the Earl had?

He wondered if the Earl would ever even mention as much to him. Certainly men were not required to disclose prior sins to present lovers.

Levi felt no guilt for it. At least, not for the deceit. He enjoyed the kisses and the playful tension, without a doubt. But he also felt somewhat detached, cold and in awe of himself for doing such things and not feeling a single moral shiver about it. It was a delicious game. He couldn't deny that. The kisses, the brush of fingertips, the racing of his heart, and the way the Earl's damning glances and secretive smirks just grabbed his desire by the throat…. Well, why couldn't he get a little pleasure out of it too?

Sitting in the dark on the Earl's balcony, or before the fire in his wide elegant room, or in the dancing shadows of St. Vincent's, they even talked together.

They talked of politics and business, and they gossiped about parties and people and the jokes of life in general. They talked about nothing. They talked about everything. They shared childhood memories, which Levi carefully edited on his part.

There was no stopping the inevitable befriending.

But Levi needed to know things.

It was vital to know things in his complex and duplicitous position.

"I find myself wondering," he prompted from below the Earl's balcony, where it was safe tonight, a beckoning bed partner like he had been when BLACK had urged him back over the wall almost a fortnight ago, "just how many men like me you've gobbled up as lovers?"

The Earl was in that oversize smoking jacket of his, the one his butler had draped over him the same night. He hoisted himself up to sit near the stone gargoyle, and it was either stupidity or an unwavering and rebellious bravery with which he left himself vulnerable on his balcony like that, stripped of formalities and security.

"I hope you're not accusing me of trickery and selfishness," the Earl called down, hooking his feet at the ankles and lounging against the gargoyle. It made Levi nervous to see him perched on the ledge like that. He did not want him to fall. "Don't be insulting. I like to think I'm rather selective about my bedmates."

"Selective, you say?"

"Yes, you should feel honored."

Levi was no stranger to utilizing surroundings, and with something just short of ease, he climbed the vines and uneven stones of the manor until he was beside the Earl's balcony. The Earl wore that ever-teasing smirk of his, the one that said Levi could trust him if he wanted to, but for all he knew, he could still just be using him for his own manly needs. The Earl slid away from the gargoyle and helped Levi over the stone and onto his balcony.

"I do feel honored," Levi replied.

"Are you jealous?" The Earl sounded eager. "You're jealous of those in my past?"

"I'm curious," Levi parried.

"Admit it," the Earl hissed, fingers digging into Levi's arm. His eyes were wide and lit by a mischievous light as he ducked out of view from the open bedroom doors, and that teasing smirk became a full greedy grin. "Admit it, you can't resist me."

Levi stared at him for a moment, not really feeling moved one way or the other, except for the fact that a natural and unaffiliated sort of lust was stirring between his hips, hardening and responding to the pure physical aspect of it all, which was numb and terrible in and of itself.

God, how easy it was to play this role. One might have thought it was his natural character. Closer, closer—he had to become indispensable to the Earl. He wasn't sure what drove him to such a goal, other than an obvious shift of power directly into his hands. He had to become a puppet master of sorts.

But all his words felt honest, and Levi wondered if he was getting too much into character.

I feel honored.

The Earl simply smiled a mysterious and distant smile, like the spider in the center of the web smiling over at the fly snared in its silk, lashes lowered on those ruthless pale eyes.

It was rather eerie. It sparked a fleeting misgiving in Levi. He thought—what if the Earl was bluffing too? What if this was all one grand chess game and neither would win because it was an endless dance with danger and dirty design?

But why was he afraid of that, if not only for the obvious loss of strategy? Certainly not because he was enjoying himself—

"I'm the Earl, for Christ's sake," the young man had scoffed another night on his balcony—reserved now for kisses in the chilly moonlight—wrapped in secrecy and bed furs. He took Levi's cigarette for a puff or two and then laughed a cold and entitled laugh, shaking his head. He was a beautiful spoiled brat, wasn't he?

"I'm the Earl," he said again. "I'll sneak around with whomever I please, and no one can stop me! Can't I enjoy myself now and again? I've romped with a few men here and there. Noblemen, hired men, noblemen's sons…. Listen, I just—I've tried to change, Levi. I have, I really have! But I can't get excited about pretty girls and their powdered cheeks and their tiny little hands. I just can't."

"It's your inclination, and you're the Earl," Levi echoed supportively, nodding thoughtfully as he took his Turkish cigarette back. "You can have whomever you please."

"Emily is to keep up appearances. It sounds merciless, but it's the truth. And one day, perhaps, I'll have to get an heir from her, but… what she doesn't know won't hurt her."

"Ah, rumor is powerful, though, my lord…."

"I much prefer men," the Earl countered tartly. "As you seem to, as well. Unless it's just another one of your 'I'll be your whatever you want' tricks. You're about as bad as a whore, you know that?"

"I love to read," Levi confessed. "I particularly enjoy darker fiction and the writings of Goethe and Paracelsus."

"Paracelsus," the Earl confirmed with a note of skepticism.

"And Aristotle," Levi added, smiling that damnable smile of his. But it felt sort of sad, so he shook it off. "And, I suppose, former acquaintances and employers saw me as *soft* because of such. My appetite for reading, that is."

"What do you think of love, Levi?" the Earl detoured, and it sounded like he was testing Levi again.

Levi's brow knotted. He smirked bitterly. He said, "Love is just another contract. A promise to devote your life to someone by their conditions. Love is monstrous. I've been in love twice, and twice alone. What about you?"

"Oh, you're as philosophical as a writer," the Earl complained wryly. "Maybe that should have been your chosen profession."

"Ah." Levi held up a finger. "But there's the catch, my lord. The key word is *chosen*."

"I don't believe in love at all," the Earl whispered, peering down his nose at Levi. "Love is a lie. We're all animals, and we submit to our instincts. We travel together, nest together, eat together, fight together, and breed together. And those of us who can't breed, well…." He blushed, smiling tartly. "Well, we still try. And we get the most enjoyment out of the lack of love in the world, now don't we?"

Levi laughed. The Earl smiled at him gratefully, like he was happy Levi agreed with him.

"Twice I've loved," Levi said again, boldly, but in a flat voice. "And twice that love destroyed me. Just another contract in a world where you find a cause and you serve it until it crushes your force of will—"

"So you've said."

The Earl cast another dark sultry glance at him, a simple flick of the lashes. Levi hated him for how much he loved it.

"Good, then," the Earl whispered. "Don't love me. It's not what I'm paying you for, anyway."

It was obvious that the Earl's self-worth and moral compass were deeply flawed, and Levi reveled in it. There was no judgment on his part.

It was from an objective sort of view that he enjoyed it all, really. Like a rook, watching from the rooftops. The Earl didn't know who he was fooling around with. That was the worst part, because Levi knew almost everything. The tragedy of the Earl's parents' slaughter, the feud between the families, the Earl's torture after being dumped into the hands of that joke Oberon and Father Kelvin, his raging and brutal thirst for revenge, while across New London, his enemy Lord Ruslaniv was growing so weary of the fighting....

All these things and their deep injustice kept Levi rapt in that sick, curious way of the aftermath. Like the way he stared at the bodies as they were taken away after a shoot-out, or the way the blood was washed off the cobblestones by boys paid to do it like they paid them to exterminate the rats in the worst parts of the city, bucket after bucket and splash after splash. Like the way he stared at his mother when his mother went off on any of her many heartbroken tangents about Quinton, and the past, and why couldn't things be like the past again?

"Why do you insist on sneaking around like this?"

"Are you an idiot?" The Earl looked at him like he really thought he was just that. "If they knew—if anyone knew—these types of things are not meant to be discussed in the daylight."

"But there's something else to it. There's something rebellious in you, rebellious against yourself, I think."

"Oh, so poetic, aren't you?" The Earl iced the words out, and there was a flat note of sarcasm in his voice. "Why must you bring it up? I'm just so tortured, I want to forget who I am before the sun rises and I'm forced to remember, that's all. You're *so* right, Levi."

The sarcasm fell away and the Earl turned a solemn gaze over to Levi, a little dimple between his brow like his pretense was faltering. Just a bit. Just enough to prove some sort of vulnerability in there beyond his rotten Machiavellian self-importance.

"Maybe," he whispered, "I'm just a normal man under all these curses, and I just want what I want and won't stop until I get it."

Oh God, was that stunning. The confession and the ghost of the frown, and the embittered pride at such an admission. Levi couldn't help it. There was that indifferent lust again, hot and ready. His clothes felt too tight. He fought the urge to rock forward. Instead he cornered the Earl in against the vines that hung down against the stone of his balcony, and with only the gargoyle as witness, Levi kissed him like he hadn't kissed anyone in a long time. Hard, and hungry, and impatient, holding his chin in place with one hand, and the Earl growled at him when the kisses bruised, so Levi let up a bit—but then the Earl's hands shot to the front of his trousers, and Levi yielded because it had been so long since he'd actually *wanted* to be touched. It was one thing to let himself be teased and pleased for a night's payment, but to be aroused for free....

"My lord—" he whispered, in a jagged and impatient way, because playing the lower class did get tiring after a while. The Earl covered his mouth with his hand roughly.

The Earl kissed his ear, such tantalizing heat in the cold of a brisk autumn night, and he whispered there in the most casual and uncaring way, "Call me Cain, for Christ's sake."

And Levi rather liked it.

SCENE FIVE

November trudged on toward December.

Like a little town of clockwork, every piece playing its rusty part, the city moved. Neighborhoods pulsed with the rattling, sauntering life of the cheesemongers and shop owners and milkmen meeting maids at back doors. In the blushing glow of sunrise, it was the same colorless, depressed, and mechanical routine. Gangs roamed the streets they'd claimed—dangerous ones and petty ones, and gangs of thieves and gangs of chimney sweeps. And the rich and elegant wallowed in their luxury, cursing the soggy weather for ruining their good fashion.

The office of the Dietrich house was flooded by business. There were annual agreements to sign, and leases to renew, and accounting to be finalized, and balls to be planned, and financial obligations to the Queen, and donations to be made to charities that reflected best on the family. The Dietrich protective services worked tirelessly, as they always had, to satisfy their young earl's demands when it came to patrolling the streets and combating the Ruslanivs. And with his slick street man Levi, Cain felt he was prevailing.

"I see you've made a new friend," Uncle Bradley commented under his breath one afternoon, when the sun peeked through the autumn clouds and he'd cracked a tall window open as he puffed on his pipe. Cain blushed and shrugged and nodded at the same time, glaring at his uncle in an admittedly childish fashion.

What was he supposed to say to that? It wasn't as if he had been keeping Levi a great secret. Weston knew what it meant when Cain said to him, "Don't knock after ten o'clock tonight," and what else were the guards supposed to think when their aloof master declared, "I have a visitor coming tonight. Don't shoot him."

"He's an unaffiliated gunslinger," Cain explained. "I can invite him to dinner if you'd like to meet him, but I'm trying to keep our house and the streets separated. You can only imagine why."

Uncle Bradley snorted in disdain. "I'm afraid of what it is—that you're using him as a pawn of yours to get him in bed, or getting him in bed to manipulate him as your pawn. And I'm not sure which is worse."

Secretly, Cain was galvanized by such accusations. But he promised his uncle there was nothing to worry about, and then his uncle just shook his head as if to say, *What am I to do with you, my outrageous little nephew?*

Aunt Ophelia and Uncle Bradley both had the unfortunate gift of being able to read him like an open book, Cain had found over the last few years. He couldn't go a single night having a little bit of fun without waking up the next day to their knowing stares, dry smiles, and suggestive looks with brows risen. Was it wrong to feel so giddy, being bad and not speaking of it with those who knew? No, perhaps it was only the way he was.

Aunt Ophelia had just *known* when he'd slept with Lord Arnaudet's son, and that dark-eyed violinist from a Christmas ball a year or so ago, and the handful of insignificant others whom he'd shared his bed with for the night and then tossed out the next morning. She'd sat him down at breakfast the next morning and shook her head at him, shameless and wanton as he was, wandering about with love bites on his throat.

"I understand you're a young man and your sensuality is something novel and great to you, but your life is not one grand pursuit of pleasure. You have responsibilities and obligations. And secrets have a way of getting out whether you want them to or not."

"It's not that," Cain had replied, casually picking at a scone. He'd been just shy of eighteen then, and like she'd said, distinctly aware of his own virile charm. "They mean nothing to me but a good time."

"You have a fiancée," his aunt had reminded.

"I'll sleep with whomever I please," Cain had argued. He'd been indignant and impertinent. It wasn't like he was a man on the prowl; he had a type, anyway. It was just that some nights, at some party or another, he drank a little more than his tiny body could handle, and he found himself chasing after someone, desperate for the final embrace that would make him feel accomplished and triumphant.

He could name his one-night flames on a hand and a half, anyway, each and every one of them from the last two years. There was Jasper, the dark-eyed violinist, who played like he'd sold his soul to the devil and made eyes at Cain from across the room more brazenly than Cain made eyes at him.

There was the Honourable Clem Arnaudet, and Julian Wellseley, who had probably been even more intoxicated than Cain the night they'd tangled together in the shadows of some Old Chelsea flat while a charity function had spun on into the night on the floor below.

There was Theo de Claire, who had wooed Cain for about a week in the code that men wooed men, before Cain had rolled his eyes and told him to get lost, satisfied with the revelation that Theo wasn't going to peak beyond the first night Cain had given in. The sex was the same and there was nothing exciting about that.

There'd been starry-eyed Reuben, who had given Cain flowers the morning after, and rugged, handsome Nicolo, who was a dancer, and there'd also been that rampsman Zane, who had made Cain feel like a stumbling little boy with a crush again, and Emily's cousin Oscar, who had gone down on his knees and smirked up at Cain like he knew this secret was just another part of the vast, unspoken, tangled and tattered web of secrets men held together.

All those little flames were disposable, and disposed of they'd been.

Ah, he was unforgivable. He knew that.

He also knew that if he'd been asked two weeks before, or two months, or certainly two years, just what he foresaw of his life, he would have readily replied, "I'll be alone, of course, because we're only ever alone in the end." And he would have believed it, and been utterly content with it.

But something about Levi was different, very different.

When was the last time he'd felt this way? Excited, and invigorated, and *alive*. Like there was something to look forward to, something worth the risk of the secret-keeping. Was it with Zane? But still, Zane had left an aftertaste in his mouth of self-hatred and fragility, the way Zane had played with his feelings and tried to reach into the pocket of the nobleman as he did so. Or was it with Clem, Lord Arnaudet's middle son, because that had been a grand game of Avoid the Servants and Lie to the Grown-ups and Laugh Too Hard When You're Red-Faced and Drunk, Because Clearly They Know Why You're Running Around the Manor Together But Won't Speak It Aloud.

The truth was that Cain couldn't remember the last time he'd looked forward to someone else's company so much, and he hated that it was so because he didn't know what to do with it.

Levi had slipped in through some chance crack in his carefully tended façade, invading the secret self that hid there.

It astonished him—and left him feeling rather weak and shy, staring at his paperwork and blushing alone with himself and his thoughts in his office at high tea—that he actually really wanted Levi to be his nighttime romp forever.

Picturing a future where he was married and content with the world seemed bleak and purposeless without Levi. Because Levi didn't judge him, and Levi saw right through him. Levi didn't condemn him. He listened to his angriest words and talked sense back into him. He didn't look at him in that quiet way as if to say, *You're severely damaged, but I can't point out just precisely how because you're the Earl.* Levi made him laugh, *real* laughter that hurt Cain's sides and left him breathless. Levi made him smile, and without thinking about it. Levi made him feel peaceful in the dark of St. Vincent's and on his balcony, and Levi was on his mind even in the daylight.

Levi was like a friend. Cain didn't want to get rid of him, ever. And that was a strange and unfamiliar longing that sank its claws into him and wouldn't let go.

"You won't want me in ten years, when I'm older and bitter and worse for the wear," Cain assumed, sitting with Levi outside his room and watching the sky change colors over New London as the sunrise struggled to shake off the blanket of night.

Levi uttered a little sympathetic sigh. "You won't love me when I'm no longer young and beautiful either," he argued, and it was the perfect moment for his confession, so Cain craned in, whispering along Levi's lower lip:

"Yes…. Levi, yes, I want you to be my dirty secret forever. I want to whisper your name to the priest day after day. That is, if I still saw the priest. I want it to be your name on my lips when I fall asleep at night and when I wake in the morning."

He was a little ashamed of the honesty, but honesty it was, and Levi gawked at him like it was slowly dawning on him in turn the brazen truth of Cain's words, all wrapped up in sensuality as they were.

Levi made him feel alive.

To feel that way was a deep and aching need, like a rebirth of hope that was cold and sharp.

"Are you trying to seduce me?" Levi teased in a whisper, with his little half-cocked smirk and hooded eyes. Cain threw back his head and laughed. Because yes, yes, for once, he was the one doing the charming, and he believed it had worked.

"I want you forever," Cain promised, breathless, wrapping his arms about Levi's shoulders.

Levi's smirk softened. A heated look sparked in his eyes.

At his touch Cain arched like a cat, lashes lowering. "I want you forever as my friend, and my fighter, and my lover."

There was a brisk silence, a tense pause.

"Only if you'll have me forever," Levi finally acquiesced, voice raw and ragged and full of surrender.

Ah, it seemed a worthy crusade now, but who could know if it would stand the test of time? Perhaps it wasn't going to last forever, perhaps it was, but in that moment the warm feelings inside felt infinite. Nothing else—responsibilities, engagements, revenge— nothing else seemed as important as kissing Levi long and soft before he climbed down from the balcony and left for his lodgings on the Rue.

And the next afternoon, utterly unaware of the dreamy look on his face, Cain smiled faintly and pointed to the papers his uncle and guards laid out before him in his office. He really needed to stop daydreaming and get on with business. Did everyone around him wonder why he was so calm and content today, so moved to smiles and nods instead of insults? Did it strike them as odd?

"St. Mikael's," Cain murmured, running a finger over the papers. Police records, documents from the Yard. St. Vincent's was so much nicer than St. Mikael's—no, stay on topic…. "Yes, the gang connected to what happened at St. Mikael's back then… I want to know who they are. Find them for me. They're going to die."

He waved a dismissive hand and turned around in his leather chair to prop his feet up against the windowsill behind his desk. Soon—but not soon enough—the meeting would be over. Thank God. All he wanted to do was look out at the brumal sun and think of Levi.

SCENE SIX

HE NEVER said, "Let's talk of the world." It just sort of happened.

"If heaven is for clean people, it's got to be empty. No one is clean. Not truly. We're sinful creatures, and that's the way it is," Cain declared, standing under the bowed face of the Virgin in the dark of St. Vincent's, where he'd wanted to meet again after Levi's task for the evening. There was something quite disturbing but beautiful about the way his guns looked along his sides. Levi had yet to actually see him use them.

"What if we all create our own hell?" Levi echoed, sprawled casually in the front pew, arms folded behind his head and one leg crossed over the other. He was rather enjoying this talk of theirs and the level of leisure in the evening, the lack of formalities between them. Was that what it was to actually court someone? Was that what they were tangled up in—courtship they wouldn't admit?

"Of course we do," Cain husked. "And we create our own demons, and our own monsters."

"Perhaps."

"Perhaps there is no hell, and no heaven either. What if the world is only what we make of it, and when we pray we're pleading with our own conscience?"

"Ah, tell me your soul really isn't as broken as that."

"Maybe it is. Maybe it isn't."

If it was so, Cain wore the misery well. He climbed onto the pew and sat on his knees next to Levi, narrowing those haunting, colorless eyes in his telltale sneaky way.

"What if we were to go at it, right here in this church, right now, like animals?" he prompted. "Do you think we'd be eternally damned?"

Levi threw back his head and laughed. Ah, it was moments where Cain was not a ruthless, vengeance-driven lord, but just a mischievous little boy—moments like that that absolutely took hold of Levi's heart.

"Turn down the lights, turn them down," Cain hissed as he led the way into his room from the balcony one night. His room was empty, of course, at his request for privacy, and he swatted at Levi grumpily a few times before conceding to his hungry kisses and reckless embrace from behind as Levi followed him into the room. Cain turned down his own lights until they were both just silhouettes in the moonlight.

"You don't want to see who you're giving yourself to?" Levi teased.

"Why the hell should I?" Cain retorted, and Levi understood that what he meant was the feeling was more important than what he saw. Or perhaps the shame and self-destruction still hovered in the light, waiting to come down upon him in the safety of the shadows.

A mess of groping hands and greedy mouths, they made it to Cain's wide four-poster bed, with its elaborate carvings in the black walnut, and the light from the fire danced under a marble mantel. Cain's skin was flawless lily-white and possibly just as soft once Levi got his nightshirt open, trailing his fingers up and down that taut, smooth chest. Toes curled in the thick coverlets. Cain clawed at Levi's waistcoat and collar with a wild and possessive abandon that just fired Levi up even hotter.

"I want you!" Cain gasped. "I must have you...."

"You'll have me, you said you always get what you want when you want it," Levi whispered back, and God, did it feel right to grind down against the stiff heat of Cain's sex.

The bedding rustled as they moved together, hips rocking. Cain covered his face with his arms when Levi dragged his thumbs over his nipples, and then he laughed and shoved his hands down the front of Levi's trousers. *Ah, release!* He was so hard and ready. Cain's fingers were skilled. With spit and more of that breathless laughter, he welcomed Levi—practically yanked him forward—and Cain rolled over on top, sending Levi in so deep, so far—

Well, it was no wonder Father Kelvin had cherished Cain so much.

Levi dreamt one night near the end of November of angels and choirboys and getting drunk on sacramental wine. Of bullets, and steam-powered gadgets, and pulling out the angels' wings feather by feather, and a little prince with a crown of thorns smiling down at skeletons. He dreamt of Finn, and at first he thought he was dreaming of the Earl.

It was a dreadful collision of feelings, of pain and an emptiness that might have been nostalgia or something else irretrievably lonely.

He dreamt of being fourteen, fresh out of training, and terrified he'd forget all he'd been taught before he could ever use it. The world had still been warm and full of sunlight back then, wandering through the stooping, sweeping, knotted old trees of the orchard, which had once been as big as the world before he'd learned a world existed outside the tall Ruslaniv walls. Finn was there, Finn in his plain tweed and charcoal-colored breeches, and Levi could still remember the way it felt to run his fingers through Finn's hair and listen to him talk about how he was jealous of the carriage hand, because the carriage hand didn't have to see the blood and the fighting like he did. Finn was one of Lord Ruslaniv's errand boys, and Levi could taste, as if he'd just tasted it the day before, that pouty lower lip. He could feel the way Finn had shivered against him and grabbed his wrists as if to push him away. But Finn, his father's errand boy, had only yanked him closer, and as the wind had rustled through the trees, they'd kissed and groaned and—and just like that, at the end of the summer, there was Levi's brother, Quinton, seething and snarling, and the way the blood had splattered across the paneled walls of Levi's old room had been strangely fascinating in the blue of the moonlight.

Levi awoke with a start, sweating and cold.

He threw back his furs and covers and moved swiftly out into the courtyard, where the stones of the patio were cold under his bare feet and the night was almost silent. He lit a cigarette and scowled up at the clouds over the moon. The Ruslaniv house was tranquil in such dead hours of the morning, when the sky was still black and nothing, no one, was stirring.

The foggy memory of Finn's face blended with Cain's, and Levi threw down his silver lighter and hissed, "*Shit.*"

He could deny it no longer.

He picked up his lighter again and slipped it into his breast pocket.

Something had changed.

It finally sank into Levi then, as he surveyed the Ruslaniv house washed in moonlight and smoked angrily, shivering and straining to shake the sick hold of his nightmare.

It sank into him that Cain Dietrich, the hated Earl, the morbid little prince wearing a crown of thorns, had become *worth* something to him. And any sense of loyalty to his own weary name could not make him hate that.

In fact, Levi *yearned* for it.

He yearned for Cain more fiercely than he'd yearned for anyone or anything in a very long time. He wanted him again and again, those damning glances and tricky smiles, and the way he laughed when they fell into bed together—and Quinton was gone, Quinton was long gone, so what was there to be afraid of?

Well, damn it all.

This was troublesome, wasn't it?

SCENE SEVEN

"HELLO, PRINCE Charming."

The Witch smiled at him over the pianoforte. The smile was harsh, just a shade or two of hate short of a sneer. Her blouse was unfastened over whalebone and leather, per usual, but the sight of too much bosom was one Levi had become well desensitized to.

He held his fingers over the keyboard, offering her the most uninterested stare he could muster. Behind her was William, looking uncomfortable as always. Eliott was nowhere to be seen. Across the hall, in the yawning threshold to the darkled salon, the Blond One and the One with Glasses lingered against the marble—Claude, Levi had discovered again the other night while cracking into his second bottle of Muscovian liquor. Perhaps it wasn't right to constantly forget the names of his own gang, but oh well.

"Yes?" Levi looked back at the Witch.

Her smile had crossed the line and become a pure simper, a few curls come loose from her tight braid and bouncing at her ears. The dark beauty mark on her left cheek made her look all the more ascetic. Gypsy, almost. She drummed her fingers atop the pianoforte, a sharp staccato of nails.

"We were just curious, darling," she purred, and it was a shame the sound of it was so untrustworthy. "It's been nearly a month and a half now. You're never around. You're gone all night. You're neglecting your own duties as our commander. You won't speak of what you do, except to say that you're a 'hidden ace' and 'a make-believe gunslinger for hire.' Whatever. So how goes plan F, as it seems to be monopolizing so much of your precious time and energy?"

"Who named it plan F?" William's mouth twisted in doubt, but it might have just been his default frown of discomfort. The Witch didn't even spare him a glance. She rolled big brown eyes around sarcastically before settling them on Levi again, talking as if he'd been the one who'd asked.

"Plan *F* for *Fake*. Faking a friendship with the Earl, and so on. Snatching up his trust like a mole. You keep telling us it's getting on smoothly, there's no suspicions on his part, but—"

The Witch's nose wrinkled in a girlish snarl. Behind her, across the front hall in the marble archway to the salon, the Blond One started laughing from behind Claude's shoulder. Claude had pulled him tight in a suggestive embrace; everyone knew they were closer than they should have been. They must have been bored with the conversation already.

"—I want a serious update, Levi. *We* want a serious update. So, what's the scoop, oh fearful and respected leader?"

Oh, he just loved it, the way she still managed to slip the mockery in there. Levi saw William fidget in the periphery. He sighed, digging around for the will to involve himself again as he met the Witch's eyes. God, they all exhausted him sometimes. It wasn't so much reluctance or hesitance as it was a simple loathing of the people around him, and a little stab of distress as he reminded himself his affairs with the Dietrich heir were being closely monitored. He was not the only master of this game he played.

But perhaps he was, because he was the leader of BLACK. Levi shifted, brushing a finger along a black key. He divulged, "A bridge of trust has been built between us—a *strong* bridge of trust. Which, I'll remind you, is an incredibly difficult task to undertake with the Earl Dietrich. It's taken this long to do so, anyway. But the longer that trust is nurtured, the easier it will be to take advantage of it."

The Witch opened her mouth, and Levi narrowed his eyes. He didn't let her speak. He was tired of listening to her.

"And," he said curtly, "I would know more than you at this point that he's a complex young man who requires much patience and vigilant exploration. I thought this was understood already. I thought that was why *I* was assigned to this little *plan F* of ours—because we all know I'm the only one of us who could manage such careful manipulation. God knows your temper and impulsiveness would have betrayed you right away, Witch. Listen, it's only a matter of time now until we can utilize this bridge of trust. It's just not the *right* time yet. I'm keeping wary, though, I promise. Are you satisfied?"

The Witch's mouth shut with a sharp *click* of the teeth and she frowned, less severely and more in honest consideration of this. Her fingertips drummed away, nails tapping. William shifted with a terse sigh behind her. Claude and the Blond One—Petyr—were fooling around near the salon, snickering and whispering like brothers avoiding bedtime.

"I don't understand you," the Witch whispered over the big pianoforte, "and sometimes that scares me. You should thank Oberon every night for convincing me to trust you."

Levi offered a thin smile, lashes lowering. He meant no real ill will as he murmured, "He crosses your mind enough, why don't you thank him for me?"

The Witch shot him a look that was supposed to be sour, but her carefully constructed mask was failing and the knot in her throat was obvious. She turned sharply on a heel, the butt of her gun showing above the pockets of her trousers. Ah, a woman in trousers. It was shocking in the best way. She hooked her fingers in William's sleeve, dragging him with her, and William sent Levi a glance that promised he'd talk to him further later.

Their footsteps bounced off the highest corners of the hall, voices hissing whispers as they met up with the other two. They all disappeared into the dark, dank salon, drifting away into other corners of the house, and Levi gawked at the keys on the pianoforte for a moment. Faded black, yellowed white, like the teeth of an old man, stained by too many fingers and years of sunlight pouring in through the vast multipaned windows around the room. What a sight tonight through those windows: the dark of night, the angry black shadows of trees in the fall, and the high, inescapable walls of the Ruslaniv estate.

Levi thought about BLACK. He thought about their lackadaisical missions, their capers—so safe and juvenile compared to those of the previous BLACK.

And he thought of his responsibility as the new leader—to them, as well as to his father and his name. *Plan F*, the Witch had called it.

Levi thought about the previous BLACK—his brother Quinton, Wolfe, Red, Vyncent, Oberon. Oberon had been the only one Levi had really liked back then. It was still scalded into Levi's memories, like staring at the sun too long, the way half of Oberon's arm had fallen on one side of the street as he'd reached for the Witch with the other. His blood had stained the same cobbles as Rosalie's. And Levi had been forced to pull the Witch away after Oberon's only hand finally dropped and the Dietrich "protective services"—done away with after the earl and his wife were murdered and the feud fell to uncultivated brutality—ran like the bunch of cowards they were.

Levi thought of the remaining heir of the Dietrichs and the way he looked when he spoke, regal and nostalgic, tragic and beautiful at the same time. *Cain.* Pale eyes, wispy layers of dark hair around a soft, perfect face, and the way he kissed, the way he smiled, the way he laughed. He was pretty like death, macabre and unconquerable, and all those unfailing truths of life thrown back in a man's face.

Levi thought about the young earl's revenge—the way his eyes flashed with hatred when he spoke of it, and when their wet mouths drew apart and breaths tumbled out after being held. With trembling fingers, he touched Levi's face. Cain was fever hot against Levi's chest, a silence between them in which Levi could feel his heartbeat.

The way the Earl had looked when he'd found his parents dead—the way he'd trudged along, dazed and stupid, to Wolfe and Quinton and Oberon with their open hands and wily smiles. They'd taken him to Kelvin's then, and Levi had crumpled down and gotten sick with guilt that sludgy afternoon above Lovers' Lane because he hadn't stopped them.

He hadn't stopped them!

Levi's mouth tightened, but he wouldn't surrender to the scowl. He slammed the cover down over the keyboard, a *bang*, which echoed in the nooks and crannies of the gilded hall as he shoved away from the pianoforte and stormed swiftly off, away from the silence, as if he might really flee his thoughts.

Finn, and Rosalie, and Cain Dietrich.

Ah, this had become something far more complicated than he'd ever expected. What would BLACK do if they knew how tangled this had all become? What would they say?

They couldn't know. They couldn't find out.

He was not in this for BLACK anymore.

He was in this for himself. And he was determined to keep it that way.

SCENE EIGHT

"WE'RE SORRY for the interruption, my lord."

"Don't be. It was a stifling luncheon. Look, we have a few minutes. We were to have a meeting after I was through with Miss Emily, anyway. Regale me now as we move."

"Yes, right, we believe the ensemble calls itself 'BLACK.'"

"BLACK. Like the color?"

Footsteps were quick, an urgent clip through puddles, across uneven flagstone, following the shortcuts through jumbled, grimy alleys and between buildings to avoid the mayhem on the main streets—the panic, the plebeians.

There'd been a gunfight.

"Yes. And, listen to this. It's a gang organized by the Ruslaniv house itself, not mere civilians! The group has been relatively inactive and elusive, most likely because they've changed members since then, but the reasons for this are unknown and the former members have been banished from New London, that we're aware of."

The grip of Aunt Ophelia's pistol matched the vibrant scarlet of her blouse. She followed Cain, and around them were the Dietrich protective services, like obedient hunting hounds—Mr. Collins, Percy, Hazel, and the Persians, whispering in that smooth exotic cadence of theirs. The newest recruit, a rough retired hit man named Dominic, tailed Cain's father's favorite watchdogs—whom Cain had inherited with the house and the legacy—Rodney and Graham.

Down by Dmitri's Pavilion, a rather brutal gunfight had shattered the eventless afternoon, erupting at a rally against the House of Lords. The House of Lords was political if only by the honor the Queen had bestowed upon them with such a title: that handful of the oldest and wealthiest noble families in New London, who kept in place the system of class the working men despised. Two Lords of the House were tangled in the bloodiest feud between noble names since the High War of the Roses centuries ago—and they were the Dietrichs and Ruslanivs.

The Dietrich party moved in like a pack of wolves. The closer they got to the scene, the louder the commotion on the street became.

Rodney shook his head, eyes narrowed. "The names of these former gang members can be traced to St. Mikael's, and if what you suspect is true, then—"

"*Fuck*!" Cain hissed, and the meeting on the go drew to a temporary close as they emerged onto Dmitri's Pavilion.

What a shoddy thoroughfare the brawl had taken place in. Cain's men circled tighter around him until he had to elbow them aside to survey the carnage. The sunlight was hot and bright on his eyes. Officers and volunteers held the hysterical throngs back, and the air was a cacophony of wails and shouts—demands for answers, demands for peace, threats and promises and shrieks alike.

The bodies still lay on the street, blood drying on the cobbles, and the scent of death and hysteria bloomed in the air.

Where was Levi?

The Rue wasn't far from Dmitri's Pavilion. Surely Levi, the Dietrich street spy, would catch wind of the news as it spread like wildfire through the city and appear on the scene. Surely he'd be worried. Surely he would understand the sense of crisis and show up, like a thief in the night, like the shadow in the crowd that he was, ready for any and all of Cain's commands—

Her Majesty's right-hand man stood with his blades and guns obvious on his sides. The Ruslaniv responders crowded around him as they spoke. Cain scoffed. He couldn't quell the rage that smoldered in him at so much as having to be in the same proximity as those dogs.

Emily had looked at him with such fear in her eyes when Security had barged in to luncheon and announced there'd been another big fight. Cain hadn't wanted to appear for it, but they'd insisted.

"Dietrichs and Ruslanivs have been killed," Graham and Uncle Bradley had urged. "It was a pointless slaughter of almost military caliber. Lord Dietrich, you *must* make an appearance. The Queen's agent is there and requests all Lords of the House."

Infuriated as he was that whatever fight had gone down had been savage enough to summon Her Majesty's agent and forced him to be face-to-face with Ruslaniv nobility, Cain managed to sustain a shred of civility as, followed by his men, he made his way forth to speak to the Queen's officer. He stepped over bodies, avoiding dark splashes of blood and ignoring the general roar of the public. The sun was blinding in the pale sky. The air was brisk and refreshing until one gave it a sniff. It was a typical December day, and Her Majesty's public agent, in the midst of the Ruslaniv responders, caught sight of Cain and curled into a disparaging smile.

"Oh, the Dietrichs have decided to join us!" he cried, clapping his hands together. Cain's scowl pinched tighter in distaste.

"Sir Graye," he returned the condemnation-coated greeting. "It's a pleasure. My apologies for being late. I was at luncheon with a lady."

He could feel glances thrown from the Ruslaniv family, but he refused to acknowledge them beyond the mutual struggle to remain well mannered in front of the Queen's envoy. He pushed through his men and circled around Sir Graye, measuring the bloodshed.

Three young men, slicked-back hair and jackets lined with red braid—a Ruslaniv gang. Two others, in navy blue with silver buttons—Dietrich citizens. Quite a few uninvolved citizens lay scattered about, and one authority caught in the crossfire, dead hands limp on the street. There was a little girl, brilliant red staining her dress. Her soiled doll lay a few feet from her motionless fingertips, and Cain swallowed a sickened thought of gratitude that she had fallen facedown, because, imagine, her eyes probably weren't even closed.

"This is disgraceful!" someone spat from their place inside the noble crowd. Cain glanced up with a vicious scowl, searching out and finding the eyes of Lord Ruslaniv before just panning the lot of them and hoping to frighten the one who'd complained. The four other Lords of the House and all their defensive men—Ruslanivs, Desrosiers, Gotthards, Arnaudets. In his periphery, the Dietrich protective services lingered attentively, observing the grisly scene.

"Do we know who opened fire?" Cain hissed. "Ruslaniv, or Dietrich?"

"It was a Dietrich gang," Sir Graye declared with a judgmental sniff, adjusting the lapels of his white suit. "What we've gathered is that it was a dispute within the rally, which turned to gunfire, and innocent civilians were caught between. When more officials arrived, the gangs had already dispersed. The injured have been collected and taken for medical care. What remains now is just the consequence of such ill morality."

Sir Graye paused briefly, and it was tacit between them all, between any who had eyes to see, that it was only the dead who remained, littered so carelessly on the street.

"So," Sir Graye sighed, "noble families, what do you suggest we do about this, here?"

"What do you mean, what do we do about this?" Lord Ruslaniv sputtered. "What are we supposed to do, *patrol the streets for you*? That's what officers are for!"

"Agreed," Cain said over the roar of the public. He met Lord Ruslaniv's eyes for a moment of brief, arbitrary understanding. "He has a point, Sir Graye. What the hell can we do? We can't control the gangs."

"Lead by example," Sir Graye announced with an offhanded shrug. He had always been far too complacent, too high above society to fully care. Cain despised it. It was the reason he always hated inviting Her Majesty to certain balls; Graye was always with her, and always sneering.

"We *already* lead by example!" Lord Ruslaniv cried in positive outrage. Some of the surrounding civilians uttered murmurs of alarm and shouts of disagreement.

"Sign another peace treaty, for Christ's sake," the Viscount Arnaudet spat, mousy mustachio twitching over a scowl of contempt.

"Just arrest any man not of high birth who keeps a weapon!" Lord Desrosiers shook his head as if exasperated. "I've petitioned for this before. We shouldn't put weapons in people's hands unless they have some warrant of sorts."

It was like an argument between brothers, and Cain was the spoiled rotten baby while Lord Ruslaniv was the exhausted first in line. All the others were the fired-up boys in between with nothing to lose and nothing to prove, and Sir Graye was the tutor who had to talk them all down or throw them in time-out. It was always like this, grumpy old men in fine suits and house jewels shuffling around, secretly envying the only House Lord under twenty-five, while that young House Lord disdained them all.

Cain tried not to feel sympathy when he noticed how weary and bruised by the weight of it all Lord Ruslaniv looked.

"What about another set of peace laws? The last was in 1881, but they've fallen to pieces now."

"Those never work, anyway," Cain reminded him curtly. The not so jolly old man squinted over at him in scrutiny. Cain returned the stare, mouth in a thin line. His eyes travelled the ranks behind Lord Ruslaniv again as his thoughts ran. What exactly did the Queen think they could do? There was no possible way to control the gangs in the city, and there was absolutely no way he'd agree to leading by example. How could one possibly carry out revenge as a role model?

Perhaps he could ask Levi what he thought about it, once the son of a bitch arrived. He could ask him his point of view, being a relatively neutral citizen and all. He could see what Levi thought was the best way to communicate with the gangs. Perhaps if he could create a solid line of communication to the citizens, with Levi as their bridge, they could work together as one united force against the Ruslaniv family instead of inconsistent, scattered ideas and savage loyalty, and then he could—

Ah, there was Levi. He stood behind the Ruslanivs, hunched deep in a fur-collared coat, speaking in a low and furtive way with some of the men and women in the Ruslaniv party as if he knew them.

Actually, Cain knew the men and women he spoke with too.

A conscious and dramatic anguish brimmed within him, evident in the sick flutter of his heart and his gut. His fingers almost slipped on his gun. His stomach dropped, and for just a moment or two, he couldn't understand what he was seeing.

Black, fur-collared militia jackets, and a little Blond One, and one with thick red hair, unique enough that Cain recognized it. He recognized it from the roof of the Dietrich manor the night of the All Hallows' masquerade.

Either Levi was a flawless spy, or—

Confirming what Cain already dreaded was true, Levi turned to cast a stormy glance back at the Lords of the House and the Queen's agent, and as subtle as it was, it was also unfortunate enough to be perfectly aligned with Cain's disbelieving stare.

Cain noticed the way the shadows of Levi's eyes were copper brown in the sunlight, and he thought it was very attractive. But they weren't the same eyes Levi had ever turned on Cain before. They widened, if ever so slightly, with subdued recognition, and then Levi looked away again, just as smoothly, as if nothing had happened, no contact made, no realizations exchanged.

Cain went rigid with a sharp stab of shock.

His ears rang. All the world seemed to quiet, to retreat from the thunder of his pulse in his ears.

A sick, rotten fury bubbled up from deep within, a harrowing sense of betrayal, of lies and deceit, and the arguments between Sir Graye and the incensed lords didn't matter to him anymore. The solution to this mess didn't matter to him anymore. He withdrew from it. He could only stare, feeling the shock make its way down his body like poison, icy and sickening.

Was Levi a spy acting as a spy?

Was he really that capable of deceit and manipulation? Surely, God damn it, and Cain had been stupid enough to fall fast and hard for it! Good God, what if Levi had been a distraction for the attackers at the ball? Worse yet, what if his connection to Cain was part of some dark collusion?

But the worst by far was—Christ Almighty, *it's a gang organized by the Ruslaniv house itself, not mere civilians*—what if it was BLACK over there?

Cain wanted to vomit.

He felt little again. Little, and senseless, and naive, and abused.

Sir Graye's suit was too white, blinding in the sunlight. Cain squinted against it as Sir Graye spoke, and he and the Ruslaniv dogs and the other selfish lords stared at Cain like they waited for him to say something, but Cain hadn't heard a single word. The howl of the world was drowned out by the lurching thud of his heart, a steady bass chord of panic. The crowd around the scene pulsed. The air bit his skin, already so cold. Everyone looked at him, waiting, waiting.

His knees shook, and the dead little girl on the street wouldn't stop reaching for her bloody doll.

Cain turned with a scuff of the heel. He almost tripped over a fallen Dietrich supporter. Rodney reached for him, but Cain shook him off. Aunt Ophelia looked at him, distraught, but she knew far better and hurried forward to take his place, talking to Sir Graye and Lord Ruslaniv. Uncle Bradley stepped up beside her, well aware of a woman's standing in politics, even if she wore breeches better than a man could.

Cain found himself back in the alleys, the rumble of the distressed public deafening even between the buildings.

But he was alone, and grateful to be alone, amid cracked walls and dripping pipes and uneven paths.

And this, this was far too close to the bad part of town for his comfort. This was where rats scurried and dead dogs floated in the mire and scabby little children begged for food while their mothers bedded for money. This was where gangs of poor men killed for more, and there was filth and disease and desperate, impoverished, broken souls.

He found himself in Lovers' Lane. What a sick tribute to the tortured soul. This was where the bodies would have been dumped, had the officials not interrupted when they had. He knew that. Everyone knew that. And on that crack, *there*, his mother had been thrown. He would never forget it, every time he saw that particular jut of broken concrete.

Step on a crack, break your mother's back.

The undertaker was there. He waddled around with his cart, and he stopped just to watch the way the head of the Dietrichs staggered through the alley, dazed and detached. The way he stopped at the crack in the ground that haunted him, and squatted down on shaking legs and held his mouth, trying to muffle the cries he could no longer restrain.

Sounds of bitter agony, somewhere raw between despair and rage, nothing more than a little man with guns on his back huddled in Lovers' Lane, sobbing from the memories and the betrayal.

The undertaker lifted a hand to his mouth and chuckled.

ACT THREE
REMINISCE, REGRET

O father, what a hell of witchcraft lies in the small orb of one particular tear.
William Shakespeare, *A Lover's Complaint*

SCENE ONE

THE ONLY child of the former Earl Dietrich was a pampered boy.

He was a beautiful baby, for one, and when he was christened, he drowned in more *oohs* and *aahs* than holy water. He grew up among butlers and maids who liked to wink at him and ruffle his hair in the hallways, and a governess who somehow caught up with him whenever he wandered off, and tutors who reveled in how he soaked up his lessons just in time for playtime yet the next day always remembered what he'd learned. The gossiping public outside the gates of the manor or flooding the halls during banquets and parties were as much part of the house as the uncles and agents who smoked in the library and called him *Liebling*. His mother and father held their chins high and wore expensive fashion and sat to either side of him at the long walnut dining table.

Cain's father was quiet in an intelligent way. He always smiled, but behind every smile there seemed deep and relentless contemplation. Dietrich business kept his schedule near to unmanageable, and yet when Cain passed him in the halls his father had always had time to swing him up onto his shoulders for a moment or two of *How are you, love?* and *I hope you're being a good boy* before returning him to Maggie the governess and hurrying on to his office again.

Cain watched him with a shy little understanding that his father was *important*, and that made him *important* too. That made him proud.

Cain's mother was beautiful and soft in every way, and sometimes she'd joined him in his nursery and made voices for his painted soldiers and wooden marionettes while Maggie sat blushing in the corner. Sometimes his mother had joined him outside, in the garden, and she'd named off different flowers and what they symbolized. Sometimes she'd just sat in her boudoir and brushed her long hair, staring out the window, and Cain had liked to sit on her lap while she did that because it made him feel like he was part of her listlessness, the private thoughts that took her away from the world for long periods of time. He liked the way her skin smelled, sweet like powder and perfumes. The way her pretty gowns with the blue buttons and the Dietrich crest felt, the cameo at her throat, and all the taffeta and brocade and folds of a perfectly white blouse. She had thin hands with clean nails and jutting wrist bones, and Cain had liked the way they felt when they ran through his hair.

Cain had wanted for nothing. He'd gotten every snack he'd asked for, sneaking around the kitchen. The manor had been a vast kingdom to explore and the big German wolf of a dog like a living stuffed animal to cuddle with. When he was scared at night, his mother and father had let him tiptoe into their room and join them in their massive bed, his father a wall of security on one side and his mother a blonde, blue-eyed guardian angel on the other, running her fingers through his hair. The dog would follow him and sleep at their feet.

They went to the church in Molching Court on holidays and feast days, with the other highborn. When they walked on the streets, the Dietrich protective services had been like a moving wall around them. Cain had sometimes liked to peek between their legs, out at the regular people on the streets, and his Uncle Bradley had laughed and patted his head and pushed him back between his mother and father.

He'd had one friend to play with, a boy with the last name Byron. But when he was almost eight, the Byron family stopped coming for tea every Tuesday, Thursday, and Saturday, and Cain had heard his mother and father fighting in his father's office, and he'd wondered if anybody knew that he saw the way his mother was crying as she stormed back to her boudoir and slammed the doors shut.

His father hired the Persians on his eighth birthday, and they were entertainers. Cain had been caught so rapt in their antics and the look of foreign culture about them that he'd forgotten about his crème caramel and just stared. The one with thick black curls was just a little bit older than him, and although many of his father's friends and members of the house had whispered in disapproval of the Persians replacing the Byron boy as Cain's friends, his father had smiled and held Cain up on his shoulder and declared that the Persian entertainers would get a room on the second floor, by the servants' quarters, like proper Dietrich men.

By the time he was ten, Cain was well versed in the history of the feud between the Dietrichs and Ruslanivs, the current (albeit precarious) peace laws, and the devilry of the filthy Ruslaniv family. The tutor, Mr. Quinn, cracked out the texts on sciences and theology.

Mrs. Colvender moved Cain from German to Latin to French. Miss Willford had announced her little pupil was almost a prodigy in the elementary lessons of violin and piano, but that his painting could use a little practice, and Mr. Ashleigh mentioned a junior fencing competition coming up in the winter.

Cain spent his afternoons in the garden with the Persians, or practicing his schoolwork, or playing in the billiards room while the men talked politics. He joined his mother in her boudoir with a book after dinner, and he liked eavesdropping on his father's meetings, curled up before the fire, pretending to read the weekly comic magazines. Sometimes he accompanied Aunt Ophelia and the others of the Dietrich protective services on an excursion to start exposing him to the grave reality of the world outside the manor. His father taught him to work with a revolver and pistol. All his father's associates laughed in proud surprise at Cain's adolescent success with a gun, blowing through target practices during hunt weekends. But that world of Dietrich business was still far away, like a fairy tale. He went out with his aunt and the protective services, but he was back in time for dinner and a bath before bed. He never shot a gun at anyone. He couldn't imagine doing so.

He was naive, and if he'd known better then, he would have fixed it fast.

There were occasional *talks* in his father's den, when he really got out of line, and once he was fifteen, Cain didn't sit on his mother's lap when she grew wistful. He just lingered in the corner of her room, feeling the sadness on the air and not understanding what it was for. The dog's fur was always warm and soft between his toes, and its wet nose pressed to his cheek woke him up in the mornings just before the servants entered.

AND THEN the great dazzling tapestry of his life had snagged on some evil corner of fate and begun to rapidly unravel, like candles snuffed out in the night or barrels emptied, sighing bluish gray smoke in sad little tendrils.

THE SKY was the color of old bones, gray and dingy. The rain drizzled. Cain's breath hung in the air like clouds of life escaping with every gasp.

He touched his mother's ruined curls, and he almost stepped on his father in the alley they called Lovers' Lane.

They were dead.

He could count the bullet wounds, singed and bloody through their good clothes. He took his father's rings and tripped in a dirty puddle, staining his palms and knees with gritty mud. It was cold, and he hadn't put on gloves or a muffler. Just his double-breasted coat with the hood and his untied shoes. He hadn't even fastened the buttons of his coat, because he'd been too scared. Too lost. Too frantic.

His voice fell in a ragged sob, but there were no tears to accompany it. No, that was just the rain, spitting down on him as if his life were as worthless as this puddle he'd fallen in. He couldn't cry. He thought maybe he should feel the emotion tightening in his throat like it always had when he'd cried before, but everything was numb.

He walked, and he didn't even feel the steps as he took them. He ambled through the wet shadows of Lovers' Lane, dripping and shivering and in a daze.

"Hey—"

Cain stopped. When he blinked, a few drops of rain that had gathered on the tips of his eyelashes fell away and he looked to the corner of Lovers' Lane. A set of dilapidated steps led up the dirty wall to a door completely boarded up, and below it was a pile of junk from every corner of life. Just garbage, a haven for street urchins and street rats alike, and beneath a crooked curtain of Bohemian fleur-de-lis and tassels that hung from the rusty landing and its laundry lines above, a man who looked like a clown smiled cordially. A graveyard clown. A resurrectionist, maybe, a body snatcher, a man of the underbelly. His hair was dark and thick, and his eyelids painted as if with kohl, though the eyes themselves were wide and full of life. His face was so pale, it was almost gray, theatrically so. The solitaire necktie at his throat was checked. Rings danced along his slender fingers. Behind him lingered a few others, and despite their abundance of black and black and more black, they looked too clean, too *healthy*, too well dressed and self-aware to really be ragamuffins.

"*Malchik malenky,*" the graveyard clown called, and wiggled his fingers invitingly.

Cain fidgeted. That wasn't a language he knew. He stared, perplexed. Disoriented. He thought about his father, his uncle, his aunt, his teachers—telling him to always be aware and attentive, especially as a Dietrich.

"Come here," the graveyard clown urged, smile softening. He looked so welcoming and warm. Cain inched over a few steps until the landing of the stairs and the broken balconies above sheltered him from the misting rain. "Don't be scared," the graveyard clown said, leaning out from the shadows of the alley, a pipe dripping above his head. Cain thought the way his hair was pinned out of his face was very handsome. Like a character from the penny-dreadful romances Maggie liked to read, a pirate or a gypsy. Behind the graveyard clown, the other few men shifted in impatience. They seemed edgy, uncomfortable. Like they wanted to get out of the rain and into a dark, dry place. Like they had no idea what to do with anyone younger than themselves and were more than content to let the graveyard clown talk to Cain. They were nobodies. He had never seen them before, not even the one who Cain had followed to Lovers' Lane. He'd just thought he'd been following a helpful servant.

The graveyard clown smiled down at Cain where Cain stopped short before him.

"Your mamma and daddy wanted you to come with us if anything ever happened to them. They said so themselves. So you wouldn't be alone," the clown said.

"I'm alone," Cain whispered as if the fact was a lesson in need of memorization, but the words were paper-thin and barely audible.

He let the graveyard clown scoop him up into his arms even though it seemed outrageous to be carried when he was fifteen. The graveyard clown and his friends wore a little bit of red with all that black, and Cain knew those weren't his family colors, but all the colors seemed to be running together into a mess of dirty gray and too, too bright whites.

"We'll take care of you, I promise, *miliya*." The clown man held him on one hip, and Cain stared over his shoulder at the others. They didn't look like people his parents would have liked. They had the feel about them that the Dietrich protective services did—good at lying and good at fighting. Rough and tumble but somehow refined. One of them winked at him. Cain heard hidden holsters creaking as the graveyard clown turned and ducked under the Bohemian curtain, and, cradled in the clown's arms with his nose pressed into his neck, Cain went with them out of the alley and left his parents' bodies in the puddles of Lovers' Lane for the undertaker to pick up.

IN A dusty corner of the rooms below St. Mikael's-on-Windsor, there were secrets—better than drugs hidden in figurines of the Virgin, better than the church's hidden tithe, better than the whispered sins collected by the latticework of the confessionals for all time.

The graveyard clown and the others took him to an apartment on Flynn Street. They sat in a dirty kitchen drinking coffee together and discussing their own business, taking turns checking on the *malchik malenky* whom they'd left in the narrow salon to read the moldy children's books they'd offered and eat the stew and bread they'd given.

They waited until dark, changed Cain's clothes, paused to marvel over his colorless eyes, then gave him a scratchy coat and a cap to wear as they made their way to Windsor Avenue, Ruslaniv territory, where St. Mikael's sat on its treasure trove of secrets.

There was a hidden door in the sanctuary, and beyond it a dark unknown hall where the next concealed entrance was a trapdoor in the floor.

The graveyard clown had held Cain's hand as they made their way through the secret corridors and down below the church, where the air was colder and danker, and the meager candlelight danced on the walls with their peeling red paper. It was like the dungeons of lore, or the gateway to hell everyone talked about. And Cain clung to the clown as the first real fear began to set in.

It was sharp and cold, but not yet eloquent of witless panic. *My parents are dead,* he kept thinking. *Why did they give me to these people?* was the thought thereafter. Then the panic set in. The panic was numb and mindless. Logic was not his anymore, just the fear and the distrust. He was not stupid with youth; he was the heir of the Dietrichs. Instinct hissed this was not right—these people had never spoken to his parents before in their lives. And yet rational thought threatened to destroy him, and a plan of escape was a rational thought.

They emerged from the secret hallway into an underground haven, and the graveyard clown crouched down to eye level with Cain and gave him a reassuring wink.

"Oberon's already getting attached," one of the others had said, and Cain had tried to shrink away, eyes wide and utterly dumb with the choking veil of confusion.

His parents were dead. They'd been left in Lovers' Lane, full of holes. There had been a hellish fray on the streets, and with the most elite Dietrichs out, distracted by such, Ruslanivs had broken into the manor. And someone had killed his dog. And the halls had been in chaos. And someone had found him hiding, and they'd said, "*Follow me, love*," and Cain had followed. Stupidly, he'd followed. He'd run through the streets, hadn't even tied his damn shoes, and there he'd found his parents, and then—why, why, why, why—

"Oberon, like the king of the fairies?" Cain asked, looking around. The dungeon-like stairs had led them down into what seemed an underground mansion, complete with ornamented ceilings, and giltwood furniture of crushed velvet, lovely paintings and gold-faced urns. Hallways branched off in every direction. A detailed crucifix sat above a bowl of holy water and rose petals. The air was still chilly.

Murmurs rippled through the others. The graveyard clown, *Oberon*, had tugged Cain by the collar over to big doors on the right. The two brass knockers there had vicious-looking lion faces, snarling and pierced by large rings. Oberon knocked with them, thrice.

It was Father Kelvin's office, and he was jubilant as Oberon led Cain into the room.

He rambled about something or another—a blessing, a score, a *perfect scheme*, and Q's genius, but who Q was, Cain didn't know. All he'd thought in the daze was that something was just *off* with the Father.

"Strip," Father Kelvin thundered, eyes wide and glittering as if he'd just told the best joke in the world, and his accent was harsh and Eastern.

"No," Cain had argued.

"Strip," Father Kelvin repeated. "Even *you* have to be deemed healthy and fit for my circus, little prince."

Cain broke off and tried to run then, as suddenly as a lock might snap to the right key. But they'd caught him before he'd even made it to the stairs—strong hands, that horrible language he knew but didn't know—and he'd tried to bite them and kick them, but that was the best he'd managed, reduced to animal instincts.

Then the graveyard clown, the king of the fairies, had whispered, "I'm really very sorry, *miliya*," and clamped a cloth soaked in chloroform over his mouth.

Out went the lights under St. Mikael's.

IT SEEMED forever he was dreaming.

The dreams hadn't made any sense at all. They weren't familiar to him. Sometimes he wondered if they were even his dreams at all. Colors and shapes swam in and out of his vision. People spoke. He stared at a wall. Someone played music—Schubert, on the violin, and Chopin on the pianoforte, and a scratchy paraffin wax cylinder of some warbling old opera or another. *Put a sock in it, for Christ's sake!*

He was awake, and then he wasn't, and he couldn't keep his eyes open long enough to see who came and went, bringing him dinner and pulling out that terrible bronze syringe with the angel faces at the knuckle holes. Apparently he was still alive, but he couldn't remember taking nourishment, or wandering around the room they kept him in, or talking to those who claimed he had, but finally the nightmarish fog lifted and Cain sat cross-legged, hands shaking over his dinner, staring across the ugly little bed at his captor. *Oberon.*

"You're drugging me," Cain mumbled matter-of-factly, eyes wide and cold with hate. Or at least, they'd felt so. But perhaps he'd still looked utterly out of it, barely fifteen and held hostage under the influence. He understood in a grave and detached way that he could not feel anything with urgency like he had the last time he'd been aware of himself. Because they'd been drugging him.

Oberon stood at the foot of the bed, hands in the pockets of his pinstriped waistcoat. His eyes were dark and inhospitable, a stark contrast to the kind smile he'd offered in Lovers' Lane. He shrugged limply.

"Morphine," he confirmed the accusation. "Tears of the poppy, put right in the veins."

"How long?" Cain croaked.

"A week and a half," Oberon replied. "Your house has all but announced you dead too, *malysh*. And that's all the good you are to them, anyway, no matter how much you fight us, because now you belong to Father Kelvin. Kelvin bought you fair and square."

All but dead. Belong to Father Kelvin. Kelvin bought you.

Cain realized then that his father's rings were missing. He didn't know where they were. It was the last detail to pierce the fog that made it clear to him his parents were dead, he was alone, and the world as he'd known it was simply no more.

It had all just ground to a vicious halt and left him reeling and dizzy and broken, abandoned by miracles.

Oberon led him to a magnificent washroom, in the style of a Roman bath for one. Cain bathed. Under the bandages, he found on his arms bruises and dried blood, and it made him ill to think they'd been using that ugly needle on him, nursing his stupor with the tears of the poppy. Oberon gave him a Turkish cigarette, in fine paper with gold arabesques and with a little silver filter that felt nice on his dry lips. The smoking woke him up a little more as the morphine dreams continued to fade away.

Oberon showed him to another room, deeper in the maze of underground halls, if they were still under St. Mikael's at all. The lodgings were eight to a room, assuming by the count of beds.

"This is your room now," Oberon said, with a cordial smile. Either the graveyard clown was mad, or defeated by the sheer madness of it all. "You get the last bed on the left."

"I'm not here because my parents set it up," Cain finally choked out, which he already knew, but it was like he needed Oberon's confirmation to fully grasp this sudden hell. Bleak acceptance was hard to swallow. He wondered where the other occupants of the shared room were—who they were, what they were.

Oberon offered a bitter shrug.

"No," he said, without even sugarcoating it. "*Rabota.*"

MALCHIK MALENKY meant "little boy." Cain learned that one fast, just like *miliya* meant "darling" and *malysh* meant "baby."

Rabota meant "work."

FATHER KELVIN'S circus was a brothel.

It was a perfect prison with no windows and seemingly no chance of escape.

In structure, it was genius. In morals, it was diabolical. Some worked the rooms hidden below St. Mikael's, auctioned off for a night or reserved for a short while between highest-paying clients. Others were rented for parties where they danced. Others yet took part in what had garnered the name *circus* for Father Kelvin's evil little business in the first place, a touring performance for clients and prospective clients who came through, wanting sights New London couldn't offer on the street level. It was a colorful exploitation of the dead-eyed and broken souls Father Kelvin kept as his own.

If Oberon had never let him wake from that trancelike limbo of morphine dreams, resentful and hardening deep inside, Cain wouldn't have cared. The world wasn't much different thereafter, anyway.

It was hazy, like the fog of early morning when a boy couldn't keep his eyes open, or the peak of a fever when the body was so cold but the sweat didn't help. Times, events, faces, and names blurred dizzily together, bled together, ran together. In the dark and chilly labyrinth of rooms, all framed up in artifice as they were, points of reference began to merge, as did the days and the nights, until it was all one big swirl of slaughtered hope.

Cain made friends with the other boys in his room. They ranged in age and price, of course. They called each other "Brother," in a secret and confidential way, and Cain had stared at them all the first night and wondered if he'd be there long enough to be called "Brother" too.

He learned their names, because they talked to him even when he'd refused to talk back, convinced for some reason that if he stayed remote and aloof, somehow he might be saved.

There'd been Larke, and Jasper, and Mordecai, who had all been working the streets of New London in various shadowy ways before they'd stumbled upon Father Kelvin's circus and decided it was better than sleeping in the gutter another night. There'd been Garrett, who had fallen into Father Kelvin's grasp after being ousted from one of the Queen's many orphanariums. There was Andrej, who had once run with gypsies and sometimes resurrectionists, and who'd been stolen away from the hanging block of Yekaterinburg by Q and Oberon years before. And then there'd been Emil, whose parents knew he was there and took a quarter of the profit he earned, which was all Father Kelvin would allow them.

That was the saddest to Cain. First he figured, well, that wasn't fair at all, that none of them got paid for the work they did. But Andrej explained Father Kelvin assumed it was reimbursement for "room and board," and Cain was struck by a void-like gloom, a sorrow for Emil. Cain was like most of the others, there only because fate had discarded them. But to be there because your family had signed you up for it? That was heartbreaking, in a cold and distant way.

Cain wished he could pity Emil, but he couldn't stop pitying himself long enough.

Without his father's rings, in this cold, dark underground place of moldering velvet and damp candlewicks, whispering footsteps and creaking beds, where the air was thick with secrets surely he was not Cain Dietrich anymore.

You're as good as dead, Oberon, the eerie graveyard clown, had told him.

After all, Father Kelvin didn't refer to him by name. He called him "The Little Prince."

NOBODY HAD ever really told Cain what he'd be doing for Father Kelvin, but he made inferences.

He started out working the rooms under St. Mikael's. One of Father Kelvin's men snapped, "Stop snarling like that, we know you're not dumb," and threw him into a festooned room.

It seemed all rational thought had dissolved into the thunderous bass chord of his panicked heart, but it was rather nice to be alone again for a short while, feeling the smooth marble floor underfoot and running his fingers over the vanity table, the clean mirror. He stooped over to smell the flowers at the bedside, and he took a moment to lay curled up on the maroon divan, pressing his nose to the cool gold frame.

He'd known what he was waiting for. And when the man was let in by another one of Kelvin's agents, there was a soft, genteel light in his deep-set eyes and his suit was of fine broadcloth. Wasn't it amazing how one's appearance and demeanor could tell the story of one's life? Lamplight glinted off the man's pocket watch. Cain stood in the shadows behind the draped bed and stared at him in bleak distaste, wondering just how much the gentleman had paid for a virgin with noble blood. Unless Kelvin's men had spun some other wild furtive lie about Cain, and in that case, what did the man think of him? Could he tell he was a noble son plucked from grace or did he just look like another one of the dark-eyed and underfed fallen of the rooms beneath St. Mikael's?

The wide beautiful bed creaked under the man's weight, and Cain's bitter acuity gave way to a vast and hopeless wasteland of despair. A cold black wave of it crashed into him as if it had just been waiting for the right trigger to elicit its presence, cresting and crashing around in the back of his soul.

Cain climbed up on the bed among the scarlet pillows, which only scattered when the gentleman dragged him down from the headboard by the ankle. The silence was strangling. Cain tried to hold his breath and maybe die of asphyxiation, but he was too chicken not to breathe when his chest felt it would burst. The man popped the buttons on his shabby shirt, and there they went, the last lingering rebellious shreds of dignity and attachment, snapping away.

The sex wasn't really the bad part, other than the way his insides felt bruised. It was more the shame and repulsion and self-hatred for giving up.

Giving up.

The gentleman dressed when he was done and would not meet Cain's eyes—as if it had been Cain's fault he'd succumbed to rampant sin. If there was any other sort of arbitrary thought exchanged between the conqueror and the conquered, Cain ignored it, because the way the lamplight bounced and swelled in the corner was more interesting to him. He didn't even care to get more decent than yanking up his breeches again.

One of Father Kelvin's men poked his head into the room after the gentleman made his leave. Cain recognized this one from Lovers' Lane, with Oberon. The fellow looked around, seemed satisfied, then said, "Up, little boy blue. Get up. Make the room presentable. Your next client is coming in an hour."

CAIN HADN'T been sure how to measure the passing of time. All he knew was that life Before was over and this was life Now.

When he slept, images of his parents in Lovers' Lane and the last glimpses of the chaotic manor haunted him.

More times than he'd readily admit, he climbed into bed with Andrej, and pretended Andrej's dozing heat was the big German hound's. Now and again he woke up accidentally curling his toes into Andrej's calves, and Andrej laughed at him and told him to let the dream fairies kiss him back to sleep.

Cain was listless with the subdued shock, the repressed grief. He was numb, but cold with repulsion. Gradually the routine became familiar. Get up in what never felt like morning, wash off, get dressed, eat breakfast, and smile and laugh with the others like they weren't all off to sell their souls in fragile little bits and pieces, meet in the underground chapel to pray to the Lord and the Virgin and kiss the little wooden Christ on Father Kelvin's rosary. And then it was time to work.

Cain worked with the same passion that he'd played and learned back at home when life had been simple, because there was a time and place for hating himself and the laughing stock they called God and for letting the bad feelings take over. Work was not that time and place. That was late at night in bed when his body ached and his mouth was dry, and whatever was left of the pride from Before splintered and fell.

Cain kept the rooms assigned to him nice and clean. He always welcomed his clients graciously, waiting among red pillows and taffeta coverlets, smiling inviting smiles and greeting them like he wasn't imagining some untimely and atrocious death for them as they dived in for kisses.

There were many ways to say it.

He fucked. He bedded. He "played backgammon" and gave "lip." Sometimes his Brothers called the clients *Corinthians*, and a few of them called Cain a *toff*, which he didn't take as an insult at all. He'd rather be considered a snob than a gutter rat.

"The Little Prince," Father Kelvin advertised.

No client had ever looked him in the face long enough to ask why his eyes were not blue or brown or green like the other boys', or recognize it as the trademark defect that had once been such popular gossip in drawing rooms and salons. The Brothers didn't ask either, but it was more out of fear of Cain's icy glances than disinterest.

If clients wanted him to scream, Cain screamed. If they liked it when he begged and cried for mercy, he obeyed. If they wanted him to recite poetry, why, he most certainly did, and if they liked it when he laughed, he laughed sweetly, because they couldn't read his mind.

They'd never know he was laughing at them and how pathetic they all were, men and women paying so much money just to exercise their filthy weaknesses without being judged.

Father Kelvin's ladies, who were older than Cain but younger than his mother had been, loved it when he visited their side of the maze under St. Mikael's, which was usually on what never felt like Sundays. They braided each other's hair and giggled when Andrej nuzzled their shoulders and necks, and they played with the young boys and winked at the older ones like they all shared some great secret. Sometimes they'd even read stories aloud and played music like they did for *their* clients.

Some regulars brought Cain candy and treats. He shared those presents with the Brothers in his room.

Mordecai disappeared at some point.

The whispers through the cold candlelit chambers said he'd been murdered by a client.

Cain hadn't even connected enough to feel fear.

And when it all got too much, which now and again it did, Cain sought out Oberon and offered his most lamenting of frowns. Oberon usually gave in almost immediately. He brought out the cigarettes rolled with opium and hashish, the morphine, the little flasks of brandy. All of it, anything to make the feelings die, because feelings were dangerous, and threatened to debilitate the instinct that got Cain by.

Once or twice, but only once or twice, Cain had wondered if Before had just been one great morphine dream, head rolling on his shoulders as a regular client left love bites along his hips.

There was a tier system of sorts, which Cain learned soon enough, like he learned soon enough that work was work and dissociation was an art he needed to perfect. There were cruel tortures masquerading as discipline for those who tried to shake loose of Father Kelvin and the crushing of the soul and the dignity that in hindsight would appear as indoctrination.

Cain found himself at the top of the class, which didn't seem surprising in the least.

"You're good in bed," Father Kelvin had said, during a routine evaluation of his "circus" workers. "That's all I ever hear of you—you're good in bed and most of your clients wish to book you again and again."

Whether he had a right to be proud of himself, Cain had never been able to tell. The pride still carried shame on its back, because why would anyone want to be proud of the things they did for Father Kelvin's factory of sin and lies?

They trained him for one circus, with Oberon, who seemed to be in charge of many aspects of Father Kelvin's operation. But Cain never traveled. Apparently he was too good. Father Kelvin wanted him always under his thumb, never too far away, forever close enough to pull onto his lap like Cain wasn't fifteen, going on sixteen, and quite aware now of monsters parading as men.

He was The Little Prince, anyway, and when he came out to dance, the men and women in the masked audience always clapped and cheered.

Surely he was the only *real* nobility there, and he was the *first choice* for some clients, his regulars. He was one of Father Kelvin's *favorites.*

A few times, even Oberon stopped by, slithering into the red sheets with him and letting Cain run his fingers through that dark and stubborn hair as Oberon surrendered to the unspeakable lust.

Cain knew that he was higher than the dirty-nosed boys and girls there because their families were destitute. He was higher even than the ones who had been kidnapped, or orphaned, or recruited, or the common-class ones who did what they had to.

He was The Little Prince.

He was Cain Dietrich, he was good in bed, and he was alive.

Six months, a year…? He was clueless as to how long he'd been there, in the clutches of Father Kelvin and his palace of pleasure.

Eventually there was nothing else to learn and even the sin and the seduction grew colorless, nondescript. He wanted to see the sun again. That was what he dreamed of, not nightmarish memories or hellish trauma, the sacrifice of innocence in a red-themed bed with roaring lion faces carved into the headboard.

There were no real answers to be found under St. Mikael's. Cain had come to dismal understandings. He'd given up on fighting before; now he'd given up on giving in. He had some questions, and he was ready to start finding answers.

FOR ONE, *How did a boy escape Father Kelvin's?*

Cain found the answer one morning in what really hadn't felt like late March.

Gunshots ripped through the pretty gilded charade of Father Kelvin's underground gentlemen's club, but they were not aimed at anyone. It was quite unfortunate for the angel faces in the coffered ceiling, which took the bullets without much resistance.

Boys and girls and young men and pretty ladies in muslin tea gowns had scattered, taking shelter in red velvet rooms. Voices rose, coarse and roaring.

There was an argument between Father Kelvin and Wolfe, one of the men who had been with Oberon so long ago in Lovers' Lane.

Cain sat in Father Kelvin's office, on the scrolled daybed in the corner of the room. He'd been called to the office for something or another, when Wolfe had started ranting and raving in the hallways, yelling about how the city authorities were snub-nosed bastards and someone had lost the assignment book and clients were waiting but they didn't know who went to what room anymore, and about how Kelvin was a worthless, brainless *piece of shit.*

In the office, Father Kelvin had heaved a defeated sigh and patted Cain's shoulder, saying, "I'll be back momentarily, *malysh.*"

They'd yelled about the bust that had happened in Yekaterinburg, that barren, grungy city northeast of New London. Cain had waited, in boredom. Father Kelvin's voice echoed, grossly placating and very passive aggressive. More gunshots had ripped through the hush. He'd jumped. There was more yelling, interspersed with bouts of that coarse and guttural language they all spoke there. *Malysh.*

Cain wasn't sure what compelled him, but he made his way to Kelvin's desk and started going through the drawers.

What was he looking for? A snack, perhaps. Something better than what they were rationed. Or money. Or secrets. Or a gun. A blade. A letter opener would do. He wanted to feel protected.

He'd found his father's rings, and *that* was when the apathy shattered.

There was more incoherent yelling outside the office, and some thuds and sounds of violence. The Dietrich in Cain's blood had never actually been corroded, and in a moment of tragic clarity, it *reawakened.*

Cain grabbed his father's rings.

He didn't even take the chance to peek around the corners outside Kelvin's office to see if the coast was clear—that would have wasted too much vital time. Wolfe and Father Kelvin were fighting, and probably with many others now. This was an opportunity he'd never see again. Nobody was paying heed to the circus workers. Nobody would see him. This was his chance. Instinct hissed in the back of his mind: *Now. Now. Now!*

Cain sped out of the office and down the winding halls. Pieces of ceiling that had been broken by bullets scraped at his bare toes. He almost tripped on a painting thrown from the wall. There were shouts, slamming doors, the echo of someone's infuriated howl, and voices from a room some of Father Kelvin's ladies had fearfully closed themselves into. Cain's breath ripped in and out of his chest, hot with urgency, and his feet pounded on the floor as he ran from Father Kelvin's.

Out of the labyrinth of halls, down the dim corridor to the stairs, and up into the secret hall behind the sanctuary.

Out, out of the church, the cobblestones biting at his feet as he ran through New London. The sunlight was blinding. It made the world blurry with tears. It hurt his head. The fresh air made his lungs feel new again.

Did he look lost? Did he look starved? Did he look abused? Did he look mad? Did someone on the streets reach out and try to stop him, suspicion and goodwill piqued by the obvious shades of *wrong*? If they did, he hadn't noticed.

Cain didn't stop until he was outside the gates of the Dietrich manor. He didn't even remember the surroundings he'd passed on his way, navigating the streets intuitively, and as the guards rushed to open the wrought iron gates in shock, Cain opened up his hand and found that he'd clutched his father's rings so tight, they'd left deep imprints in the skin of his palm and fingers.

He was Cain Dietrich, he was sixteen by then, surely, and he was an orphan. He was good in bed, he was alive, and in March of 1887, he was home again.

SCENE TWO

"TAKING YOUR coffee in the garden, I see."

Levi looked over his shoulder, all bundled up in fleece and a fur collar.

His father stood behind him, smiling small but cheerily. His graying hair fell loose about gentle, liver-spotted jowls. He had his walking stick, clutched in old fingers that trembled this morning. His many jewels and rings looked as if they might cut off his circulation. His breath hung on the air, as his son's did, and Levi licked the taste of coffee off his lips and offered a polite smile. He really didn't feel like talking; he hadn't felt like talking to anyone for days now. But he'd known it was only going to be a matter of time before his father approached him, ready to ask questions again after so long.

"*Dobroye utro,*" Levi murmured. *Good morning.* "I'm sorry, did you want me at the table for breakfast?"

His father waved a hand dismissively as he moved up the flagstone steps to the patio. Levi reached over to pull the chair out for him, but his father swatted his hand away, frowning. He eased down into the chair with a loud sigh. Crow's feet branched from his eyes.

Levi frowned again, deeply. He lifted his coffee to his lips and glanced away, because he didn't like seeing his father on the days he seemed to feel his oldest.

There was a small silence, comfortable. Neither required much conversation, anyway. They were very alike each other in that way. Morning fog rolled along the Ruslaniv grounds, and the orchards and trees were gray in the pale light. Birds chirped somewhere, hesitantly.

"You haven't been out all night lately," his father declared. He took some fresh fruit from Levi's breakfast plate. Levi smiled faintly, pushing the dish over to his father.

"I haven't," he confirmed.

"Not even with BLACK?"

"No."

"You've been going out by yourself quite often, anyway, I've heard."

Levi shrugged listlessly. "I have…."

"My son, the romantic."

Even his father's chuckle commanded respect. Levi let him make his assumptions. From the few fountains, birds scattered.

My son, the romantic…. Levi's smile softened just a bit. His lashes lowered on clouded eyes. His father always spoke as though Quinton had never existed—or, at least, wasn't his blood son. But Quinton had been much older, almost thirteen when Levi had been born, and he'd left with the other senior members of BLACK. Nobody had heard from him since.

Levi frowned around his coffee. Besides, Quinton had never *acted* like a son. Or a brother.

Levi, the romantic. Quinton, the monster. Maybe he was dead somewhere, banished from New London.

"How are you feeling today, Father?"

His father skirted the question easily. "Do you remember what I told you when I designated you as the new leader of BLACK? That I was confident in your being levelheaded? You are, Lawrence. That's what's good about a fighter being a romantic at heart."

It was meant to be a compliment, surely, but it stung him, just as it stung him to hear his first name fall from his father's mouth. He was so accustomed to being called by his second name. In fact he felt sometimes he didn't even know who *Lawrence* was supposed to be. "Father—"

"The Dietrichs have been digging around in documents and records related to St. Mikael's."

Father's eyes met son's over the table as these words sank in like claws.

"I'm still a little angry about the incident in October," his father eventually went on, meaning the gunfight at the Dietrich masquerade, "but I think you'll be able to persuade the others to honor the gravity of the situation. This isn't a game, Lawrence. BLACK is not separate from me, and I've made sure of that by making you leader. Remember that you may be such, but you still answer to me."

"What exactly are you getting at, prefacing with such a lecture?" Levi propped an elbow on the table, cradling his temple in his hand. *My son, the romantic....* "I told you, our little joke at the All Hallows masque was pointless and ridiculous, and I've already taken all the blame for even letting Eliott talk me into it—"

"They're digging around, Lawrence, and I don't know why. Surely the stunt BLACK pulled in October didn't help any. You know how murky our history with St. Mikael's is. Are they searching for blackmail, or is there some secret I'm not aware of? I just don't know. It makes me nervous. But I'm too old to play this game of war any longer, so I want you to watch them. Watch the Dietrichs like a hawk. Anything suspicious, anything uncovered.... Just keep an eye on everything. That is all I'm requesting."

The weight of guilt was almost enough to crush Levi right then and there. It had been so long since he'd heard his father mention St. Mikael's, so long, and still it pained him so much to know that he knew more than his own father, the head of their house. He knew more about what had happened with Quinton and St. Mikael's than Lord Ruslaniv himself!

Levi cleared his throat, slumping down on crossed arms like a brooding child. "That's all?" he mumbled.

"Yes." His father shrugged, and it too was somehow regal even in his weariness. "I'm asking you as your father *and* the head of this family, so please do your best. No—I know you'll do your best, Lawrence. You wouldn't allow anything less."

Another silence fell, but Levi was not at rest. He shifted in his chair, rubbed his aching head. He dug in his pocket for his engraved cigarette case and closed his eyes, pulling his scarf down to feel the cool December air on his skin.

The Dietrichs are digging around.... Yes, yes they were. Levi had no doubt of it. In St. Mikael's, nonetheless. God, if Cain found the incriminating past of St. Mikael's—

Well, Cain had been perfectly honest about his intentions once he found the killers of his parents and his bastard kidnappers, who had all seemed to drop off the face of the earth once the missing Dietrich heir had returned home that wondrous day three years ago.

And Levi didn't doubt Cain's fortitude or his ability to keep his word. He didn't doubt any of it in the *least*.

And now for his father, he was to *keep an eye on everything.*

If only they all knew.

SCENE THREE

IT WAS 1882. A set of peace laws had been established the year before, but the Ruslaniv family wasn't taking any chances.

"My lord, your sons are the most well protected in all of New London," they said, the guards, the men who watched from the fringes of sight to make sure Levi and his brother didn't get too close to the manor wall.

"Both of my sons will know how to take care of themselves, regardless," their father had declared from the head of the long dining table, and Levi had frowned at his soup and Quinton had raised his glass in a toast of agreement.

Quinton was always thinking about guns and bullets and strategic perfection, so when he'd been of age, he'd had no problem leaving the manor to be trained.

But Levi hated it.

They had to bid *adieu* to the comfort of the Ruslaniv estate and stay at a militia camp outside Yekaterinburg. They were drilled on loading guns, aiming guns, shooting guns, cleaning guns, running, dodging, hiding—running-dodging-hiding with guns, running-dodging-hiding-*aiming-unloading-reloading* guns—instincts should a gun jam, the best guns for the best situations, and too many other useless lessons that Levi retained and excelled at but did not prefer.

He was twelve years old. It was fun, but he had other inclinations.

Like finishing *Gulliver's Travels* and the treatises on the four humors he'd found in the library.

The militia camp was small. They'd all slept in one room, lined with cots—Eliott and William, and those others, the manic Blond One and the smug One with the Glasses. The beds were uneven and the blankets scratchy, and sometimes Levi had tried to read with a lighter to illuminate the words at night. Eliott's bed was next to his. They'd lie awake at night and make exciting shadows with their hands and talk about what kinds of girls they'd marry, and other times they'd exchange funny faces and muffled laughter every time they heard Petyr taking someone new to bed. Some nights it was Claude, some nights it was Wolfe, or Red, or Vyncent, and once or twice it was even Quinton.

"How old is he again?" Levi had mouthed to Eliott, and Eliott had shaken his head, bedtime ponytail bobbing in the darkness, eyes wide and face aghast.

The senior members of BLACK ran the training. The militia camp had been abandoned by the Queen's soldiers long ago and served more as a shooting range for the Ruslaniv family, after they'd bought it.

With the absence of real military, the atmosphere of stifling formality was gone too. There was training, and then evenings were spent in the cafeteria, while the senior members smoked cigarettes and played cards and led by gangster example.

Levi and the others graduated from the training as junior members of BLACK.

Lord Ruslaniv rewarded his youngest son with an ivory-gripped Merwin Hulbert, the word *R O O K* engraved on the barrel. He presented it to him rather ceremoniously, sitting in red velvet in a cherrywood case. Levi blushed about it, but not really because he was honored. He was kind of embarrassed by the pomp and procedure of it all.

Being officially trained did not at all mask the truth about BLACK.

BLACK carried themselves with a royal pride, but Levi knew they were hardly any better than the gangs of the commoners. BLACK took advantage of their anonymity, of nobody on the streets knowing they were comprised of members of a House. They gambled and drank and fought and partied. It was all magnificent fun to them, like bullies out of view of the nurse.

Levi turned thirteen. His hair was long. He wore it tied back, high off his neck. He walked with the grace of a privileged child and the distant eyes of a saint. He met with private tutors twice a week, but he was at the age where anything more to learn would be found in the experiences of life—which, for him, was a life of gold and bright flowers and indulgent parents, and the random and erratic "assignments" with BLACK that felt more like simple troublemaking.

They patrolled the streets and kept other gangs kissing their feet. They spied on Dietrichs and terrorized Dietrich citizens the same way they terrorized the general public, parading around in honor of the "greatest house in all New London." They hit the scene when a street gang in Ruslaniv colors was in a fight, and they protected Ruslaniv supporters and Ruslaniv family at all times and at all costs.

His first real gunfight happened in the August before he was fourteen, when the air was sticky and heavy with the end of summer.

The thrill of it was distinctly addicting.

He was good at it, and he knew it. But Levi got bored of it quickly. It became tedium: the senior members gave him orders, Levi obeyed, and then he returned to his secret corner of the library and tried to immerse himself in the words and the fantasies, not the blood or the sounds of bullets hitting flesh, the shatter of glass, the way people screamed as if demons from Hell had just crossed over and into their world.

His mother despised his reclusive attitude. But his father wouldn't let her bother him, so she'd return her focus to Quinton and smile and bat her lashes and remind Quinton of what a good job he was doing for the family.

Only when Levi came back from an assignment with a dislocated shoulder and his temple bloodied by the butt of a gun did his mother ever sit and fawn over him, bandaged up in his big room with a stack of books at his bedside next to his soup. And it wasn't even that bad, he'd insisted, but his mother wanted to believe it was.

She wanted her younger son to stop being *a romantic* and start being *a fighter* like Quinton.

Levi met Finn then.

Assignments were tedious. The peace laws had been unofficially revoked by the public. The Ruslaniv gunslingers had picked up the daughter of Lord Ruslaniv's cousin, a girl they immediately started calling *the Witch* because of her hostile demeanor. Levi's forehead was still black and blue but his mother's affection had already returned to Quinton, and Finn kept peeking in on Levi when his bedroom door was open, so Levi finally gestured for him to come in.

"I'm sorry, Master Levi."

"Don't be sorry. Why are you sorry?"

"I shouldn't be staring."

"You're an errand boy, aren't you?"

"Yes, sir. I was just worried about you."

"*Worried?*" Levi's face puckered in disbelief.

He'd laughed. Finn had blushed cherry red and then knocked his fist against Levi's head, intentionally hitting him where it hurt as if to get him back for laughing. Levi had just laughed some more, because he was tired of servants kissing his feet.

Levi loved Finn for exactly eleven months.

Finn had big brown eyes and honey-colored curls, and while Levi was still restricted to bed, Finn snuck in to read and talk and keep Levi company. He was a bold and vivacious little errand man, fifteen but with the charm of childhood still intact.

Once Levi was out of bed, Finn avoided him. Finally Levi trapped him in the darkest corner of the library and said, "So now you're not my friend anymore?"

"I can't be," Finn had replied curtly, trying to escape Levi's narrowed eyes.

"And why is that? Because I'm the son of Lord Ruslaniv and you're one of his runners?"

"No—"

"Ah, well, excuse me, then! Why not?"

"Because the more I'm around you, the more I want to kiss you," Finn sputtered, and Levi had sat down on a leather armchair like he'd been pushed.

He didn't do anything about it. He didn't say anything about it. He hadn't the slightest idea *what* to do or say about it. He'd never truly thought about affection before, and relationships—and while quite suddenly he was conscious of himself as a man to be wanted, he sure as hell wasn't prepared to accept someone else's devotion. Especially a boy's. Especially when that boy's devotion made him feel rather proud, because look, anyone could land a lady, but to be chased by a *man*....

However, Finn was his friend, and surely his only real friend apart from Eliott. Levi knew a little something about making someone happy when they were sad, and anything else he knew of romance he'd learned from stories he'd read. So when Finn came to him two weeks later, shaking and crying about a particularly troubling errand he'd run, dodging bullets and watching blood spill, Levi grabbed him by the wrists and gave him the kiss he'd so been coveting.

It was a sweet and harmless and utterly fulfilling secret romance.

"Why aren't you more involved with BLACK?" Finn asked one night, when Levi had snuck him into his room from the servants' quarters and they sat at the window pointing out constellations in the velvety sky over New London.

"I am," Levi replied, dubiously.

"No," Finn pressed. "Not the missions, but the carousing."

"Because, I think it's boring," Levi had insisted. "What's not boring is being with you."

Lying nose-to-nose together in his bed, Levi thought that as long as Finn was there and filling his head, he'd be happy. Finn did not demand Levi be anything but himself. Finn didn't think Levi was too quiet or too thoughtful. He certainly didn't think Levi was *too romantic* either.

Finn made Levi feel light, and warm, and free.

But Quinton suspected. He'd been suspecting for some time, and when he barged into Levi's room one night, the moonlight had rendered him an absolute tyrant as he cried, *"Are you an idiot, little brother? Are you completely moronic, brother of mine? Sharing a bed with a domestic, firstly! Sharing a bed with a boy, secondly! You bloody little fairy, get out of this house before you sully our name any further! Lawrence, what would Father say? What would Father say if he knew what you've been doing? You'll break his heart! You'll give him an early death if this shame were ever to be uncovered—"*

"Stop, Quin!" Levi had choked out, and the real fear of his own kin had far outcolored the humiliation as the whole house was awoken by Quinton's outrage. "Stop, please, brother! I'm begging you… I can explain… just don't tell Father—"

"You're a monster!" Finn hissed, and he threw Quinton an obscene gesture, the rebellious little imp that he was, and Levi's heart fell because it was all over.

Quinton killed Finn right there, a perfect shot. Finn's blood splattered across Levi's bed and the paneled walls over the table. Finn's eyes rolled up, and he fell like a thrown doll to the blankets, and Levi had fallen down to the middle of his bedroom floor and just sat there, gawking, utterly stupefied by the shock of the betrayal.

When the guards and servants came running, Quinton explained that Finn had been hired by a rotten hit man sent to slit Levi's throat in his sleep. The lie made no sense. Quinton attached no enemy to the hit, no House to hate for it.

But Levi had nodded dumbly in agreement, crippled by shame and heartbreak. And worse yet, everyone believed the story.

Word spread fast. Quinton partied with Wolfe and Oberon afterward. The Witch offered Levi her condolences, touching his hand, saying, "It's terrible, the worries you have to bear as an heir of the House."

Levi shrugged. "Are you a guest?" he asked, and the Witch looked ready to tear him limb from limb as she screamed:

"I've been living here for months; I've been *talking* to you for months, you *bastard*! *Rot in hell*!"

Levi thought that maybe he'd start getting more involved in BLACK.

SIXTEEN WAS a big year for Levi.

He shot his eighth lethal bullet in a time of alleged *peace*. Lying and smoking and drinking and gambling had become second nature. He finished reading his 103rd book; he got knocked out during a fight and woke up cold and in pain on the cobblestones just as Petyr, the Witch, and Oberon returned for him. He met Charysse, who was a whore, and he slept with her because she was BLACK's birthday present to him. He put more effort into his assignments with BLACK. One night he got unintelligibly drunk for the first time, and Petyr, the Blond One, made a move on him, and he and the Witch got into a wrestling match neither could win in their state of intoxication, and he gave Eliott a more than friendly kiss or two across the billiards table.

It was also the year that Levi thought of fondly as his last year of forgivable naïveté.

"YOU'RE A genius, Quinton. A goddamn *genius*."

Levi stared.

Wolfe clapped Quinton on the back, and the others around the drawing room uttered a chorus of concurrence. Guns were spread out, polish and rags on the table. A fire roared in the elaborate marble hearth. Levi shifted where he sat in a wingback chair, one leg tucked under the other. Oberon sat across from him, on the sofa, and a similar look of doubt and dread pinched up his face too.

No, Levi wanted to say. *He's not a genius. This is a bad, bad idea.*

But he didn't even have to bite his tongue. Years of silent obedience had taken their toll. His fingertips brushed over the letters on the barrel of his gun—*R O O K.* He heard his mother in his head.

Quinton, you're such a good boy. We're so lucky to have you as our own. It made him sick.

Levi was twenty. He was the only junior member of BLACK at the gun-cleaning party. Quinton had asked him to come after dinner, and that had made him uneasy to begin with, but now Levi felt very small and vulnerable. He felt in the spotlight, somehow, even though he was close to a wallflower in the upholstered chair. Across from him, Oberon rubbed at his temples and gawked at his feet as the others gathered around Quinton and spoke in excited tones about his latest *genius* idea.

Levi wanted nothing to do with it. He hoped he wasn't involved. He cleared his throat, and first Oberon looked at him, and then the others did. He knew Levi was going to say something.

Levi met his brother's eyes, trying to ignore the fact that everyone else was staring too.

"Am I part of this mission?" he asked softly.

There was a brief silence, swaying on the threshold between awkward and just plain precarious. Quinton seemed to chew on the words before they came out, his eyes sharpening. He laughed, harshly—and the others laughed along, grown men but as brainless at the moment as any crony.

"Of course not, baby brother," Quinton said. He sounded as if he were trying to comfort Levi, a curious lilt to his voice as if Levi had just asked if there were monsters beneath his bed. "No, Lawrence. This is a job for *experienced* members only."

It was ridiculous, the way he said it. Like they were kicking him out of a club or something.

There was a second or two in which Levi stared in disbelief, before the rage burned in his throat and he looked away, because if he saw the way the senior members of BLACK were looking at him any longer—eyes sparkling, faces alive with subdued laughter, patronizing and condescending—he might do something rash that would get Quinton angry.

Levi looked up. Oberon offered a thin smile, and he looked like a very sad clown.

Quinton and the others struck up their impatient conversation again. Levi gawked at Oberon in silence before gathering his weapon and leaving the billiards room. Oberon was a good guy. He was sweet, and kind, and he always made the Witch happy after Levi hurt her feelings, which seemed to happen quite a lot for some reason. Levi thought that Oberon would make a better leader than Quinton.

Quinton was *not* a genius, but apparently nobody thought that besides Levi. And maybe Oberon, but Oberon would never speak up either. At least, Levi didn't expect he would, unless he underestimated the fellow.

Whatever. In a gang like BLACK, majority ruled over integrity no matter who spoke the most sense.

IT WAS early January 1886. Levi gawked out one of the multipaned windows in the hall, feeling the chill from outside creep in through the glass. The orchard was soggy, and the light was dark gray. Petyr and Claude were playing a very questionable game of tag down in the other corners of the gallery. Eliott had wandered by once or twice, but maybe there was something in Levi's face that told him to stay away.

Quinton and the senior members of BLACK had left an hour earlier.

The genius plan was to ruin the Dietrichs once and for all, and to enervate them to the point of forfeit.

Forfeiting *what*? Levi wanted to scream.

Levi had the strangest quiver of intuition that right then, at that very moment, as he stared out the window, his brother and the men whose morality his brother had poisoned were murdering the Earl Dietrich and his wife.

What a *genius* idea.

The intuition was an odd sensation, a low tingle in his muscles, a current of clarity shuttling deep down—he just knew it. Levi just knew it. They were killing them now. And they were going to dump their bodies in Lovers' Lane, like they'd said.

"What about the boy?" Levi had asked Quinton later in the night of the gun-cleaning party, lingering in his brother's bedroom doorway as the clock struck midnight. Quinton had smiled an insane smile and assured him:

"Don't worry, baby brother. We're not killing him. We've got a better plan. Father Kelvin will take care of him."

Peering out the window, looking out at the day that seemed to mourn for him because he could not bring himself to, Levi wished he could tell his father what was going on, right there under his nose but unbeknownst to him. He wished he could walk away from the window, but his feet would not move. He wished he could talk, just to anyone who would listen—but he could hardly swallow.

He felt hollow, and numb, and a little overwhelmed by the gnawing dread that something volatile was building in the air.

But what could he do?

He was only Levi, the romantic, the baby brother. And there was no power in any of those things.

SOMEHOW LEVI made it from the hall window to the rooftops over Lovers' Lane. There, broken and bloodied on the ground, were the Earl and Lady Dietrich.

It made his skin crawl.

His stomach lurched.

It was different when the reality wasn't numbed by the rush of fight-or-die.

The rain misted, dampening his clammy skin, but his neck was sweaty under his fur collar. Levi was about to leave, obviously too late—not that he'd really had a *plan of action* or anything. Nobody cared what an *inexperienced* gunslinger thought. And then his eye caught on the boy staggering into the alley from the streets.

Levi was rooted in place overhead, watching, and he could hardly breathe.

Beautiful little thing, getting wet in the spitting rain. Beautiful because his lashes were long and his eyes were big, and his hair fell about his face in a perfect wispy laurel. He wasn't small; puberty had been kind to him, but he was a fragile Ganymede swimming in that big coat as he just stumbled along with no real purpose whatsoever. He looked dazed, disoriented. He almost stepped on his father. He stared for a long moment, and Levi watched him as he stared. Levi watched him as he dug in his pockets, then stared some more as if completely at a loss.

Levi's mouth was dry. It occurred to him then, bright and painful, *the Dietrich heir*. That was the Earl Dietrich's son, Cain Dietrich. But why was he alone? God, to find your own parents' corpses....

Levi's throat locked. His heart hammered. He wanted to go down there and gather Lord Dietrich's orphan son into his arms and rock him and run his fingers through his hair and kiss his wet cheeks and tell him, *It's okay, they haven't gotten you yet, and I'll make sure they don't. I'm a romantic, and Quinton's the fighter, but a romantic man can be a force to be reckoned with too, because love is insanity and obsession, and I'll teach you that.*

Levi watched Cain Dietrich fall in a puddle. Up on the rooftops, Levi's fingers shook. He watched Cain Dietrich stand up and continue forth, mindlessly, squinting up into the rain. And then there was a familiar voice, down in the alley, calling out to him.

It was Oberon. Sweet, sweet Oberon. The guy with the big heart.

"Don't worry, baby brother," Quinton had said. "We're not killing him. We've got a better plan. Father Kelvin will take care of him."

Cain Dietrich crumpled into Oberon's arms, in the corner of Lovers' Lane. And Levi knew Oberon would take him to St. Mikael's, Father Kelvin's pride and joy.

Levi scraped down the side of the building, where the sagging old fire escape was. He wavered a few steps, down off the roof now, before he turned into a nearby alley and got sick. An expensive Ruslaniv lunch didn't taste as good the second time around.

He pressed his face to the cold stone of the building next to him and closed his eyes. *Father Kelvin.* His own father called the man a nut, but what church leader wasn't?

God, he couldn't shake this sense of *desolation.* It wasn't exactly guilt. It was more like intense anxiety, a hate, a maelstrom of everything from pride to helplessness—

Levi knew one thing for sure, shivering in his militia jacket, and that was that this genius idea of his brother's was not going to end the feud any time soon.

THE SHORT period of peace shattered.

There were months on end of brutal bloodshed. A breath of war was in the air again, civil war, and rioters were on the edges of their seats as men slept with guns under their pillows.

Levi met Rosalie not long before a fight in Pavlov's Place. He sent her gifts; she sent him smiles. For the first time in forever, it seemed, he'd found a safe haven for his weary mind, and his cold heart was warmed by Rosalie's laughter. He went to sleep thinking about the way she looked in the sunrise, sitting in her open window in just her muslin dress, shoulders bare and hair swept loose and untamed up off her white shoulders as she read or wrote or smoked a cigarette she'd stolen from Levi's silver case. She read the papers like a man would. She wrote poetry and stories about ghosts, and she was the kind of privileged whore one would call a practicing *mistress*. Her pale legs always looked so delicious in her black thigh-high stockings.

But the streets were dangerous. Gangs roamed in the name of the ruined Dietrichs, baring their fangs at anyone who looked at them wrong. Gangs fought in the name of the Ruslanivs, instigating brawl after brawl in a state of crazed triumph and invincibility now that the Dietrichs had been practically destroyed. And BLACK was no exception, of course.

The Queen wouldn't get involved. The web of bloodshed was too tangled. Some feared Her Majesty would ask New London to secede from the province, to become its own troubled state.

It was far too effortless for BLACK to frame a group of radicals for the murder of the Dietrich family, but worse yet, nobody cared. Nobody remembered the radicals' names or any travesty of justice that might have been displayed. The world was in uproar, and for BLACK there were gunfights, poker games, victory raids, and pride. Too much pride.

The biggest fight was the fight between the jaded Dietrich Security and BLACK. The Dietrich Security surprised them on the scene of a fray between street gangs. The Dietrich Security was ruthless in the wake of their family's tragedies, as the remaining heirs tried still to untangle the Dietrich legacy and fortune and name a new earl.

Oberon fell victim to hidden blades and bullets. Rosalie had come running as soon as she'd heard of the battle, and she'd begged the fighting to stop and was shot three times in the chest, then once in the head.

The Dietrich protective services were virtually slaughtered.

But Vyncent was injured; he died later in the hospital. Petyr wavered on the verge of a psychotic break, and Eliott cried because so many people had died, so many innocent civilians caught in the crossfire.

Days later, news surfaced that the Honourable Cain Dietrich had somehow reappeared at the gates of his manor, a changed creature but alive and ready to take over as the head of his family almost a year after his parents' deaths.

Quinton threatened Father Kelvin's life if he didn't dismantle his circus, and off Kelvin and his boys went even farther north than Yekaterinburg, to the cities along Muscov Bay. It was another flawless cover-up on Quinton's part—and just in time too, somehow. The man had the devil's luck.

Not even a week after Levi's father sent Quinton and the remaining senior members of BLACK away from New London until further notice, hoping their absence would mean less violence, the new Earl Dietrich's first order of postdelegation business was to seize St. Mikael's under suspicion of all sorts of illegal activities.

The story of the season was that nothing was found there, and the little Earl Dietrich who had shown up at home so mysteriously went to the country for a few months to "recuperate mind, body, and soul."

Levi's father was quiet for weeks. His wife wore mourning colors even though her son was technically still alive.

The chaos was a chaos with system again. Levi found his old collection of Poe.

Levi read.

SCENE FOUR

IN HIS mind, Levi could walk the halls of memory in the dark with all the sure faith of a blind man on familiar turf.

But narrowing his eyes at his reflection in the mirror, he suddenly felt a shortage of surety. He felt like he didn't know himself at all.

Who was he? Lawrence Levi Ruslaniv, heir to the Ruslaniv House, captain of BLACK, the Ruslanivs' secret gang. Blond hair, brown eyes, a gentleman's build, and the quick glance of a trained killer.

His father was dying, either of life's grief and regrets or vicious old age, and his mother insisted yet on mourning black despite having one son still alive and in her arms.

His only brother had been a maniac, and Levi didn't know if he was living or dead, banished from the city as he'd been.

A romantic, they all said, pitying him behind those false smiles of appreciation, but the truth was that after his only two loves had been ripped away from him, Levi had become a gambling, drinking, guns-blazing mockery of a romantic, because his heart had closed up and left him hollow and cruel and jaded. Undeserving of such a title, anyway. *Romantic.*

The world was an ugly, stinking, disappointing machine, and he was just another rusty cog, wasn't he?

Levi hated it.

Suddenly, and passionately, Levi hated everything about his life and the way it was. The opulence, the indulgence, the luxury, the lies, the evasion of accountability—

Rather, the way that it had been before he'd become the Levi Cain Dietrich knew. Or had known. The lone wolf gunslinger who had sworn his loyalty on his life and who had inevitably committed the ultimate betrayal anyway.

God, why did he have to be another pawn of this feud started so long ago, too long ago to even pretend anymore? Why couldn't he just follow his whims, and shake free of the bondage of witless, unquestioning loyalty to some antiquated and forgotten maltreatment?

It dawned on him then, like the sun breaking free of a morning mist.

I've decided to follow my whims, he'd said.

Following my whims, he'd told Cain.

And when the words had fallen from his lips then, he'd believed them to be a fib, an invention of this solitary gunslinger charade, an utter fabrication to get himself on the Earl's good side.

Levi gawked at his reflection with wide eyes. He felt sick with the sudden realization. God, it was maddening, how it had hidden there in the depths of his soul and he hadn't seen it. How could he not have seen it! How irretrievably *stupid* was he!

Living for himself was all he wanted and had ever wanted!

Through this character he'd played for Cain, he had stumbled upon warped self-discovery in the pit of cold, heartless violence that had become his life.

What left him in an even worse state of utter despair was not that fact, but the chilling idea that he had never adopted a character in his games to garner the Earl's trust.

He'd just been himself.

Levi threw himself up and away from the mirror as if his reflection threatened him. He paced. Thought threatened him, on the contrary. Cold thought divorced from emotion, shoving the bold and stunning truth in his face.

He had only been himself!

That was why the guilt was crippling. That was why he could not stop thinking about Cain, about the awful hatred that had darkened his face in Dmitri's Pavilion and seemed to leave him mindless and trembling. That was why he couldn't move on from the frozen feelings of that day and carry out these sloppy and irrational plans BLACK had formulated based on Levi's first accidental run-in with the hated Earl.

And for the first time in forever, it seemed his heart *ached*, and he *cherished* the feeling because he was simply being himself.

He had to see Cain again.

He had to speak with him, explain all these things. Desperately and obsessively, he needed to taste Cain's forgiveness. He needed to know that there was redemption for these things, and he just hoped the revelation had not come too late. He felt manic with the urgency. The truth sank its teeth into him and wouldn't let him free.

Love was monstrous, wasn't it?

It struck him then, cold and vivid.

Levi wanted to end this feud once and for all, but Cain needed to agree to it.

"Levi! Levi, where are you headed?"

Levi turned in a tense and guilty way as if Eliott could read his thoughts or the inner whispers of his pounding heart. But Eliott was too dense for all that. Eliott knew him well, but surely not that well. Levi stood in the dark hall, all bundled up in his street wear, and he regarded Eliott in impatience.

"Out," he replied tartly.

"What did your father want, earlier today?" Eliott asked, strolling to a stop at Levi's side and speaking in a low and confidential tone.

Levi's stomach tightened. He hated these hellish butterflies, the vicious gnaw of real feelings. "For me to keep an eye on the Dietrichs," he husked, cutting Eliott a pointed glance. *This is my task*, that glance said. *Stay out of it*. "They've been digging around about St. Mikael's."

Eliott didn't seem to catch Levi's drift. "Perfect!" he breathed, eyes all but dancing excitedly in the dimly lit hall. "You've gotten close enough to the Earl, haven't you? You could distract him, and we could take a peek around his offices and see if we can't find what he knows."

"Whose idea is that?" Levi hissed. "Yours, or the Witch's? Or William's, even?"

Eliott's face soured. His scowl was deep, uncharacteristic. It only gave away that the idea was not his. It was all Levi had to see to understand. "The hell's got you all tangled up?" Eliott spat back. "It's BLACK's idea," he stressed, rather bitterly, as if to prove Levi's recent withdrawal from their work together. "Your father wants this infernal vendetta put to rest, doesn't he? That's what we're trying to do. We're trying to put your father at ease before the fighting sends him to his deathbed!"

Levi knew Eliott. He knew Eliott well. He didn't want to be reminded of Quinton and Quinton's warped ideas of justice, because he knew in his bones Eliott was not a cruel and devious mastermind like Quinton was. But still Eliott's offended speech stabbed him right where it hurt the most, and Levi shoved roughly past his cousin and friend. He shook his head, a sneer darkening his face.

"Right, because the whole world has my father's best interests at heart," he cried over his shoulder, ashamed of how spiteful and full of hatred he sounded but unable to stop the venom. "Don't make me laugh, Eliott!"

"I guess I'll just ask you again tomorrow, you moody bastard!" Eliott called after him.

Levi didn't reply.

It was probably for the better if he was asked tomorrow.

Presently he was filled with a refreshed purpose. Other matters meant more to him at the moment. Like the freeing sense of renewal and his own plan to put the centuries-old feud to final rest.

SCENE FIVE

EMILY WINCED.

Aunt Ophelia dodged the slam of the doors just before she was shut between them, and, just as she had three times already, without another moment's thought, she jerked them open again and stood in the threshold, hands on her hips.

"I've had enough of this!" she roared.

Her coarse and unsympathetic voice echoed in the halls. Servants cowered around corners, casting apprehensive glances when forced to pass the scene in the master wing of the house. Emily stood at the nearest turn, with the Persians behind her, whispering in their bubbling brook of a language. Aunt Ophelia's words were hasty and fierce, and the retorts that met them from inside the master bedroom were not much better.

"All I've asked for is to be left alone, Auntie!"

"You've been slinking around the house like death itself, Cain, and frankly, I'm sick of it! I'm not asking you to let me into your little kingdom of trouble, but good Lord, you can't just decide to be a moody spoiled child again without any sort of responsibility for it. Your father wouldn't have had it, and I certainly won't either!"

"Then leave me be."

"It's been *ten days* of this, my beloved nephew, ever since you stormed off the scene in the Pavilion—"

"*Just leave me be, Ophelia!*"

"We're a week into December, with many business items to consider before the end of the year. We've received letter after letter from the public and other lords, including Lord Ruslaniv, regarding God knows what. They've just been added to the rest of the pile in your office because business cannot proceed without the word of the Earl!"

"I don't *care* about any of that right now. I refuse to so much as *read* the names of those filthy, flea-ridden dogs!"

"You don't *care*? Are you ill? If you're not delirious, you're *mad*, and I'll be forced to—"

"Please, Auntie. I'm just in a foul state of mind. There is nothing you can do about it, and it's not like you're my nurse or my mother, so just *let me be!*"

There it was, a firm and hateful statement cold as the pit of Hell according to Dante. And there, again, the crack of Cain's palms against the door and the rush of air as he heaved them shut. But this time the movement was halted by the powerful smack of Aunt Ophelia catching the thick, masterfully carved doors in ready hands.

Emily could see it all from around the corner, hands clasped worriedly against her chin. Cain glowered up at his aunt, and Aunt Ophelia returned the murderous scowl. Cain seemed to falter for a moment. Emily thought about the way he'd been the last week and a half, after he and all of Security had rushed out to Dmitri's Pavilion at short notice.

He'd been sullen, and brusque, and vile, eyes damning everyone and everything they observed. He'd pushed one maid to tears with his insufferable attitude. Emily had caught her in the hallway after elevenses, trying to weep in secret, and Emily didn't want to admit that her fiancé was being such a despicable monster of a man, but it was the truth. He was almost intolerable, and despotic. And he wouldn't speak to her, and he wouldn't even look at her. Even when he sighed and touched her hand to bid her good night, he wouldn't meet her eyes. It pained her.

There was a hush in the hallway that lasted perhaps one simple second before it soured, warping into something dangerous. Aunt Ophelia's nails scraped against fine dark wood as her hand left the door in a flash, slapping across Cain's face.

The sound of skin on skin echoed in the corridor, sharp, and what followed was a deathly silence. Even the eavesdropping servants quieted. The last Emily heard before Cain shrank away into his bedroom with head hanging, his aunt following him in and closing the thick doors, was Ophelia's voice, low and menacing:

"I won't have you acting like such a fool in front of your future wife. Now get your spoiled ass inside your room, so we can talk without the whole house listening in...."

Sometimes Emily felt like she was alone in the big Dietrich house—with the servants, sure, but also with the ghosts and secrets of the noble family.

Sometimes she missed the country.

Sometimes she wanted to learn to shoot a gun.

SCENE SIX

HE FELT bruised, all over. Inside and out, like he had when his father had disapproved of something and taken him into his den for *a talk*.

Cain knew that his aunt had been able to see the injured pride, the subdued rage burning in his eyes after she'd slapped him, but a childhood of *talks* with his father had taught him that, even as the earl now, and even as the earl in the future, there would forever be times when elders dominated. His ego ached just like his cheek, and he remembered the way his head would spin after a number of chastising smacks in his father's den.

In front of your future wife! she'd said. It was only salt in a deep and unhealing wound.

Cain was alone in his room now. Aunt Ophelia was long gone, but the power of her words still sizzled in the air, hanging over him like a fever.

He paced at the foot of his bed, rubbing his eyes. They felt tired and glassy and sick. The silence was alive, it seemed, and suffocating him. The distant rushing of water in the house pipes, the tick of the giltwood clock on the mantle, the soft whispers of his bare feet in the white fur of his rug. Mocking him. *Silly man, silly, silly man, falling head over heels for the snake in the grass....*

A Ruslaniv.

A Ruslaniv supporter, at the very least.

A *liar* and a *thief* and a *spy*!

Or maybe none of those things, but that was the worst part—the *not knowing*. The tangled, crushing questions and the emptiness where answers should have been. Levi sure as hell hadn't come around to explain yet, had he? And he hadn't sent any sort of courier wondering why Cain had halted all correspondence, an obvious sign of guilt. Nothing could convince Cain otherwise.

Whatever the answers or pathetic reasoning, he just couldn't get over it.

He was sick with it; his body ached with it. The betrayal, the sting of something akin to abandonment. All too like the death of hope under a misused church.

It wasn't fair!

The fury, the shame at being deceived, and the disgust that he had opened himself up to someone who quite possibly held the key to his demise in the same hands that had loved him, *ooh*—

And yet, the seething anger was not enough to blanket against the cold of despair, the chastened pain.

Because he'd been fond of Levi.

He'd *let* himself be fond of Levi.

And the lying, abominable bastard had just yanked all of that out of his grasp again, reminding him of the disgrace and revulsion that had *killed* him a few years ago. To be used and discarded… it *hurt*!

He had duties. He was the Lord of the Dietrich house. He had responsibilities that did not belong to his aunt, his uncle, his cousins, his feeble old grandmother out in the country, or any of the others who had tried so hard to run the family in the absence of an heir years ago. He was Cain Dietrich, engaged to Miss Emily Kelley. He was nobility, and of course he was not given the freedom to seek happiness on his own. He lived for the Dietrich name, and that was it. That was the ball and chain.

But he couldn't say that to Aunt Ophelia. She wouldn't understand.

All he'd been able to do was sit on his bed and stare at his feet while she reminded him of his place, of his reputation, of his *responsibilities*. Sometimes people as important as him could not afford to have a time of foul state of mind, she'd reprimanded. There was too much to take care of, and if he wasn't capable of accepting these responsibilities as a young man still plagued by adolescence's lingering erratic moods, well, something might have to be done about that. It was a threat.

Alone now, Cain climbed onto the foot of his bed and sat cross-legged, dropping his face to his hands and struggling to remain in control of his emotions. He'd never had trouble with it before, not after coming back home after his parents' murder; but this *hurt*!

No matter where his mind was, it always ended up coming back around to Levi, his ace in the sleeve. Or so he'd thought. *Levi*. Damn, it *hurt.* It hurt deep inside, heart hot and chest tight with anguish. Cain's jaw tightened. His fingers fisted in his hair.

He hadn't taken dinner again. He was vaguely hungry—or at least in need of some kind of nourishment. Maybe he'd wander down to the kitchen and make Weston fix him something to eat. Something that went well with scotch, because that's what he wanted more than anything else. Something to burn and numb at the same time.

The double doors to the balcony were slightly ajar. It was cold now that he'd calmed a little. Cain slid off the bed, trudging over to close the doors—but he stopped, picking up on the scent of tobacco. The aroma was sweet and pungent, and it came from out under the balcony.

Cain shoved forth outside and leaned over past the stone gargoyle, his granite friend who held so many of his secrets behind those austere, unseeing eyes. Full of rancor, Cain fired down below: *"Oh, you're a bloody bastard fool!"*

Levi stood under the balcony with one hand on the vine-covered wall of the house, perfectly out of view from any surrounding windows. He knew the routine too well, unfortunately. With his free hand, he smoked a Turkish cigarette, and as he stared up at Cain in this casual posture, Levi certainly didn't deny that he was a bloody fool. He smoked his cigarette a moment longer, then put it out on the wall and slipped the remaining half of it into his pocket. His brow knotted.

He said—in a perfectly reasonable tone and that damnable lovely voice""I'm no bastard, I'm afraid. Sorry to disappoint you."

Cain glared down at him with a rage far too easy to offer. It didn't seem right, to send such scathing hatred that way, at that wonderful blond hair and those dark, expressive eyes. The fur of that collar framed Levi's face so handsomely.

"I don't want you here," Cain hissed.

"I don't believe you," Levi returned coldly.

Cain clenched his teeth against a shiver, the December night nippy. He could feel himself getting all sorts of worked up. "I should have upped security. I can't believe I failed to assume that something as dirty as you would come sneaking around again."

"Hey," Levi countered briskly, "maybe you didn't up security because you *wanted* something as dirty as me to come sneaking around. My lord, don't forget you've been *kissing* something as dirty as me."

He grasped the vines along the wall with both hands as if in silent threat that he'd climb up if he felt the need. He didn't smile. There was a spark of something predatory and tenacious somewhere in his narrowed eyes. He clearly held no intention of leaving. Cain scoffed.

"Please, I've already vomited and confessed twice because of such filth. Listen, my hatred is boiling, but my will is weary. I'll give you five minutes to get as far away from here as you can before I send my—"

"You've been *talking* to something as dirty as me," Levi added, effortlessly evading Cain's insults. "You can't deny it," he said, voice falling softly to a more intimate volume as he started to climb up to the balcony as easily as he had many nights in the last month. "Cain—my lord—Earl Dietrich, I'm just going to explain."

"You're so certain you're going to explain! You don't even ask, you just assume I'll listen? Ha!" Cain offered a few rude gestures, backing up against his balcony doors. "What is there to explain? I've been exploited. I've been used. You've been hiding things from me, which is quite clear and irrefutable, and I won't accommodate a liar and a snitch. I'm going to call Security! Better yet, I'll shoot you myself!" Cain scowled as Levi's head crested the floor of the balcony. "*Why are you still climbing up here*? My gun is right—"

He shut up as Levi climbed over the top of the balcony, and he winced away a few more steps as he saw the look in Levi's eyes— confusing eyes, eyes that could be soft in one moment and sly the next. But in that breath, they looked dangerous with hardened guilt. Cain's hands shook.

"Who are you? Why were you there, in Dmitri's Pavilion? Why didn't you come talk to me right away? What is your connection to the Ruslanivs?" Cain demanded, jaw tight, and he was ashamed to hear the emotion ripe in his voice.

Levi drew a tiny breath and seemed to hold it for a moment the way he held Cain with his stare, strung somewhere now between that heavy guilt and something a little more irredeemable.

Finally, in a slow and empty way, Levi confessed, "Lord Ruslaniv is my father."

Cain dodged for his Rapier.

"*You son of a bitch! You infernal lying son of a bitch! You—*"

Seemingly without a struggle—and whether that was due to Levi's skills or the way Cain's fighting spirit was being burned to ashes by the blazing rage, or due in part to both these things—Levi snatched Cain by the wrist and threw him up against one of the balcony doors. It rattled and thudded behind him. Levi's hand sealed his mouth shut, and his eyes were aflame with every last bit of his merciless resolve as he hissed, "You be quiet, little earl, or do you *want* to be found like this?"

Cain felt a devastation of will. He went rigid in Levi's grip. He contemplated biting his hand, but he was frozen in place. The onset of tears was a cold and helpless feeling he hadn't surrendered to in what seemed like eternity

"I am not an unaffiliated gunslinger," Levi's unbelievable testimony continued. "I am the last son of Lord Ruslaniv. You are one of the perhaps handful of those outside Ruslaniv walls that know that now. And I assure you, I swear it on my life, that that is the only lie I've told. Everything else has been the truth—"

"*Versions* of the truth!" Cain snarled, but it was muffled behind Levi's hand.

"I am a trained fighter," Levi went on. There was no plea for sympathy in his voice, just raw and ragged honesty and a fury on his part that was more like self-hatred. He was practically brimming with it. "But like I told you in St. Vincent's, it is not my *chosen* path. I simply want to do as I please, damn it! I want to 'follow my whims'! I *wanted* to be talking with you, to be visiting with you, to be carrying out the demands you gave me! Alas, I'm tied down by my own name, and I'm tired of it! That is the truth, Cain. This, between us, has *nothing* to do with my family, only me and my own wishes! Can you not trust that?"

He let Cain shove his hand away. But Cain didn't let go of it. Instead, he dug his fingers into it, needing a place to channel the violence he felt inside. "Trust? *Trust*! You throw the word around like it's worth something here! I don't know what to believe anymore, Levi. Or is that even your name? Why? Why did you come to me pretending to need a contract that night? Why have you been working for me? Why should I not kill you on grounds of suspected treason? Ugh, why am I even still speaking with you! You're the fucking *Ruslaniv heir*, the sheltered faceless prince Lord Ruslaniv has kept so protected, and lo and behold, against all logic, you've always been here, and there, and everywhere, a thief in the night, and *I hate you!*"

Strange, how he really just wanted to say *Come back, I need you and your broken promises, the you I know that I know.*

"I'm well aware of that," Levi seethed, teeth gritted. "I know very well how you feel about my family. But just believe me when I say it was all of my own volition. I needed a purpose in life. When I met you at the masquerade, when you were 'the Death of the Ruslanivs,' damn it, Cain, I wanted you then and there and didn't even know you were the earl. Did it change the color of the flame of desire once I knew who you were? No! Cain, ask me to do anything for you! I'll become an outcast. I'll extricate myself from my family. I'll be only who you want me to be. You know as well as I do that I don't really hold influence anywhere, so who would mourn my disappearance? I bring valuable insight to the table, love—I'll betray my own family for *you*, all for *you*, Cain!"

Cain dug his fingers deeper into Levi's arms. "Don't call me 'love,' and don't call me by my name either," he spat through his teeth, stubbornly. "Levi, you lied to me."

But he could already feel himself giving way.

The way Levi looked at him... It was harder than he'd anticipated, seeing Levi again. Because God, he wanted to forgive him so badly.

Levi's face seemed to curdle with more guilt. Cain wondered if Levi could see things in Cain's eyes that went unspoken from his tongue. He swallowed, casting his aggrieved glance elsewhere. "You lied to me many times," he reminded him briskly, then shook Levi loose and retreated into his room.

Levi gawked after him. Surely he was torn between following or staying put. He visibly relaxed when Cain returned to the balcony with his father's old smoking jacket. He crossed his arms to hug it closed. The balcony stone was like ice under his feet.

"This is me, acting on what I want," Levi husked again, indignant and insistent and penitent, in that swoon-inducing voice like burnt silk, and he was utterly more convincing than Cain could wish. Ah, Levi, even in the throes of heartache, charming and elegant, and so eloquent of a lustrous and angst-ridden longing.

Levi frowned, lashes lowered on those tortured eyes, mouth in a somber line; he straightened up, pressing a fist to the balcony stone. Cain wondered how long he'd lain awake at night rehearsing this, how long he'd fretted over this conflict. But the real wondering was—did he care if it was rehearsed, if it was anything but truthful?

Who had once said hate and love were two sides of the same emotion?

"I want you," Levi vowed, voice brittle with helplessness. "I don't care that you're my sworn enemy. Mind, body, and soul, I want your everything. Your hatred, your revenge, your cursed name—and if that gets me disowned, *so be it*. If you decide to hate me anyway, *shoot me right here*—like you said you would—and I'll never haunt you again."

"Levi, the gravity of these things—"

"Cain, you're freedom to me! My need for you is undeniable! It has been from the moment I laid eyes on you, 'the Death of the Ruslanivs.' Maybe even before that."

Even before that....

"I have so much hate, I don't know if you understand," Cain whispered fiercely. "And I absolutely *despise* myself for feeling this way about you."

Levi stared. Cain fumbled with the sleeves of the old smoking jacket. And then there was the concession. The concession to fate and all its puppeteer's strings, the yielding to honesty and raw, desperate need.

Cain slipped forward to the edge of the balcony. He let his head hang against Levi's chest. He could feel the ridges of hidden holsters, the beat of Levi's heart beneath his militia jacket. His own heart throbbed in his ears. Every emotion rattled through him, one at a time, as if collected in a line. The shock, the distress, the rage, the disgust, the fear, the pain, the pining. The crumbling of an iron will at the feet of what would not change. Anger and pride fell into the pit of longing.

Levi's arms closed around him possessively. Cain stood stiff and rigid against him, but he stretched up and sought his mouth in a firm kiss.

"Do you believe me?" Levi pressed.

Cain kissed him again to shut him up.

"Do you trust the things I say?" Levi begged.

"Yes! Yes, damn it!"

Levi kissed him back then, presumably to keep him from saying anything more and ruining the conciliation.

"You make me so very nervous," Cain whispered as their lips broke apart, and it was the truth. Levi was dismantling his bruised and battered heart piece by piece, and he hadn't a clue how to protect himself against it.

Levi stared down at him, eyes heated and glassy with words unspoken.

Cain licked the taste of his kiss off the corner of his mouth. Christ, there was nothing he could do about the way this felt, because there was nothing that would win against this natural inclination. There was no denying this intimacy, this need, right or wrong or whatever it was. It was simply there, and indisputable.

He was *content* in Levi's arms. He wanted to be there.

The realization knocked the wind out of him as Levi went searching for another kiss with a hunger that did not waver, open, gasping mouth and desperate hands. Cain shuddered. Levi tasted like metal, like nervousness. And when Cain pulled away for a short breath, his gaze moved over Levi's face, and it pained his heart.

Levi's features bore the pinch of a most lustrous sadness, a brightness to his eyes that threatened to shatter in the darkness of the night. Cain felt a pang of guilt for it, sure, because this was only Levi's frantic quest for redemption. But oh, even in such exquisite unhappiness, Levi enchanted him. That dark intelligence of his, that misleading decorum and the seemingly cunning fox that slept beneath, the stunning, well-bred virility and that beguiling, almost dangerous mystery of his that kept such deep, dark, vulnerable depths of soul protected behind his worst of smirks.

Cain was terrified that petty words would destroy the burgeoning truce, too fickle and unpredictable and regrettable. But Levi spoke, clinging to a tender pride as he whispered in a jagged way, "I was a fool to deceive you."

"You were," Cain allowed, folding his fingers on the back of Levi's neck to keep their faces nose-to-nose.

"I've fallen for you," Levi confessed, with all the feel of an apology.

Cain bristled. Why did those words alarm him so, the same as they warmed him? Why did they make his head light as if spinning giddily, while his heart leapt to his throat in a sick lurch? He wondered if he looked as full of desperate raw emotion to Levi as Levi did to him. It was a lovely sight.

"Have you, now?" Cain husked, and then he smiled because it felt natural to do so.

The ache was deep and sweet in the chest, like all the best songs and loveliest paintings. Levi's need was contagious. Surely their two souls shivered together in the same cosmic continuity, and Cain's fingers curled as he pulled Levi closer, closer, closer yet, but never close enough it felt.

"Please say something," Levi hissed. It was so discomfiting to see him stripped of his normal strength of character. What many traumas hid behind such a plea? *Forgive me.* What insecurities, what secrets?

"I hope people hate you, because I can't," Cain croaked. He tried still to pull Levi closer and closer. "I'm livid, don't doubt it, but I can't hate you. I hope your *family* despises you, but don't ever leave me. Just don't. I wouldn't be able to stand it, being alone."

Don't ever leave me. Cain was terrified both of the fact and the fear itself. Shameful, but true. Yes, somewhere along the way it had become the truth. It was so uncomplicated and clear, he was shocked he hadn't realized it before. But that was just the art of the soul changing colors, wasn't it?

Levi was silent, nose buried in the nape of Cain's neck. Warm, present, real. His breath was a soft tickle behind his ear.

Gently, Levi whispered, "*Now* I swear by the moon."

The stars were dim little pinpricks in the December blanket of clouds, and the moon was a soft, quarter-full glow. Midnight had come and gone. The time was nearing one in the morning. The echo of servants bustling in the big Dietrich house had finally settled, the last of the bedroom lights had been extinguished, and secluded on the balcony in the bitterly cold night, Cain chased body heat, clawing tighter against Levi's chest. That was nice.

There was the rustle of clothes and a startled gasp. The stone gargoyle watched as Cain arched into Levi's covetous touch. The kisses were stolen with indulgence and abandon. They made Cain's hips want to dance. And Cain wondered about Levi—about just what had happened to him that made him into such a child at times. His eyes were pools of honesty in the moonlight. He was sarcasm and cynicism transformed, but all the complexities and subtleties that had captivated Cain at first suddenly simplified as Levi buckled under the weight of seemingly tangled thoughts. After all, it wasn't an unconditional and unquestioning clemency. Cain just didn't feel like asking yet. There was reason to doubt anything Levi had said before, under that fabulous pretense of his. Unless in the way of the most effective lies, he had just told the truth, and all the stories of childhood memories and feelings and experiences he'd entertained Cain with were indeed the building blocks of the man he was.

Levi smiled. The flash of innocence was gone. The lusting fiend was back with a vengeance in the sore wake of forgiveness. His hands moved up Cain's legs and gave a little squeeze where he knew it would trigger a wonderful squirm. Cain's stern scowl dissolved into little sighs of defeated delight.

He surrendered. He gave up to the swell of passion and let it infect him, let Levi walk him backward into his room. He fell easily into the collection of pillows on a wide, sky blue daybed, and when Levi's hand dived between his knees, Cain uttered an impatient groan. His toes curled tight. His heart jumped, the desire sparking in all his nerves.

"Leave the lights down, keep them off," he pleaded on a shivering sigh. "I can't bear the shame of witnessing all this in the light, just let me love you the best I can...."

Fingernails dug into skin the way teeth grazed a lower lip. Knees twitched apart. Levi clawed greedily at Cain's naked chest, reaching up under his waistcoat, under his shirt. He left a trail of hot kisses all along Cain's throat, teasing and pleading until Cain dropped those obstinate defenses and begged for what he truly wanted. Ah, how great was this collision of feelings, to have the son of the enemy in your arms and the foreign taste of pardon on your tongue!

The desire was a burning need, leaving him feverish as he ripped at Levi's clothes, longing for the feel of skin against skin in this secret ritual of theirs that had become so vital. The lovemaking was nearly brutal, an awkward but worthwhile twist of limbs on the daybed, like the drunken, impatient trysts of youth's wildest romance. Tears of concession dried sticky and cold on his flushed face as Levi's fingers prodded and pried into intimately sensitive places. The flesh of an arousal was so torturously sensitive it was sweet, throbbing in long, hot fingers. The swirl of Levi's thumb at the tip of his sex nearly yanked Cain over the edge into the shuddering depths of climax already. God, but Levi drove him nearly mad with the sensations!

It was a culmination and outlet for all their subjugated anger at the world, and a safe place for the knotting of fear and lust and trust.

Small scuffles of hands and elbows and knees were nothing but foreplay, interrupted by guilty gasps for breath as wet teeth grazed nipples and the stiff heat of Levi's sex brushed Cain's thigh, tantalizingly close and daunting.

The closeness was dangerous in a thrilling way, sure destruction in the inevitable end, like all reckless indulgence always was. It was pleasure and relief and terror rushing through Cain's body all at once, like the luscious daze of a bone-deep fever that leaves one smiling and giddy.

Out the open balcony doors, winter clouds passed over the moon as gauzy as strips of sodden muslin. There were the quivering, heated shudders of orgasm, and then Cain's incensed insistence that he dominate in the same fashion, trying to salvage the ragged shreds of control in the wake of utter surrender to feelings. He finished Levi off with his hand, silky skin as sweet and hot as the smooth satin of his eyelids. It dazed him fiercely to touch the hard, flushed length of Levi's cock and know it was his.

Cain couldn't stop shaking, even when Levi discarded the dirty glances to drop kiss after loving kiss down his back. His entire body trembled like the last leaf on a tree in the advent of winter, and when he couldn't stop shaking, he cried. He cried like a damn child, for all his lost hopes and dreams and convictions, and the fact that there was no light at the end of the tunnel for an earl who slept with the adversary's son. There just wasn't any more room for excuses for those who promised themselves they'd never give in to the weakness of love, only to crumble as every whisper of undiluted affection destroyed their defenses.

"Those big beautiful eyes...." Levi whispered, and even his touch was a little different now, like a nervous boy's, slightly awkward and rough as he thumbed away Cain's tears. *Beautiful eyes.* Cain knew he did not mean to patronize him at all.

Ah, this tender poison was more dangerous even than malice or vengeance. *Love.* The need for that loved one knew no subtlety or restraint in the face of stubborn denial. Because even in the wake of betrayal and revelation, he was still desperate to find a way for Levi to have his way with his heart, and he was determined to a fault.

The heady fragrance of sex lingered on Cain's hands and in the bed. The moonlight kissed Levi's bare shoulder as he fought sleep, his lashes fluttering, some sort of delicate and tortured Adonis fallen and lying there next to him in Cain's tangled bedding.

"Would you really want me to kill you if I didn't forgive you?" Cain ventured.

Levi stirred as if woken from a dream. He cut Cain the most crestfallen glance, all the darkest shadows of his soul in those grave eyes. "Yes," he confessed in a low, grim voice. It was the cold sophistication of guilt. "I couldn't ever trouble you, and I can't bear troubling anyone anymore...."

"You could never trouble me," Cain whispered, his eyes heavy. "You anger me—you anger me *greatly*—but somehow, you can't trouble me. And I'm forever damned for it."

What noxious beauty in that quiet truth.

LEVI FELT like a ghost, perhaps the only soul still awake in the most secret corners of the Dietrich manor.

He watched Cain as he slept. Cain looked utterly vulnerable there, nestled up in the blankets, his hair still disheveled from their coming together in those expensive sheets not too long ago. His shirt was unfastened halfway, and his eyelids just looked so silky and soft, Levi wanted to run his mouth over them and those long lashes.

Did everyone look so defenseless and simple in sleep? Eyes shut, mouth parted, warm slender fingers curled limply on the pillows? So capable of trust, so devoid of hatred and compunction?

There was something so dark and sad about Cain, so very dark and sad and tragic that it became lovely and fascinating, as was characteristic of all disasters spinning out of control. His very name spoke to his character—*Cain*. The murderous brother, the brother who surrendered to sin.

Welsh for *fair*.

Levi wanted to lie down next to him and fall asleep in that pocket of warmth, pressed against his side and smelling his hair, but he couldn't. He had to get back home soon.

He was frustrated he hadn't gotten a chance to voice his idea, the core reason he'd come seeking forgiveness in the first place. The reprieve had simply been too great and distracting, and the sex had been sticky and long. He was sore from it, deliciously tired and sore. Maybe it had been the culmination of the last week and a half's self-torture, which they'd both submitted to after Dmitri's Pavilion, a crucifixion of feelings finally relieved. That was just what happened when a man pent up his desires, anyway. They consumed him and took control of him, and when his knuckles brushed tempting skin, nothing else mattered anymore but the need.

The last of the fire under the marvelous mantel popped and spit embers at him. Levi's frown tightened. The room had warmed up once they'd closed the balcony doors, but he was still cold.

THERE WAS movement in the room.

The curtains danced at the open balcony doors. Morning light spilled into the room and tried to burn through his closed eyes. Cain grimaced, burying deeper into his pillows. Cool air tickled his cheeks. He shifted in his blankets, curling in on the pocket of warmth sleep had created. His head hurt. He didn't want to get up. What day was it? The thirteenth of December. And last night he and Levi had fucked, and it had been perhaps the most intimate coalescence of feelings and lust that he'd ever encountered—

Perhaps Levi had never left. Cain smiled as the morning kissed his eyelids. Maybe Levi was the one moving around, parting the curtains, opening the balcony. Was he leaving? He'd be seen, the fool. It was broad daylight. Cain's smile widened. He tried to smell Levi on his pillow. What did he smell like? Sweet hair, hot skin, tobacco smoke, gunpowder, and expensive cologne.

Footsteps swept across the bedroom, muffled by the white fur of the rug. Cain opened his eyes, and immediately his smile fell.

It was just a maid crossing his room again, carrying his clothes for the day, stirring the coke in the hearth. Not Levi. He'd left in the night of course, like the lying sneak he was. Flitted right out like a rook off the eaves.

"Good morning, sir," the maid said.

"Morning," Cain grumbled in return, and hid his face in his pillow again.

ACT FOUR
RED

Although I joy in thee, I have no joy in this contract tonight. It is too rash, too unadvised, too sudden; too like the lightning, which doth cease to be ere one can say, "It lightens."
William Shakespeare, *Romeo and Juliet*

SCENE ONE

THERE WAS a strange sense of liberation in the filthy secret.

Cain hated himself for allowing it to happen, the return to normalcy—whatever had been "normal" about the world at all before the untangling of Levi's lies and regrets. But he didn't want to cut loose his contracted gunslinger, because, conceivably, what other spy could ever be better than the son of his family's enemy?

He hated himself for melting under Levi's eyes, and he hated the way all the reasons to distrust Levi bent and broke under the instinctive understanding that Levi's admission of guilt was nothing but true. He hated himself for smiling gaily when Levi complained that it was difficult running around for Cain with his household breathing down his neck about where he went at night.

"The prodigal son," Cain hummed gleefully. "You bad thing. I like that."

"That this liaison is ruining me?" Levi pressed, with a little knot in his brow.

"Yes," Cain whispered, privately understanding the strain of loyalty and personal need, a series of relatives' condemning glances passing through the back of his mind. Levi leaned near and Cain mumbled, "Don't touch me. Don't kiss me. I need time, Levi. I'm still mad."

Time. Yes, time to sulk and time to capitulate. Because by the end of the night—a business meeting in a church, a rendezvous on a balcony—his head was on Levi's shoulder, and they shared a Turkish cigarette, and Cain knew with a cold little shiver of clarity that Levi's allegiance to his own family was fraying and uncoiling.

He found a greedy satisfaction in that.

What better way to destroy the Ruslanivs than by weakening family fidelity with kisses and longing glances?

Ah, little did he know that Ruslaniv loyalty was unraveling on its own.

Aunt Ophelia met him at his bedroom doorway one December morning, and Cain pretended not to notice the way her eyes roamed over him as if searching for signs of errant affairs among his mess of uncombed hair and wrinkled nightshirt. "Cain, my nephew, New Year's is approaching."

Cain flashed a dark glance in her direction, silently combatting her nosy frown. He knew what she was getting at. New Year's and its delivery of updates and Dietrich decisions.

"Yes, Auntie. I know that."

But first there was Yuletide, which was magical per usual, and New London was alive with red velvet ribbons and holly and carolers tromping through the slush on the streets. Bells rang from tower to tower. Hymns and lovely voices caressed even the dirtiest of storefronts, and gifts were exchanged midmorning Christmas Day, after the Mass the night before.

It was all so rampant with tradition to Cain, and always slightly tedious and uncomfortable in that sense. Casting wishes in the bread pudding, telling ghost stories around the fire, and avoiding the mistletoe lest Emily be waiting and watching for the perfect moment to expect a kiss. Sneaking out of his own family's Yule banquet to run off with Levi to Brackham's House of Variety was perhaps the most reckless and illogical decision he'd made in a long while, but it felt so good to escape the manor like it wasn't his and he wasn't himself for the night.

"We'll wear masks and be perfect nobodies," Levi had sworn, upon requesting Cain's company for the soiree at Brackham's. "Nobody has ever recognized me as Lord Ruslaniv's son, Cain. *You* didn't even know—"

"You hush up," Cain had hissed, and he felt as though Levi just didn't understand things like responsibilities because he had none— because he was not the head of his family, because he was safe under the cover of carefully constructed mystery. Because apparently he'd always run around playing outlaw and had never been required to grow up.

But Levi had convinced him a little sinful play couldn't hurt either of them, and Cain wasn't going to pretend he was averse to a little defiance.

Brackham's was holding glamorous holiday festivities, and nonpartisan ones at that. The kind of fêtes that those of higher class in the crowd would deny attending the morning after, as they pinched their noses and drank their coffee without milk to soothe the hangover. It had nothing to do with Dietrich or Ruslaniv, nor the feud between them, because it was a rowdy bash and frankly, to Cain, the thrill of really sneaking around was too much to deny.

Over the wall they'd gone together, and Cain had never felt more exhilarated in his life.

"You've made a vagrant lord out of me!" he scolded, swatting Levi away when he tried to steal kisses in the shadows between the streetlamps.

"Lies! You've already got a wayward streak in you. You just throw the blame at me," Levi retorted. Cain couldn't argue that one.

Cain had slicked his hair back and worn the dreariest clothes he'd been able to find in his wardrobe to complete the disguise. And oh, these discolored eyes? From a fever years ago, sir, more common than you'd think.

"How cleverly you lie," Levi purred.

Cain gloried in the praise but gave Levi no credit for it.

The crowds moved like a sea in the yawning shell of Brackham's in all its Bohemian splendor, with its velvet-tasseled curtains and private lounges. There were handsome men in silk shirts, gorgeous ladies with lace fans, and beauties in drag showing off too much flesh, ostrich plumes, and scandalous little ruffled shorts. Voices and music collided in one great tumultuous sea of sounds as citizens danced and gambled and drank.

They'd run into a few of Levi's associates on the great open floor of the club, under the dancers on their swings. One Levi called *the One with Glasses* and the other he called *the Blond One*. At first they'd spoken together in low voices that seemed confidential and somehow significant, but Cain hadn't paid attention. He probably should have. He didn't want to. The vodka burned his throat as it went down, but it warmed him up and set his smile free. As if by a spell, the last of the pain of finding Levi in Dmitri's Pavilion was dwindling away in all the glory of being disguised as just another *nobody* among the other *nobodies* at the theatre. No wonder Levi reveled in this.

The adventure of it all, and the disregard for general inhibitions, sitting about the green-topped gambling tables and sharing a chair with Levi as the men around them smoked ship's and Persian blends and Levi bet along with them in hands of *Cassino*. And Cain didn't care that others looked at him like he was a Cleveland Street specialty or some other rented love, the way he sat half draped across Levi's side like that Blond One did with Levi's bespectacled friend, because nobody saw him for what he really was. Fooling them all was grand fun. Wasn't it about time he acted like all the other noblemen in New London, with all the *grand fun* they had under the cover of night?

Oh, the lovely duplicities of the privileged and the rich. There was a certain uncomplicated comfort about it.

"The first time we met, it was like this," Cain declared. "In a sea of bodies, dancing like idiots. And you chased me."

"No, you chased *me*," Levi corrected with a bitter smirk, like the idea of talking family versus family was a detrimental one right now. The room seemed to buckle and sway, if only for a few tipsy seconds. Levi hummed along to the voice of the violins as he led Cain around the dance floor in dizzying steps.

"How is it you're the son of Lord Ruslaniv?" Cain asked, swallowed by the roar in Brackham's as the dancers burlesqued *Vakula the Smith* and men roared and hollered over their cards. He didn't mind having to lean closer for Levi to hear him.

"Well, he's my father," Levi replied in a merry, sarcastic way. Cain elbowed him.

"How is it the world doesn't know?" Cain pressed.

Levi's eyes darkened. He shrugged and shook his head at the same time, casting his gaze off elsewhere as if annoyed by Cain's questions. And perhaps rightfully so. Why did these things have to be brought up to poison the purity of the night's leisure?

Levi cleared his throat. "My father struggled to keep my brother and me secret from the world, lest we get all caught up in the fighting and the politics when it's not necessary. He didn't want anyone to know who we were or what we looked like, to protect us from possible plots against him that might involve us in a bad way. Ransom situations, blackmail, exploitation. He wanted us to live a happy and carefree life… while we could, I suppose, sheltered from the bloodshed and darkness of the legacy."

Cain was left winded and vaguely mortified. The commotion at Brackham's swirled around him, but for a moment he didn't hear it. There was an awful ringing in his ears and the colors and pulsing crowds melted together like hot wax.

For all the reasons the Ruslaniv heirs had been kept hidden from the world, his own family had suffered pain at the hands of their foes, and that seemed a dreadful and laughable hypocrisy. A jab at his pride, a pinch to his soul.

"So that's why you're free to run around playing on the streets like a vagabond and a vigilante?" Cain hissed.

Levi narrowed his eyes as if he sensed the subtle insult in that, but he said nothing. He combed his fingers through Cain's hair and kissed his temple.

"What of your brother?" Cain asked, hoping to distract the underlying throb of confused fury that had sprung up like a bad taste on the back of his tongue. "Does he run wild like you do, pretending to be someone he's not?"

"My brother is dead," Levi said, so flatly and indifferently, Cain couldn't even find satisfaction in upsetting him.

"So you really have no power in your family's politics?" he hissed, desperate to understand just how serious his sins were. "What were you doing in Dmitri's Pavilion, then, that awful day?"

"I hold no accountability, and no responsibility, and do nothing for my father but kiss his rings," Levi spat back coldly. "I was in Dmitri's Pavilion by chance, and those who recognized me wanted my input. It's far less shady than you want it to be."

"And what about BLACK? It was disbanded once I returned home, but I catch whispers through the city as if it's still around. I just don't understand how it escapes me if it is...."

He spoke more to himself, under his breath, tipsy as he was, but Levi listened to every word. Something dark and monstrous flashed in his eyes, fast.

"BLACK?" he echoed.

"Never mind." Cain shook his head. "Never mind, it's something my higher security has their hands on. No more of this. No more talk of terrible circumstances," he said, winding his arm about Levi's waist in a gentlemanly fashion. He felt bad now for picking at open wounds for his own pleasure. "No more, darling. Let's go find those friends of yours and forget the world for the rest of the night. As far as *my* family knows, I'm in bed with an awful headache, and they all know not to disturb me when I get in a mood like that."

Levi kissed him against the wall in the darkest corner of the upper floor, as the burlesque went on and cheers flooded the air, laughter and song and shouts of drunken gentlemen, and Cain gave way completely.

He was distinctly aware of a void between them, a small shadowy stretch that neither would brave, and what slept in that dark place were intimate things. It was an awful pit of cause and effect. In that place, Cain would have to tell Levi about everything he'd done and what had been done to him for that abysmal length of time he'd been Father Kelvin's captive. But if he told him that, he'd have to confess the connection he'd discovered between a dismantled Ruslaniv gang called BLACK and St. Mikael's and how everyone had thought him manic when he'd ordered the church stormed and found nothing but dusty hymnals and baroque candlesticks. Then they'd shipped him off to the country for a short vacation as if he were a raving lunatic.

If Levi told Cain everything Cain didn't know about him, he'd be forced to recognize again and again that this was the son of his family's sworn enemy, those Cain fought to seek vengeance against. In lieu of those things would spring up again the vicious circle of doubt and distrust and the struggle to dissociate self-inflicted worries and undiluted feelings. What did Levi know, if he knew anything at all? What awful truths were just waiting for the right question to fall from Cain's lips?

Was he existing obliviously right beside a trove of information, all the answers to all his questions?

Was he keeping himself in perpetual ignorance because he wasn't sure he was prepared to know the truth should it be accessible?

Could the romance really be that detrimental to the revenge?

Levi was a bloody Ruslaniv. That was the best part, just unbelievable enough to be perfect for his wry humor. Where was the family honor in all that? Cain was quite a disobedient son, he'd come to find, but his parents were not there to lecture him, so what did it matter?

It was all too complicated for a tipsy mind, anyway, and Cain needed to get back home.

On Old Year's Eve, the Venerable Mary marched through the masquerade crowds, and *"Oranges and lemons, say the bells of St. Clement's.... Here comes a candle to light you to bed, and here comes a chopper to chop off your head!"* chorused the people.

The bells clanged from church to church, songs and folk tunes pulsed through the streets, and Aunt Ophelia gave Cain an earful for retiring early and not counting down the last moments of the year with his household and fiancée.

Clove-stuffed oranges and gilded nutmegs would have been exchanged around the fires, and the hearths were all being scrubbed, and they would have gathered in the salon to consult tea leaves and scripture for predictions of what the New Year would hold.

But Cain had claimed that headache, and nobody wanted to contend with a possible nasty temperament, though Aunt Ophelia and Uncle Bradley too, had cast Cain their narrowed, suspecting glances, silent castigation for an antisocial attitude they should have been accustomed to already. They could see right through him. *I know what you're up to*, those disappointed glances said, and rightfully so, but Cain didn't care because as Levi returned him home, he bid him a happy New Year, and the sweet parting was all right because it stoked the fire.

Levi left him on his balcony, as the first moments of morning began to breathe life into the icy world. Cain stood in his coat, breath dancing on the biting air as he watched day break over New London and its stained chimney pots and crooked towers. And there, far past the city, windmills and black trees and country stone.

A tempest of thoughts came to visit him in his solitude, inspired by the wanderlust of drink.

How indiscreet and pure it all seemed in the dark, and utterly easy and right—*love*. It was such a delicious and indiscriminate ache, like the heart knew the feelings were warped and irrational by design. And always in the morning came the inevitable condemnation of self.

But Cain was conscious then, as New Year's morning broke over New London, of the ties between him and Levi that nothing seemed capable of severing. Strange ties, powerful invisible threads knotted tight in the intimate depths between them.

It was a little bit of meaning to the otherwise tiny and meaningless little patterns of life, while other things could be so easily tattered, like a spiderweb broken by the wind, indifferent to its delicate, gossamer beauty. But his and Levi's souls shivered on a kindred tonal plane, where tragedy did not break spirits but lit a fire beneath them that came from the same great flame of life, in the endless flow of time. A carnival of rust under a pale bruised sky.

The conviction left Cain reeling like he'd never felt such communion before in his life, only pitiful cousins of it.

Imagine, if he married Miss Emily Kelley and kept the son of Lord Ruslaniv as his secret lover. He could see it, actually, a lavish house and wearing imported brocade and many splendid rings. Parties would no longer be drags, and candlelight would flicker from glinting baroque sticks. Maybe he and Emily would produce heirs, and maybe Emily would be content with blissful ignorance as her husband, the tragic earl, conducted "business" into the latest hours of the night.

But eventually Levi would inherit the Ruslaniv fortune and be decorated Lord of that House. And what then? Well, Cain's hatred suggested he'd just have to find a different suitor. Surely this romance couldn't survive under the weight of revenge.

But he didn't want to. *He didn't want anyone else.*

Watching the sky turn colors for the sun, Cain was vaguely aware that there was no such thing as a peaceful ending.

Someone was always bound to be hurt, or betrayed, or destroyed by tragedy. There would always be injustice in the world, and those who sought to avenge it. There would be those who let life destroy them, and those who fought back against the hand of cards they were dealt. It was a lesson in strength of soul, perhaps.

The inner turmoil between good and bad, and right and wrong, and love and hate, was a war that would go on for eternity.

Cain didn't mind it.

He rather liked the pain when all those things collided inside, because it made him feel alive.

He didn't think he'd ever like real peace. He just wouldn't know what to do with it.

He didn't know what to do at all, right then, about anything. Everything inside felt jaded and faded and dulled, like it all had under St. Mikael's in the solace of morphine dreams.

And he didn't like it.

It was New Year's Day, and he felt no farther ahead of life than the New Year's Day before it.

SCENE TWO

RUSLANIV LOYALTY was indeed unraveling, bit by bit.

"What say you?" William demanded, and Levi wished they'd chosen to confront him after his morning coffee and cigarettes.

"I beg your pardon?" he spat, glowering up at his comrades where they'd circled around him in the garden. It was the first of January. He'd been enjoying the peace, bundled in furs among the ice-laced private grounds of the Ruslaniv estate. He hadn't even combed his hair yet, for Christ's sake.

Eliott lingered behind the Witch and the One with Glasses, avoiding Levi's damning stare. *We could take a peek around his offices* Eliott had suggested what felt like so long ago, after what had happened in Dmitri's Pavilion, when Levi had been in his most despairing state of mind. *It's BLACK's idea. Your father wants this infernal vendetta put to rest, doesn't he?*

But Eliott had only been the messenger, hadn't he?

"Claude told us about Brackham's," the Witch hissed, leaning low over the round table and meeting Levi's eyes directly. But there was no intimidation in her face; no, what there was was a singular and desperate plea for acknowledgement. "This has gone on long enough, Levi. You've built a strong bridge. It's time to cross it."

No, that wasn't the point anymore. But he couldn't say that aloud.

They're digging around in the past of St. Mikael's....

William slammed a hand down on the garden table. Levi watched his coffee jump. "*You're lost in a dream world again!*" William cried. "Tell me, *my lord*, what are we to do when our leader no longer seems interested, no longer seems *fit* to guide us!"

Levi stared at him, darkly, wondering if they could see written all over him that he could not find a point in the games anymore. They remembered Finn, anyway. They remembered Rosalie. They knew him better than perhaps he was comfortable with, and maybe, judging by the Witch's words, they even knew what was really going on between him and the Earl Dietrich. The words unspoken were more potent than those that hung in the air.

"We don't want to kill him. We're just going to end the feud," Eliott finally spoke up, in a tiny and remorseful way. "Levi, with or without you, we're going to end this damn feud for your father."

Something seemed to snap in Levi. Something cold and inveterate, and utterly raw with a renewed inspiration.

"It won't be without me," he husked, flashing them all a reproachful glance. "I want this feud to end too, you know."

"Prove it," the Witch hissed. "Be a *fighter*, Levi. Good Christ, *fight for your family*!"

Eventually they all dispersed, leaving him to his thoughts. And Levi could feel the breaking away, the shattering of a brotherhood that before had seemed worth it.

They'd given up on him.

Be a fighter.

He wasn't, though. He wasn't a fighter, or a romantic, or any murky shade of the two.

He was just Levi, son of Lord Ruslaniv, and that was all he could ever be.

SCENE THREE

THE DIETRICH banquet of New Year's Day was for family. The grand ball would follow thereafter.

Emily looked beautiful, per usual. She sat at her place with her tight-mouthed mother on one side and her spineless father on the other; simpletons come in from the country for the holidays. The Persians sat across from them. They seemed to be making Emily giggle, much to her mother's dismay.

There was Uncle Bradley, beside Aunt Ophelia. Graham and Rodney, and Mr. Renton, and Cain's grandmother, and all the other family who had braved the city limits of New London for just this event. Hazel and Mr. Collins stood grimly near the doors of the dining room. There was the chorus of silver and crystal, and the smells wafted and the laughter rose, and even the servants seemed jolly and at ease in their hurry to and fro with marvelous dishes.

Cain wished that Levi might have been there to see him looking so elegant—cambric shirt with full sleeves, brocade tailcoat with its little black buttons, and Dietrich crest. Maybe he'd just leave it on for later, when Levi came to visit after the rest of the world retired and it was just the scoundrels and thieves and lying noble sons who moved through the shadows of the streets.

"To my nephew!" Aunt Ophelia cried out, lifting her third glass of scotch. She climbed to her feet, and she looked wonderful, for once done up like the stunning lady she was. All the noise around the table attenuated, focus falling on her. Cain wilted, knowing just what sort of sentimental speech was coming.

"To the head of our house, my wonderful nephew," Aunt Ophelia went on, "a testament to our endurance in the face of continual adversities. You see, my brother and his wife tried for years to have a child, and for a short while we really feared there would be no legitimate heir to the name. And then along came Cain, so perfect and beautiful. Miracle the first...."

There was a murmuring ripple around the table. Cain covered his face with his hands at the leading seat, feeling quite humiliated already, although his aunt's tipsy speech meant no harm.

"Then those filthy *dogs*—" Aunt Ophelia gestured spiritedly and almost spilled her drink. There was a quick hum of assent around the hall, a few quiet chuckles at her passion. "Those filthy Ruslaniv *dogs* took my precious brother and his wife, and they *thought* they could steal my precious nephew as well—but no, nobody was stealing him! Not even death! Nothing could steal my little nephew away. He came back. Miracle number two. And now here he stands, two years—almost three! Running our house with a hand as capable as his father's, and Cain—"

She leaned forward, imploring Cain from down the table. He gawked back at her from below his fingers, steepled against his forehead. His cheeks were on fire. He didn't want his aunt to say too much in her state of intoxicated inspiration.

"Even if you think I intrude, I love you very much," Aunt Ophelia went on, her voice dropping to a slow and heartfelt tone. Her eyes shone bright with the feeling. "I want you to know that I find you a very responsible young man, and even if you never tell me what has happened to you, even if you never let any of us in on the turmoil behind those lovely eyes of yours, even if you *never* trust us with the most private knowledge that keeps shadows over your soul, I support you in whatever you do. And I know everyone else in this court will too! If any of those Ruslaniv bastards knew what was good for them, so would they. God have mercy on them, *the fools*! They don't know what a man they oppose. So *to my nephew*! To you, our lord! To the Earl Dietrich on this New Year's Day—"

Uncle Bradley touched her arm, to gently signal a close to her loving, inebriated discourse. Aunt Ophelia sputtered on a word or two, tearing up, then held her drink high again and repeated in conclusion, *"To the Earl!"*

Applause rose in something like a roar. Cain could only stare at his plate. He smiled, faintly, because sometimes this was too much for him to handle. He was embarrassed by his aunt's slips of the tongue and the reminders of secret pains. Praise was not really what he searched for.

When he finally did look up, it was under the stares of his household—his *court*—and even the servants were clapping, silver trays tucked beneath their arms. The ovation drifted up to the ceiling. He could see Emily, glowing radiant between her mother and father. She looked so grown-up and lovely with her hair tied back in a loose, lustrous chignon, so much so that Cain actually felt the first pang of indecision for the day. It had to come at some point, and it came at that moment, meeting Emily's admiring eyes and exchanging a smile with her from down the table.

Running our house with a hand as capable as his father's…. I find you a very responsible young man.

Cain's throat tightened. His aunt's words had touched a shy and secret part of him, and she knew it. She was still beaming at him from her seat.

Yes. *Responsibilities*. He had those. They ran deep in his blood, on the backside of loyalty and pride, deeper even than love. Responsibilities, love, vengeance. They were all powerful and primitive forces. The question was, which one deserved more attention, and was he a monster for sleeping with the enemy's son?

Cain took hold of his wineglass and stood with a scrape of his chair on expensive checked floors. Rapier-A227 was a comforting shape against the small of his back, beneath cambric and brocade. The applause had died down into a mingling of voices, but as he stood and thrust his drink in the air, an eerie silence fell again—respectful, worshipful.

"Thank you, Aunt Ophelia," Cain said. His words felt too little in the vast dining hall. He cleared his throat. His eyes burned. His stomach knotted. His heart was pounding and his fingers were clammy. He lowered his wine, holding it in both hands, eventually setting it on the table before he dropped it altogether. It wasn't guilt he felt, or shame, just a strange and unsettling torn sensation.

"Thank you, all of you, for coming tonight," he began. "I know many of you are anticipating my decisions about the family, about the Dietrich house, for the next year. I'll begin by addressing my status with Lady Emily Kelley."

A murmur shivered down one side of the table. Emily hid behind her crimped bangs, staring at her plate. Cain knew everyone was on the edge of their seats, expecting a date to finally be announced for the marriage.

Cain smiled. It wasn't a pretense. His heart hurt, but he couldn't help smiling, bitter and aware. Emily's mother stared at him hard, with eyes burning like fire. Aunt Ophelia stared; his grandmother stared; everyone stared, and Cain couldn't speak for a moment. The words were stubborn.

"I've thought long and hard about this decision, and I'd like to announce that I will not be marrying Lady Emily Kelley."

The silence on the air buckled. Instantly, gasps sounded.

Cain went on, ignoring the interruptions. "At this point in time, with the world as it is, with the feud between this family and the wretched Ruslanivs still going strong, I feel the protection of the Dietrich family will be calling for one hundred percent of my time and effort. I refuse to keep my cousin Lady Emily hostage in the midst of that bloodshed. The center of New London is too dangerous. I would feel much better if she returned home to Essex with her mother and father, until the air here has settled a bit more."

Cain let the hush hang, heavy and tense. He could feel the hatred from Emily's mother and the other, less involved cousins, the urgent confusion from many others. Cain searched for Emily's eyes. They shimmered with the emotion she struggled to keep at bay. Her dainty chin was held high, blonde hair falling in dreamy curls at her ears and temples. She smiled, but she looked like it was the last thing she wanted to do as everyone stared at her and everyone stared at Cain, and the gossip started up already in the middle of dinner.

"But, my lord—" It was Emily's mother, of course, pompous Lady Kelley. "Don't you think we've been more than generous, allowing her to stay with her future husband *unwed*? Don't you suppose she could continue to stay, and be trained to protect herself *as your wife*? Why, Ophelia could train her. We all know what Ophelia finds *proper*."

More whispers, more gasps, and the contention of a family divided—between the simpletons from the country, with their subtle insults and judgmental remarks, and the world-weary ones from the heart of New London, whose views of the world were colored a bit grimmer.

Cain uttered a scoff, casting Emily's mother a scathing glance. He wasn't going to have her undermining him, whether her suggestion was reasonable or not. He didn't want to deal with the tears and heartbreak and questions. He just couldn't handle it. They all knew he was their mad earl, so why did they still expect things to go the way they wanted them?

"Your audacity is remarkable," he hissed. Uncle Bradley elbowed him. Cain sighed, saying with a bit more composure, "I've made my decision, Lady Kelley. At this moment, it's unchanging. Now, can we move on? I have *plans*, you see."

This was the part he'd been waiting for. Reigning over the discord around dinner, he declared, "I'm sure most of you are dying to hear news on the feud itself. We've come upon some information that is particularly incriminating, involving the Ruslaniv family. Our next move in this game of bloody tag is undecided as of yet, but please do be assured that *we have dirt* and we're going to *use it*. The real murderers of my parents will be caught, and the old schemes and deceptions will be brought to light so that the Ruslanivs will be *forced* to submit! With so much evidence, the Queen won't allow anything but justice! They're going down, I promise you! They won't escape this one, *the rats*. We've reached the beginning of the end, family!"

Again there was applause, and the Kelleys' grievances were forgotten in the wake of this new promise.

It was mayhem, beautiful mayhem, harsh on Cain's ears but comforting to his soul. He lifted his wine, grinning.

It felt good to say those things. It felt good because he knew it was true. It was the beginning of the end.

"To the Dietrich house!" he cried, and a number of glittering gold-encrusted goblets were thrust into the air around the table.

"*The Dietrich house!*" they echoed, which was followed by a chorus of voices, excited and urgent. Rejoice, the end was nigh! Centuries of ill will were drawing to a close!

Cain met Aunt Ophelia's bright eyes. He gave her a wink and tossed back a mouthful of wine, joining his household in their good cheer as his breath escaped in a burst of relief and laughter—

"*Oh, how sweet. Did your little spy tell you all that?*"

The voice came from the servants' balcony that hung over the dining room, and it was shrill and belittling and dissolved into wild, harrowing cackles from a dark-haired female gunslinger.

And as the rest of the scene registered in a matter of instants—the fur collars, the black masks, the red-haired man and three others rushing the walkway above with arms already out—the sound of gunshots rattled the air, and shells rained down on the dining table as bullets gnawed the ceiling and that awful cackling laughter rattled on and on.

Good God, it was the masquerade in October all over again.

Dishes shattered. Screams rose. Chairs and drinks were thrown over as guests and family members ran for the doors or ducked under the wide old table.

Cain chose the latter, yanking out his revolver. It wasn't going to do much in an ambush, especially not when the attackers were at that distance, but it was something, and it was there for instinct and defense as his thoughts raced with the icy resolve of panic.

They were the same ones from October. That he knew for sure. Again they'd somehow found an entrance into his home. Somebody was going to die, and Cain's heart gave a sickening thud. Who was it to be, then, fate?

"Earl Dietrich!" someone crooned from above. *"Come out and play!"*

Cain lifted the silver-embroidered tablecloth, searching the few faces beneath. Emily, her father, his feeble and shaking grandmother, a few country cousins. Most of those capable of fighting had left the dining room, maybe to corner the attackers upstairs.

Aunt Ophelia crouched at the other end of the table. She met Cain's eyes almost immediately.

The infiltrators shot at the walls, at the floors, at anything harmless to lure someone out. There were voices, and Cain recognized the slang. He was acquainted with the accent. A revolted shudder rattled through him, and a dawning fear that this was somehow his fault.

The voices in their foreign slang summoned forth the memory of Kelvin—*Ooh, miliya, raspidaty, precious boy, potselui menya....*

BLACK.

Aunt Ophelia jerked her head to the side. *Go,* she mouthed, motioning firmly beyond the table.

Cain hesitated at first, then made a run for the kitchen doors. A few bullets followed him, but by how worthlessly they were aimed, he knew they were nothing but intimidation. The popping of shells was like a tintinnabulation of bells from hell.

His breath ripped from his chest, sharp. His heart thundered. The floor tipped and swayed beneath him, all the hallways lengthening like a funhouse. Cain ran, and the urgency—the instinct—was different this time around. This part wasn't like the October masque. He was cold with panic.

This wasn't a regular fray. This was a sneak attack, a waylay; this was a true invasion of *his home*.

The horror was rusty, like he'd felt it before. It tightened in his chest, making it hard to breathe. Running, running—

Around every corner, behind every door, it seemed there were members of his household scattering. *Hiding.* He was sick with rage. He skidded into the servants' wing, climbing the stairs there to breach the second floor unseen.

To make his family fear for their lives like this—oh, these fools were going to pay!

Cain cocked the hammer of his gun before he opened the door to the second floor, peeking between the hinges first. He nudged the door open with his toe, following the wall down the corridor. Slowly, one step at a time.

Good God, the gnawing horror that he had somehow set this up for himself was too much to swallow. The intuition was dark and bruising, ripping at his fighting instincts like the hungry wind before a very bad storm.

The silence on the air was ominous. He wasn't sure where Security was, but he was confident they were on the move somewhere. His steps were soft, padded by the long imported rug in the hallway, and his fingertips shook.

The doors to his bedroom hung open.

The air was still as Cain crossed the hall, searching the corridor opposite for any sign of life.

There was nothing.

Open doors here, open doors there—but no movement.

Cain crouched down outside his room, hidden from sight from within but able to peek through the doors to inspect at least one corner of his bedroom.

There, he could see his long mirror. How convenient. He could see the other half of the room in it, and there was the rustle of clothes, a flash of black in the mirror. It wasn't a servant; that wasn't the sound of livery. It wasn't a guest either, because nobody could have made it to this part of the house that quickly unless they knew their way around.

Cain smelled the crispness of winter air. The chill of it drifted inside, which meant his balcony was open.

In one quick and jerky motion, Cain stood and threw one of the doors open, thrusting his gun into the bedroom as he crossed the threshold and confronted the intruder within.

Levi stood at the side of his bed, and there wasn't even a glimmer of shock in his eyes. He just looked as dark and lamentable as sin itself.

Cain almost dropped his gun. He pulled the trigger, in fact, and his heart stopped and he cried out in terror because he really hadn't meant to, it had just happened—but the primer backed out, thankfully, and the gun did not fire. The wave of massive relief did not mix well with the conscious and dramatic outrage. Cain needed a direction for it.

He threw his revolver to his pillow and clambered atop the bed, grabbing Levi by the front of his militia jacket and spitting the words out inches from his pretty face.

"*Levi*? What are you doing here now! What do you have to do with this! *What the hell is going on, you bloody fool*!"

Cain seethed. His throat burned as his voice tore loose from it, his knuckles ached where he clutched Levi's collar, his knees quaked where he stood on the edge of his bed. He knew there was all the animosity of murder in his eyes by the way Levi stared back at him, blankly, unmoved as a pretense. His brown eyes were cold and unaffected, but the bitterness of his frown was enough to give him away. He gave no immediate answer. Cain shook him the best he could by the collar. His voice was hoarse with fury.

"*Answer me, God damn you*! Levi, *what is going on*?"

Levi took hold of Cain's arms, yanking his fingers from his jacket. The same hard stare pierced him, and Cain burned with the onset of irrational desperation.

He didn't understand, but he wasn't stupid. Levi was there, and he shouldn't have been, and there'd been another attack.

He thought, quite twistedly, *Well, now Levi can see me in my good clothes*.

"You *monster*," Cain spat, hissing it into Levi's face. Levi cringed at the hot puff of breath, at the bark of the words, but he maintained his complacency, wrestling Cain down off the edge of the bed.

Cain's fingers hooked into claws, searching for something to grab as he stumbled down, snarling up at the Ruslaniv before him.

"You nasty, rotten, disgusting *fiend*, you *demon*, you downy *bastard*! You aren't even *denying—say something, for Christ's sake, Levi!*—you aren't even explaining yourself—you did this—you're part of this—*you filthy traitor*!"

Levi's face changed; expression flowed into it. His eyes sharpened and he scowled. "How can I be a *traitor*?" he insisted. "I'm a Ruslaniv."

"Me!" Cain broke one hand free for just a moment, clutching his chest emphatically. The desperation wrote itself across his face now, curdling with his hatred. He let go of his chest and threw his fists at Levi in a barrage of smacks and elbows. "You've betrayed *me*, Levi! You said you'd leave your family, and I believed you, but perhaps that was just me being love's ultimate clown, and all you wanted was to attack my family—"

Cain choked off into a startled burst of breath and voice as, with one swift kick, Levi swept his feet out and brought him down to the bed, one wrist still in his grip. Cain's eyes widened. Levi crawled forth, pinioning him.

But there was a crack in Levi's perfect indifference, a shimmer of something in his hardened eyes, and for just a moment, Cain felt a little regret for exploding so suddenly. His chest rolled. It hurt to breathe.

It wasn't that he despised himself for falling for more lies, because there hadn't been any more lies. It was that this was true betrayal of real trust, and he couldn't grasp why or how or....

"The less you fight me, the less time they'll have in your house," Levi said in a low, cold voice, and Cain shuddered in abhorrence at the affirmation of Levi's involvement.

Levi's hand was hot on his arm. Cain thought that, maybe, he was getting a real glimpse of the part of Levi he'd been using for his own means—the dark side. The trained side. The unemotional side. The *killer* side.

"So you *are* a part of this—"

"I've betrayed myself, as well."

"Don't get *romantic* on me now. I've walked a very fine line, trusting you, and you've just destroyed it all. I hope you're happy."

"For the love of God, Cain, *shut up*!"

Cain fell silent, eyes widening.

"I am a member of BLACK," Levi confessed, and somewhere down the hall in the southern wing of the house, gunshots exploded again.

Someone had clearly stood up to the abandoned challenge in the dining room. Cain felt himself sink lower into his bed as the breath left his lips in a sigh of cold consternation.

Levi went on. "I have been a member of BLACK since I was thirteen. I purposefully requested BLACK to stay under the radar once I learned you were sniffing around. After your parents were killed, the old members of BLACK who still lived were banished from New London and I was made the leader. My subordinates—no, my *fellow members*—are just doing what they feel is appropriate as loyal Ruslaniv men and women."

Levi paused, and Cain grimaced. He could hear screaming from somewhere else in the house.

Levi shook his head. "I'll tell you everything about that later, but for now—"

"*You knew!*" Cain's jaw tightened as a new stab of betrayal ripped open his heart. Steeling himself, he focused on a part of the ceiling to the left of Levi's head, eyes wide and cold. He felt the snarl transforming his face. "So the list of names I have, Father Kelvin's men, they're my parents' killers too, then. Oberon, Wolfe, Vyncent, Red, Quinton—"

Levi's patience seemed to wear ever thinner with each name that fell from Cain's lips, but at *Quinton*, he snapped. He grabbed Cain by the chin, redirecting his stare to meet his eyes, and Cain bristled at all the vulnerability there—*panic*. Pure panic. Levi was manic with it.

"Let's make a treaty, you and I," he demanded. Cain squirmed beneath him, loathing the way he held him down. "A pact, another *contract*. One that commands the feud come to an end under *our* conditions—yours and mine. The names on that list, you can imprison them all if any of them are still alive. And this contract, we'll both sign it and mark it with our blood, and the rest of our families will *have* to agree to it after that, as well as the rest of the House of Lords. It'll work. It will have to work."

Cain had confirmation now.

As he'd suspected, his kidnappers were the murderers of his parents. Three years of searching for the bastards without telling anyone exactly why—three years of injustice and secrets—three years of the fire of revenge burning in his chest, forever unquenched. Levi confirmed it all for him, and for one luscious breath, it was brilliant.

To have the answers was *brilliant*.

A pact, Levi had said. A pact wasn't exactly a new set of peace laws, but more like a petition—with both their blood on it, ending the feud under *their conditions*. That sounded brilliant too. That sounded like such a logical solution. Why hadn't they thought of it before?

Maybe it was the way Levi's voice was—level, and convincing, and confidential. Cain wanted it. He didn't want to hate him. He didn't have enough hatred in him for it, surprisingly. He pressed his cheek to Levi's arm, closing his eyes tight.

Surely if Levi was behind the attack, he wouldn't be going to such lengths to appease Cain, to quell the wrath, the hostility, the need for revenge. Right?

Cain turned his eyes up, meeting Levi's—and there must have been something in his stare, because Levi visibly softened.

A pact with the Ruslaniv who'd known the secrets all along, but who wanted the end of the feud too.

Cain wondered if his father would be proud of such a decision. He wondered if it would even last for very long.

It had been hardly five minutes since Cain had noticed his open bedroom doors, and in those five minutes, the standoff in the dining room had broken. Suddenly, there was commotion in the hallway—banging doors, loud voices, the bustle of a group—and as the sound of Aunt Ophelia's voice cut through the tense silence, Cain struggled to free himself from Levi's grip lest he be found in the arms of the enemy.

Less than five minutes. And in the next sixty seconds, the world became a blur.

A blur of time, relentless and fast, but seeming to stretch forever, as time always did in such vital moments.

The seconds ticked by....

Cain kicked Levi away. Levi complied. He moved to the side as Cain grabbed for his Rapier, scrambling off the bed and into the hallway. The red-haired attacker was there, the one who'd danced around a spray of bullets on the roof back in October, the one whom Cain had seen Levi talking to in Dmitri's Pavilion.

BLACK. To think he'd been lying with the leader of the wretched gang, the culprits who'd inherited the crimes. To think he'd been *so close to them* and yet so very far.

A blood-sealed pact to end the fighting....

Would it satisfy him?

In an opposite wing, Dietrich Security collided with intruders, it seemed. Voices and chaos sounded down the opulent halls.

The red-haired one was squaring off with Aunt Ophelia in the hall outside Cain's room, and he told her how someone named "the Rook" had told them how to get in. How the Earl had practically invited everyone, how this ignominy of the Dietrichs was going to go down in history with all the other embarrassments, how this was what happened when the Dietrichs went snooping around in Ruslaniv history. And Aunt Ophelia aimed her gun and told him that if he didn't give up by the count of three, he was dead and so were his pals. It became painfully clear to Cain then that there was some sort of misunderstanding between Levi and his despicable men.

Fifteen seconds passed.

Cain decided that if they were trying to pull another stunt like killing his parents, they would have shot people down already.

Levi touched his shoulder. Cain shook him off, thinking about how Aunt Ophelia shouldn't be there because she'd had four drinks already, and talented or not, her reactions were going to be dulled. Gunshots were all he heard, maybe only ringing in his ears, maybe far away in the house and ruining the walls and expensive furniture.

The red-haired gunslinger wasn't buying Aunt Ophelia's threat. He pointed his gun right back at Aunt Ophelia and told her that in the last few months, the Earl and the Rook had gotten so close, there'd never been a single hitch in the plan. Aunt Ophelia saw Cain by his doorway, and the dread on her face, the betrayal, the confusion, the disappointment—none of it could measure up to the crushed sound of her voice, sobered and defeated, as she husked:

"Cain.... What he's saying.... Can't be true, right?"

Twenty-two seconds now, and Cain opened his mouth, searching for the words. He stared. His heartbeat was too loud in his ears. What was he to say? Everything was being thrown into the light now—his own secrets, his own guilt. How was he supposed to mend this now, in this moment of conflict? How was he to convince her that what he had with Levi, the Ruslaniv heir, was good and true and worth the disloyalty?

The staccato of gunshots and shouts echoed from across the house. Footsteps pounded down the hallway, and yes, the rest of Security was coming, he hoped. They'd come and get this red-haired gunslinger, and Cain shook his head, brow knotting, opening and closing his mouth dumbly.

How did he tell her? What did he tell her? This was his fault. He'd let this happen.

Around the corner, the footsteps scraped to a halt. There was laughter—laughter dancing to the ceiling from below the full-face mask of a blond man. Cain recognized him almost immediately from Brackham's, and again he felt rather idiotic.

Another few rounds of gunfire shattered the air, discordant, lead scattering in close proximity. A maid at the other end of the hallway screamed, cowering behind a palm in the corner.

Thirty seconds.

Red.

Red, red, red.

The voices of Rodney and Graham were closing in on the corner now, and Cain didn't even care about the masked few that darted past him where he'd crumpled down against his bedroom doors to avoid getting shot. The red-haired one had opened fire, and through Cain's bedroom Levi's gang went, probably just as they'd come in, throwing themselves over the balcony in escape.

The curtains fluttered. The noise carried. The red-haired gunslinger stared in shock, then bolted, brushing past Cain and monkeying out over his balcony like the others.

Cain watched, mouth open, as Aunt Ophelia sagged to her knees, and the imported rug caught the blood as it rushed from the hole in her neck, just above her collarbone. The hole in her chest, just above the line of her bodice. The holes in the rest of her, gushing.

Thirty-six seconds was all it took.

Levi was behind Cain, and the smell of gunpowder and metal and the stink of blood permeated the air.

The silence in the absence of the intruders rang in Cain's ears. He was grateful. He didn't want to hear the sounds of his aunt struggling for her last breaths. He didn't want to hear the roar of hysteria from the rest of the house.

The blood stained the pearls and silver-nested rubies on Aunt Ophelia's breast.

Inept. They were all inept. When had they gotten that way? When he'd ensured security would still be lax on his wing of the house, so they wouldn't find suggestive footprints in the snow or perhaps hear the gasps between kisses or the secret laughter of gunslinger and earl? Or was it before that? Was it when Cain had gone missing, or when he'd returned mad and bloodthirsty and changed? Was any semblance of security only to humor him?

Aunt Ophelia was a ball of bloody brocade and satin on the floor, and if she was still clinging to life, it didn't matter at all, because she was unconscious and fading fast. She looked like a flower ripped from its stem, thrown to be crumpled underfoot.

The Rook, the red-haired one had said, over and over, and it occurred to Cain rather peacefully that that was Levi. He'd seen the word engraved on Levi's gun: *R O O K, and that was Levi.*

Cain rocked to his knees and climbed to a shaky stand. He turned. The heel of his shoe squished in the soggy carpet.

He hit Levi.

He punched and slapped, just hitting as the tears filled his eyes and doubled, trebled his vision. The world seemed to sway. His chest was tight.

"*You bastard!*" he shrieked. "*You* did this! This is all *your fault!*"

He sought out Levi's eyes as the tears blurred his own. He shook him, hit him, stomped his feet and begged for it to be different. He trembled in his hatred.

"All you wanted from me was a way in to my family! That was it! You're a liar and a sneak and a devil, and you played me! You took advantage of me! I thought—no, I didn't think. If I'd thought, I wouldn't have fallen for your tricks, you.... You blasted.... *You dirty Ruslaniv, I'll kill you!*"

Cain smacked Levi across the face. Not a slap but not quite a balled fist, just the butt of his palm with clawed fingers. He felt his nails scrape into the soft skin he loved to touch. His hand stung from the impact.

Levi stared at the floor, skin reddening. There were little marks from Cain's nails, bleeding in fragile, glittering beads on the apple of his cheek.

Uncle Bradley and Mr. Renton rounded the corner and stopped short, frozen in place by the scene they found in the western wing. Aunt Ophelia, Cain, and a Ruslaniv.

Sixty seconds had passed by the time the curtains fluttered and Levi was climbing down the side of the Earl's balcony, and only after he'd scaled the stacked-stone wall and left Dietrich grounds did the first man speak.

It was Uncle Bradley, sending the other two off to search the house and then the estate, and to meet with Security and the one attacker they'd managed to catch. Uncle Bradley would follow not long after to gather everyone in the drawing room, count heads, and get them all something to drink. "Cain?" Uncle Bradley ventured.

The bloody hallway spun. The tears spilled over, but Cain kept his face straight. With the wave of numbness flowing over him, forcing all thoughts and emotion to recede like the tides, it wasn't very difficult to look blank. Cain grabbed one of the doors to his room for stability, but it moved on its hinges, and he sat down heavy on the carpet and reached for his uncle to help him up.

SCENE FOUR

THEY'D ALL reveled in a sense of rebellious accomplishment as they'd retreated, but Levi didn't.

It was happening again, this inevitable pattern of tragedy in his life.

There was a knot in his throat and a clenching around his heart, and it wasn't really remorse so much as a feeling of emptiness.

The same spiraling, unquestioning submission to apathy he'd succumbed to in his younger years, tucking away rational thought and just *obeying*. It was easier that way. He didn't have to deal with the gravity of things that way. The regret, the responsibility, the pain of his heart.

The rest of them were so obviously cowed by his sudden change of disposition, reverent of him as they'd never been before. Not out of duty, perhaps, but out of awe. Like gossip-loving children, it seemed they finally came to terms with the extent of their leader's involvement with Earl Dietrich, and they were dumbstruck in wonderment.

All you wanted from me was a way in to my family! You took advantage of me! You dirty Ruslaniv!

Yes. Unintentionally, yes. That was what he'd done.

"You left William," his father surmised, and the placidity of his voice was unnerving.

Levi licked his lips, gawking at his father's broad back. "Yes," he whispered. "They'd already gotten him, though, Father. There was nothing we could do."

The tea set was imported silver, handcrafted. It crashed to the floor as Lord Ruslaniv's hand swept the table, and the tea and the sugar spilled on the carpet. Silver clattered. Candied fruits and nuts scattered from their shining dishes.

Levi didn't wince. He held his face straight, a mask of bitterness. The weight of everything settled, precarious, on his shoulders again— of being inane, of his brother's shadow, of the foul play three years ago, of the nights spent with the Dietrich earl in his arms. Something leaden—maybe shame, maybe anger—coiled in his stomach and crawled beneath his skin.

Across from him, his mother sat with her back rigid and her hands clasped in her lap, lace gloves wrinkled as she clutched at her little fan. She stared down her nose at him. If he'd been younger, he might have shrunk down at the scorn in her cold, contemptuous frown, but he'd learned to brush these things off.

The lounge filled with the sounds of rage. Levi's father paced, footsteps heavy and breaths heavier. He lumbered to and fro, around the sofas, past the spilled tea, beyond the marble mantel with its blackened grate and stone lions carved in the corners. He muttered things beneath his breath, colorful sentences incoherent but trembling as they fell from his red face, and only after he'd made his rounds through the lounge three times did he stop, fist his hands behind his back, and stare out the window into the snowfall. Thin, watery. It wouldn't stick. It hit the ground and melted, but it was still snow.

Levi reeled. He could just *feel* the others eavesdropping in the hallway. His mother's eyes sharpened, the condescending old hag. There was silence. The clock in the corner ticked the seconds away. The tension was thick.

"Yes, nothing you could do." His father's voice rumbled. The words weren't acidic, but they stung. "Because now *I* have to go and beg for him back. It's never anything *you* have to do. You're not the head of the family, you see."

"Father, can I—?"

"No." Lord Ruslaniv turned, sharply. He leveled a despairing frown on his son, eyes narrowed. "No, you may not. I'm not through speaking. I can't even *find the words* to tell you what I feel at the moment. I'm furious. I'm saddened. I thought you'd be different, Lawrence. I thought you'd be a better leader for BLACK than Quinton, with your level head."

His mother shifted loudly as if to remind her husband she was still there and favoring her eldest son. Both Levi and his father easily ignored her.

"*Father—*"

"You're instigating the feud with these deplorable actions. That debauchery in October, this needless ambush. It's New Year's, for Christ's sake, can't you take a break? The old BLACK—they were nothing more than a street gang given too much power, and by the time I realized that, it was too late. They had filthy motives and were run with filthy morals. But you…. Lawrence, my precious son, I thought you'd be able to govern my gunslingers with honor, and respect, and *chivalry*. Does chivalry exist no longer?"

Levi couldn't breathe for a moment. The shame was crippling, numb but sharp at the same time, sneaking up on him like poison. "I let them do it. I didn't speak up."

"*God damn it, son!*" The painting near the window—Ruisdael, *Bentheim Castle*—jumped as Levi's father slammed a fist against the wall. Levi bristled for the first time. "*God damn it—*" his father sputtered again, face reddening all the more. "Lawrence, you're the leader! You *have* to speak up! It's your responsibility. You're the sound mind that leads them, and if you're not sound enough to do so, *of course* they're going to wreak havoc like a bunch of little punks!"

Levi wilted into the sofa, staring at his hands. He felt like a child again, callow and incompetent. His mother's eyes seemed to gain power; her stare grew more and more uncomfortable as it pierced into him. His ears burned behind his clenched teeth. *A bunch of little punks.* He was still the leader and that still hurt his pride. *Not sound enough.* Yes, how could a traumatized romantic be sound enough to lead a pocket of organized crime?

Levi let out a slow breath, hoping to release some of the tension inside with it. He met his father's eyes, miserably, and whispered, "I was being selfish, and it made its mark."

"If this continues," his father said as if he hadn't heard, "I'll have to ask all of you to leave New London, like I asked the others. I'm sorry. I'm too tired for all of this. I've fought enough in my lifetime. I'm old and I'm tired. If you want to play war like a little boy, then you'll have to wait until *you're* the face of this family, because while *I* am, I won't stand for it. There is absolutely no appeal to me in starting fights with no point. That's just bad taste."

There was silence. Then "Think on it, my son. I banished your brother, my firstborn and the heir superior. I can banish you if need be, as well."

SCENE FIVE

Lady Ophelia Dietrich's funeral was on a Sunday, at the church in Molching Court. White flowers and satin filled her casket, the same blank canvas as her dress, so Cain took a blue bloom from someone's bouquet and put it in her hair. She looked too much like his father for him to look at her long.

Weeping relatives and friends reminisced together. Cain didn't join them. He stared at the stained-glass window over his aunt's casket and wondered if his parents had been given a funeral, if anyone had found them in Lovers' Lane, or if they'd been mutilated by the undertaker. He'd been gone for so long after. He had no idea what had gone on without him, and nobody had really told him because he'd never really asked. He didn't think his soul could bear any more incurable heartbreaks.

Aunt Ophelia was not the only casualty of the ambush. Three Dietrichs were severely injured, two of them being members of the protective services. Hazel had been shot in the shoulder and breathed her last that night in the royal hospital. A country cousin or two sustained wounds.

Bullet holes ravaged the dining hall, most of the good china ruined. All the polished wood of the table and chairs was pocked and slivered. The upstairs hallway bore similar scars. A sconce had been knocked off the wall and statuary shattered, paintings marred.

They let the culprit they'd captured go home the night of the whole affair, when Lord Ruslaniv himself had arrived at the front gates with weary eyes, asking peacefully. It turned out their prisoner was his nephew.

There was no ball that night.

For the first two days, Cain spent his time at the window in the library, a book in hand. But he didn't read; he just stared outside at the snow. Its purity was a mockery. Nothing was as good and clean as snow.

Emily tried to sit with him a few times, but after endless silences, she retreated and tried to find someone she'd have the guts to abide her worries in. Aunt Ophelia was gone, after all, and now Emily was even more alone in the house.

The Persians abandoned English to speak urgently in their melodic language. They might have been the only members of the household that talked beyond whispers. Lady Kelley gave quite a few angry sniffs, and then she and her husband took their daughter and returned to the country after Aunt Ophelia's interment, clearly feeling unsafe in New London.

It was a stretch of time that seemed a dream.

Security was tightened around every wing of the house.

Messengers from the Ruslaniv family arrived periodically, frightened and fidgeting on the front stairs as the Dietrich footman relayed the Earl's intense desire *not* to speak with them.

These tentative attempts at peaceful correspondence were unbeknownst to the public, but a sensation of numb despair still seemed to fall and blanket the rest of New London. There was sudden stillness. Not peace, but gloom, soured the air, turning it fickle with tension. It was a quiet anguish, as some citizens mourned and others couldn't shake the feeling that it was *not the right time* to hate.

A fortnight passed with no real trouble, no real fray between the families and their supporters, and it was a record in the last few years. It was an eerie state.

Cain didn't have an appetite. Emily was gone. He drifted around the house as walls and floors and furniture were mended, new frames and china ordered. He did not report the men on the list of names connected to St. Mikael's. He did not report BLACK. The authorities couldn't accomplish a single thing that would satisfy his thirst for revenge.

He wanted to take care of things himself, in due time.

He kept the list of names close on his person and refused to speak about the secret connection to BLACK that had brought their attack upon the house. His uncle grew darkly frustrated with him, but could do nothing about it. Cain was the earl, after all, and without Aunt Ophelia, it was harder to break through to him.

Cain ignored his office during the day, wandering around lost in a state of melancholy. He didn't talk. He was silent and solemn. Nothing angered him and nothing pleased him. He paused by windows and stared outside into the sun, into the night, into the drizzling sky, into the white afternoon. He took a bath and stayed in the water until all the steam had faded from the mirrors and glass. He walked around in his nightclothes, trailing his fingers on the embossed walls, feeling the posh carpet beneath his toes.

He couldn't sleep. He went into his old nursery and touched the globe and books and old figurines; he stopped at his office and gawked at the broad doors, hands clasped behind his back. He sat cross-legged at the window in the lady's boudoir, which had once been his mother's. He smoked with the Persians and welcomed the younger, prettier one into his own room, letting him shower him with kisses and affection that really meant nothing at all to Cain, detached and dissociated as he was, and well practiced with it. He was a man; he had needs. Or at least he went through the motions of having needs as if seeking to convince himself he was still himself somehow.

Except that he wasn't.

He went into Emily's old room and touched her porcelain clock, her footstool, her vanity table, running his fingers down the mirror and thinking about how pretty she was. He hedged every day, but finally went into Aunt Ophelia's room and laid down on her bed and smelled her pillows, went through her clothes and jewelry and every little trunk of her things. He sat in the silence and wondered if, like Shakespeare's *Hamlet*, her ghost was around, and if it could hear his wordless plea for forgiveness.

By that time, Cain had reached a cold and emotionless place like apathy.

Love was meaningless in the barren wasteland of logic and fact, where all feelings and thoughts were mechanical and uncomplicated.

Cain went into his own room and curled up in his bed. He closed his eyes and wished he wasn't alone, that he could feel the warmth of the old German hound at his toes, the swell of his furry chest as he breathed, or that he could run down the hall and into his parents' room and bury into their comforter while his father was a wall of protection that smelled like spicy cologne and looked like omniscient smiles, and his mother ran her fingers through his hair and warmed him with her angelic touch.

But that was not so.

Not now, and not ever again.

SCENE SIX

HE SMELLED the zest of smoldering tobacco, brought up on the breeze and into his room where the balcony doors were cracked to allow some fresh air.

Somebody smoked below his balcony.

Cain didn't acknowledge it. The butler was still there, gathering the day's dirty clothes, respectfully turning his eyes away as Cain dressed for bed, toes curling in the white fur of the rug. He stood in front of the long mirror, staring at his reflection. The skin below his eyes was rather dark, now wasn't it?

The butler left. Cain drifted around the room to peek out between the curtains, wondering if he could see the trespasser beneath his balcony. He'd returned security to its previous lenience, and the invitation had quite clearly been accepted.

Cain slipped out barefoot onto his balcony, the stone slimy with snow and slush. In an instant his feet were numb with cold. His fingers brushed the head of the little stone gargoyle, and Cain stretched over the side of the balcony and met Levi's stare where he stood, looking up, a distant, poignant look on his face as if he'd never expected Cain to come out.

It meant something, didn't it? There Levi was, back again. Was he a masochist or just stupid?

Cain motioned with his free hand, white fingers dancing in the moonlight. "Come up here," he called down, and the biting wind drove his hair in and out of his face.

Without waiting for Levi's reply, he turned and walked back into his room, drying his feet on the fur rug. There was silence as Levi killed the last of his cigarette and climbed the icy stone.

Cain waited on his bed. Surrounded by goose-down pillows, amid bedding of smooth cotton and comforters embroidered with blue and silver, he sat with all the languid, elegant apathy and complacent finesse he'd had when he worked for Father Kelvin and was simply waiting for the next client.

Levi closed the balcony doors when he entered, but there was still a chill in the room. His very presence filled Cain with a sense of desperation as if he'd summoned a demon against all warnings. Ah, God, was Levi splendid. But Cain's resolve was stony. He was a Dietrich, after all. He was quite possibly the only Dietrich that mattered anymore in lieu of recent events.

"Hello, Levi," he murmured.

The fire in the hearth popped.

"Cain," Levi returned, nodding his head as his form of obeisance.

Cain didn't resent him for informalities. His militia jacket hung open, and Cain just wanted to wrap his arms around that narrow waist, alluring as it was. Sophistication and sin, standing there in front of his balcony doors. Sophistication, sin, betrayal, and love.

"Sit by me," Cain insisted. "I want to talk."

Levi moved with the precision of one accustomed to caution, and his eyes were hard and critical, silently scrutinizing to try and piece together a possible outcome to the situation. The surroundings, Cain's mannerisms, his bizarre calm. Cain smirked as Levi sat down, loving the way the mattress shifted with his weight. His toes curled in the sheets as his nerves began to tingle. He reached beneath his pillow.

"I don't want you to explain yourself," he whispered, and Levi held his stare. Cain pulled his revolver from beneath his pillow, took Levi's hand, and opened his uncooperative palm himself. He lifted his gun from his lap and placed it in Levi's fingers.

"Kill me," he said, meeting Levi's eyes again. "Kill me, if it's what you intended to do all along. Like my parents. To kill me would be to kill off the last direct heir of the Dietrichs, and then your family would win. You'd be a hero among your followers. That's what you want, isn't it? To get close to me and then bring my family down. So I'm letting you. *Kill me.*"

There was a moment where the coldness in Levi's eyes left and he looked absolutely stunned as if Cain's nonchalant dare had really thrown him off. And that made Cain falter, made him wonder about everything again. Was Levi really the villain here or not? Levi's fingers curled on the revolver—but he just set it down at the foot of the bed, grabbed Cain by the wrist, and pulled him forward. There was a strange composure about his face, replacing the bitter scrutiny.

"You love me," Levi guessed, barely audible below his breath. "You do. You just admitted it. If you didn't love me, Cain, you certainly would never have offered your life. You'd have killed me even before your aunt was stiff and underground."

Cain's resolve wavered at Levi's touch, his stare, his voice. He tried to protest, but the words all died at the back of his throat, coming out in choppy little grunts. Levi's words struck notes of alarm in his heart. So Cain batted at him, like a spoiled child, unable to get the words out and using his fists instead. Levi rocked with the motion. Cain's brows knotted above harsh, narrowed eyes. Levi wasn't fazed at all.

"There were never intentions to follow in the shadow of the old BLACK," Levi edged out, rushed but collected. "Never. If anything, it was a childish game of tag, of hide-and-seek. And I didn't entirely grasp the… *gravity* of what we were doing either. I'm sorry for that."

Cain hit him again, gritting his teeth. Levi's head wagged with the blow. He kept Cain's gaze, mouth drawn in a terse line. His cheek was bright red from Cain's smacks.

"Bastard!" Cain hissed. This wasn't what he'd expected to hear. Never mind that he wanted to hear it, it wasn't how it was supposed to go! Things never worked out in the end. "Liar! Kill me. Just spare me these dumb, romantic tales and *kill me*!"

"It's not what you think." Levi's hand tightened on Cain's wrist, jerking him closer. "I made mistakes. I gave my fellow members too much freedom, too much influence over me, when I should have been the one directing them. It was my fault, Cain."

Cain kicked this time, ruining the blankets. "Don't call me by my name, damn it!"

Levi craned in, searching for eye contact again. Cain gnashed his teeth, his breath quickening with the pace of his heart. He hated Levi. He hated Levi for confusing him when he'd finally accepted the way things had to be. And his words—they seemed to reach right into him and pluck the truth out, no matter how well Cain hid it. God, he wanted him! He needed him! It made no sense to deny himself. He just couldn't stop, and how could it be that he, the passionate and driven Earl, was cursed with a love damned by the very stars that had bestowed it upon him?

"I never wanted this to happen," Levi whispered. His breath shivered on Cain's skin.

Cain smelled it. He could summon its taste from memory.

Suddenly Levi pushed away, swung off the bed and stood, pacing to and fro. He was stricken with urgency now, it seemed. He scowled, pressured.

"I swore, over and over," he reminded. "You trusted me even when you knew my wretched name. Why can't you just believe me *now*? You're so *stubborn*! Our contract to end the feud, you agreed to it. It can still happen, it can still work. It will be worth even more now. Certainly they'll see that you and I have been peaceful together for the past few months and that it *is* possible for our families to live together in harmony. Or, at least, a cousin of harmony. Tonight, Cain, let's draw up an agreement and present it tomorrow."

Cain clambered to stand on the bed, glowering down at Levi. He scrambled for Levi's hands, pressing them to his throat. "I did trust you!" he blurted, voice jagged. "I *did*—but now I would rather be dead than be betrayed again, to be abandoned by those I trusted and consigned to love." His throat was tightening. He was too worked up. He'd had such a perfect plan too, and Levi just had to come in and tip it upside down on him! And did that mean something ineffable, that Levi could just work his black magic on him so effortlessly?

There was a slight scuffle then, Levi wrenching his hands from Cain's throat and casting a frustrated hiss in his direction. Cain almost lost his balance and struck out at Levi again because he couldn't find the words. There was a wrestle on the edge of the bed, tangled arms and trembling fists, like two children in their first fight in the schoolyard. Bitten voices, struggling limbs, fingernails catching in the fabric of clothing. Finally Levi sent Cain tumbling back to the blankets and followed to pin him down. Ah, Levi's favorite move, apparently.

Cain recaptured his bearings and flung his arms about Levi's shoulders—and then he felt the cold metal of his own revolver pressed up to his skin.

His eyes widened. His mouth fell open, and his heart raced as his chest rolled with frantic breaths. Levi peered down at him. It was obvious he read all of Cain's shock as just what it was: disbelief, alarm, the first real panic, because he'd never expected to somehow end up pinned to his bed with Levi holding a gun to his temple. So maybe he'd never expected Levi to really accept the offer. Maybe it had all been manipulative.

Cain's fingertips twitched at Levi's shoulders. He couldn't talk for a moment—could hardly breathe. Levi regarded him coolly, a handsome gangster who meant business and business alone, mouth in a thin line.

"Is this really what you want?" Levi asked, and his voice was silky and smooth. "To die? I can deliver as much right now. I suppose it *is* very much like you to want death by the hands of your only real friend."

"You *are* my friend," Cain confirmed, breathless. He swallowed, mouth dry. He couldn't help but shake like a leaf with the gun pointed to his head, because he'd never been on this end of such a situation before and he didn't like it. He rolled his eyes up, meeting Levi's. He tried to compose himself. He licked his lips. Levi stared down at him, waiting, as if for something in particular. Cain didn't know what he wanted, but he knew what he was going to give him.

He let one hand sag down, off Levi's shoulder, and touched it to his face. Levi softened with the brush of skin. Cain smiled thinly. Levi was so pretty, clean-shaven in the morning and still soft by evening. Cain's smile faded.

"There will be no peace," Cain whispered, and it hurt his heart to say it because he didn't want to see the disappointment in Levi's eyes when he shattered his beautiful vision of justice and ceasefire. The Rapier-A227 was cold on his skin. "Even if we draw up a contract, there will be no peace. Ever. It will be fake, a pretense, a shroud of play-pretend. Gangs will rip it apart again. We'll have no control. The people will forever want more. There will always be hatred—like with God and the Devil, people are always searching for somewhere to place the blame. And better yet, there will be no peace inside *us* because nobody will ever understand what *we* want."

"You have got to be the most cynical man...." Levi's face darkened. "Listen, I want to teach you a lesson here. I may not have the right name, but I have twice the guts."

Cain scowled in turn. "Don't you understand, Levi? Morally, you and I are ruined! We're sinful. We're going to burn in hell for so many transgressions! And we're *noble*. We're forever in the public eye and forever will be, and they don't care if we want to be left alone to each other. The only way we can be together is if our families stay divided in hatred."

"That's ridiculous," Levi hissed. "We'll find chances to be together whether they are or not. Whether people *judge us* or not. Why does it matter to you? Is reputation that important?"

"Christ, Levi, we're the faces of our families! We have *responsibilities*."

"I don't understand how responsibilities could stand in the way—"

"Why give up what we want for the good of the people? They never do anything for us, anyway. Why just give up and say, 'All right, it's a truce?' *I*, for one, will never have peace, Levi. The betrayed blood of my family will never allow me to have peace so long as it flows through my veins. And maybe, if there is peace one day, and you and I *do* get what we want, maybe I won't have peace even then, because every time I look at you, I'll grow to hate you for your family's past wrongdoings. Or what if I avenge my family's pain, and every time I look at you, I grow to hate myself in guilt? What if the treaty we draw up works, and the feud ends, and we can be together freely, what then do I do about Emily? What do I say to those around me? She'll be devastated to know I can't love her that way, and neither of us will be happy in a forced marriage. There is no way, Levi! There is no peace. It does not exist. It will never exist—"

Cain cut off, choking on his breath, eyes widening again as Levi's hand moved. But the sounds of the gun he heard were not of the hammer cocking or the trigger moving. It was just the click of metal as Levi lifted it, unlocked and swung out the cylinder, and dumped the bullets and the empty revolver on the bed. Cain stiffened as one rolled down and touched his knuckle—cold, smooth metal. Like the tooth of a monster.

Levi thumbed hair out of Cain's face and pressed a kiss to his forehead, just above his gray eyes. Cain flinched back from it, squeezing his eyes shut instinctively. Levi's lips dusted his eyelids, the bridge of his nose, his cheeks, his chin.

Levi hovered over him, the seriousness on his face no longer cruel and hostile, but heated, desperate. Human, and only human. Cain tried to fight the emotion swelling in his chest, thickening in his throat, but he locked his arms around Levi's shoulders and pulled him down closer, giving in to everything. There was just no fighting it.

His heart jumped. A shiver rattled through him.

They made love.

ROBBING THE cradle. That was what Levi was doing, wasn't it? Cain was five years his junior, all angles and raw craving. But he was hardly innocent. So, then, it wasn't really robbing the cradle, so much as it was robbing a bed of red sheets and experience.

Bullets rolled in the bedding. Below him, aching and alluring, Cain looked vulnerable and yet somehow in control, hard and hungry, like all of this was happening just because he allowed it.

Guilt and injured pride coalesced with rampant desire, and the kisses started out biting. Maybe, at some point, Levi would be able to tell Cain that he knew where he'd been those long months, held captive under St. Mikael's, and that he'd seen him in Lovers' Lane, and that he knew who had been the mastermind of the plan in the first place. That he knew what kinds of sins had lionized his everlasting soul. But there was a smarter part of Levi, the part of his mind unaffected by things like emotion and impulse, and it reminded him that Cain had a pride he would carry to the grave. If he was aware Levi knew those things....

Cain didn't seem affected by anything of the sort, though, freed for the moment from the greedy clutch of the grudge that haunted him.

His fingertips were cold where they touched Levi's face. Levi kissed them. He rolled over, bringing Cain over to straddle his lap. Oh, the tempting heat of the places between his legs—and Cain was otherwise so loud and indignant, so cold and sarcastic, but the moment Levi's hand brushed his cheek or gathered him close enough to feel his heartbeat, or reached down between his thighs, he melted into a tangle of flushed limbs and stubborn glares as if ashamed of his weaknesses and still hiding behind that dark scowl. The words "clinging to the last shreds of dignity" sprang to Levi's mind.

Cain sat up straight and prim, still sitting atop Levi and arching like a cat in the middle of a stretch, and he regarded Levi down his nose like a prince should. Levi smiled faintly.

His jacket and his leather—*the Rook*, pistols, cartridges, holsters and weapons belt—all of it lay on the floor off the side of the big bed, beside his boots. The dying fire sizzled. There was intimidating quiet and the shift of clothes, the rustle of bedding, and tentative little breaths of calculation.

"Leave the lights up," Cain hissed, finally, for once begging to be seen in the hot dance of the lamps. "Leave the room lit so I can look my shame in the face."

"So be it," Levi whispered, "because I want to look my love in the face."

Cain crumpled down at that, grimacing under the weight of his own failures as vengeful earl. He couldn't keep up the front any longer, Levi knew. He was trying so hard. He buried his nose in Levi's neck. Levi loved the feel of his teeth on his skin. Ah, the sensations were surreal. The smell of Cain, the feel of him, the sound of him, the taste of him.

Levi pulled him into an openmouthed kiss. Cain held to him by the collar of his shirt and Levi shuddered. There was the press of him down against his sex again, titillating, and bracing, blood rushing every direction as his breath quickened. His passion stirred hotter and hotter. He ripped at the buttons of Cain's nightshirt. Ah, perfect skin, the warm pressure of his ass against Levi's hips.

Levi threw Cain back to the blankets, and Cain gasped like he was actually startled—but when Levi looked up, Cain was stoic again, and lying there fever hot, chest heaving, his eyes aflame.

Levi hovered over him with a racing heart. He'd never wanted someone so desperately before in his life, not even as a lusty adolescent. He'd never wanted to hurt someone and hold them in his arms at the same time, never wanted to come together so hard and fast that the pain bled together with the pleasure like colors running on a wet canvas. He felt like an animal, driven by primal need.

Cain glanced at Levi demurely and licked his lips. "You look a little lost," he teased, dryly and indifferently, but the joke itself died away as Levi sputtered, "I've fallen in love with you."

Cain's act as prince of passion seemed to falter for a moment. His brow knotted with the wordless question: *What?*

"I have," Levi pressed, breathless.

Cain ran his hands down his back, and Levi shivered. Cain's hands drifted around to unfasten his trousers.

"I know you have," Cain whispered. "But *show* me."

They romped, kicking blankets off the side of the bed. Bullets lost in the sheets fell to the floor. Cain led the hot press and awkward friction, the way an experienced set of hips shifted to ease the initial pain of penetration. Sticky skin, flushed sex. Toes curled as gasps married with muffled cries of pleasure. Hips cramped. Muscles quivered. Cain dug his nails into Levi's naked chest, scraping his nipples, and Levi wasn't sure whether he should like it or not.

"You'll be the death of me!" Cain gasped, clutching Levi's face in his palms.

Levi kissed his nose and tightened his fingers on Cain's cock. "You make me feel alive," he countered tenderly. But shuttling into those sweet, sensitive, secret places hard and fast, Levi was terrified of not feeling worthy of any of the delight at all. Not the carnal, not the spiritual, not a single bit of this closeness Cain gave him. Ah, surely he was a masochist. He would take a bullet for Cain even as Cain smiled behind the trigger.

"Cain, what do you say? Shall we make the pact? Shall we seek to end the fighting together?"

"I can't be without you," Cain moaned, perfect surrender, and Levi didn't care that it wasn't a straight answer.

Levi came with a sharp dance of the hips. Although he'd finished, he kept going—numb, tender, slick—but he was determined, and he didn't stop until Cain pulled away, and Levi reached around his sides and brought him to the climax of pleasure in turn.

And maybe… maybe those were tears shimmering in Cain's eyes, or just the glaze of sex. He didn't smile. He didn't look soft. He looked as dark and morbid as ever, but the love in his pale stare was obvious, heavy, overwhelming, and Levi buried into his chest and ignored how pitiful that was. He, a grown man, gunslinger and gentleman, and he was blushing in the arms of a man hardly twenty.

Cain ran his fingers through Levi's hair. Nothing was said, no questions were asked. They lay in silence, bodies tingling. The fire had gone out. The flames in the lamps shivered.

Cain drifted off. Levi resituated to hold Cain to his chest again, looking up at the notches and designs on the coffered ceiling as the need for sleep burned at the backs of his eyes and he thought about everything, without really thinking at all. The recurring thought was *Just a little longer, and then I'll leave. Just a little longer….*

Daylight broke, and the son of Lord Ruslaniv was comfortably tangled with Cain Dietrich in one arm and the other flung out, hanging off the side of the bed, like a little boy passed out for a nap.

He was asleep.

ACT FIVE
REQUIESCAT

SCENE ONE

MAGGIE WAS a strong woman. Full lips, an oval face, and a straight nose made her a very staid-looking maid, but there was a tenderness in her eyes that created a sort of gypsy-like beauty out of it all. Dark hair contrasted with her smooth olive-colored skin lusciously, and she was far from the frail, petite, birdlike thing girls and ladies struggled to be. She was voluptuous and broad shouldered, and there was something of an accent to her words that was familiar and nostalgic.

It was Maggie who had been Cain's nurse when he was younger. He remembered her face from his earliest memories, in the background of foggy recollections, floating behind his parents, his aunt, other workers, and servants. She had taken care of him: snacks, naps, playtime, a careful eye on the prodigious only son of the Dietrichs. Cain remembered her sitting in the corner while he played. He remembered her looking sad when he disobeyed, maybe because she knew she'd be punished, because how could she not listen to her young master, even though he was simply a temperamental three-year-old?

Cain remembered Maggie sometimes tucking him into bed when his mother was talking with his father in the den. Maggie used to make little flowers out of folded paper for Cain and his friend, the Byron boy. Maggie had been stern, but never reprimanding. As Cain had gotten older, he'd tormented her with questions about the world (most she couldn't answer), and managed to manipulate his way out of her watchful eye for an hour or two before she came bursting through the door, red-faced and panicked, only to sink down beside him, kiss his forehead, and whisper something like, "Thank God, thank God, the Lady would have killed me...."

And it was Maggie who found them then, the son of Lord Ruslaniv and the Earl, tangled comfortably in expensive sheets as the January air trickled in through the grate and daylight pried through the curtains.

Cain wasn't fully awake yet when the door opened with a weak whine of hinges. The silence that followed was quite loud enough. There was the echo of the house waking and, dark hair in its usual plaits, Maggie stood wordless and staring.

Shit.

Cain's heart fell. For a moment he was confused, even though the dread was thick and familiar in his gut. He looked from Levi to Maggie and back, brow creased. It wasn't the first time someone had walked in on him and a bedmate, but this was Maggie, and she'd never witnessed him in such a scandalous state. This was not something he could fix with a finger pressed to the lips—*shh*….

Levi was waking gently. His tousled blond hair fell across his temple in such a lovely way. His muscles flickered beneath bare skin. He looked childish and soft as his eyes opened and then closed again, not yet past the horizon of sleep.

And Maggie stared.

Cain looked down the length of the bed, at the way Levi's limbs lay tangled with his own. He could smell Levi on his fingers still. Levi's body was hot and limp. Cain realized with a jolt of the heart that he was not wearing anything, and he cursed himself as the shock set in so deep he hardly felt it.

Cain sat and pulled a blanket around him like a cloak. His face burned. He braved Maggie's eyes, hoping to come across far calmer than he actually felt. She didn't know who Levi was. She couldn't. Everything would be fine, if he handled it properly.

"Good morning," Cain whispered. His voice was scratchy. He blushed to know why—the night of arguing and groaning. He glanced from Maggie to the bed and back again, struggling to keep a mask of complacency, although he longed to push her out of the room and start the morning over.

"Good morning, sir," Maggie returned in a tight voice.

Her eyes were dark. They moved to the man in his bed and back to Cain again.

Embarrassment crawled under Cain's skin. He'd grown up before her, and now he fell from pride before her, and perhaps there was something meaningful about that. He didn't quite know what to say.

Maggie politely began to pick up the clothes strewn about the room. When she uncovered Levi's guns, she froze. She looked to Cain in a great panic, eyes bright. Cain's heart fell again, if it had much more room to fall at all.

The rumors had circulated. They'd infected every house in New London that mattered. *The Rook* and BLACK, the Ruslaniv gang, had killed Lady Ophelia Dietrich. Talk was vicious. Gangs stalked each other on the streets like packs of territorial wolves. A brittle tension had settled in the air that threatened to give way at any moment, and now—

Maggie was breathless. "This man is one of *them*!" she gasped, just loud enough for Cain to hear it.

Cain shooed her out of the room. "Would you let me get decent!" he hissed. He threw his doors closed and scrambled back onto the bed. Christ, was there no end to the complications?

There was a moment of struggle, a panicked voice, and sleepy grumbles as Cain ripped the blankets away from Levi. It took a round of vicious shaking before Levi fully comprehended just what had happened while he'd dozed like a lazy lion over his pride. He scrambled out of Cain's bed as fast as he could, suddenly very awake.

A kiss, quite a few worried kisses, and that was it, and over the stone and down the balcony Levi clambered while Cain watched from behind the gargoyle at the corner and tried not to gag on the emotion as it clotted in his throat. Raw, staggering emotion—humiliation, dread, regret.

What was to happen now? Maggie wasn't stupid. She'd heard the talk. Everyone heard the talk. BLACK had killed his aunt, and now he'd been found in bed with one of them. When those who knew who Levi really was found out about *that*, well....

There were love bites on his neck and bullets on the floor. Cain, with an ever-thickening lump in his throat, made sure Levi was safely off Dietrich grounds before scampering back in from the balcony.

The winter chill was still present even after he'd closed the french doors. He washed his face with the fresh water in the basin on the sideboard. He dressed himself carelessly in a linen shirt and plain tweed and threw on an old banyan for good measure. His hair was a mess. He opened his doors again and coldly met Maggie's stare from across the hall. She'd waited for him.

Whether she knew or not the degree to which Cain was veritably *screwed* at this point, she'd spoken. There at the corner, was his Uncle Bradley, and his Uncle Bradley did not look very happy at all.

Dear God, I'm dead.

SCENE TWO

THE BRISK winter air was purifying to Levi.

New London was awake and bustling. Market stands were alive; streets were busy; men and women hurried on errands and to work; church bells tolled. Levi finished buttoning his shirt as he walked, militia jacket draped on his shoulders, holsters clicking and clacking. He winked and smiled at those who met his eyes as he passed even if they didn't have any inkling who the hell he was and how exhausting it was to court a number of reputations.

The Ruslaniv manor greeted him with the smell of breakfast wafting through the halls. Servants hurried by through the vestibule, as insignificant as little mice, bobbing their heads at him as he entered and hopped up the stairs to find his father, who was right where Levi had expected him. In his office, looking regrettably worse than he had recently.

"Hey, *chto novogo*?" Levi doffed his jacket as he strode into the office, passing granite busts and upholstered chairs to stoop and press a reverent kiss to his father's temple. "How are you feeling?"

His father reached up to pat Levi's hand. He laid down the papers he'd been sifting through, reclining for a deep breath. "Older than usual. Do you know how much it cost me this time to keep everyone's noses out of this recent mess with Lady Ophelia? We're lucky the Queen hasn't involved herself, what with the second ambush on the Dietrich household in less than six months."

Ice spread through Levi's veins and he closed his eyes for a moment, searching for the proper composure. He looked down at the papers before his father, newsprint and bills and bundles of labeled banknotes. "Yes," he mumbled. "Sometimes I believe she's finally given up on New London. The authorities certainly have. They hardly intervene anymore, unless nonpartisans are in danger. Perhaps we could declare ourselves our own republic, Father, for as little as the Queen involves herself in our politics anyway."

"It's possible...." His father heaved a sigh that seemed far too difficult for him. "And it's a sad, sad world that it is so."

Levi was quiet, knowing that his father was well aware of the guilt this layered upon him. He was lucky his father was still talking to him, he supposed, after the distaste he'd expressed the other night in the drawing room, throwing the tea set and pacing about in a rage. His mother, on the other hand, had taken to talking about nothing but Quinton again, and the entire household was tiring of her.

"Lawrence." His father motioned him closer, frowning sternly. Levi leaned down respectfully, lashes lowered. His father murmured, "I do believe those are the same clothes you were in yesterday. I see you are not so overcome by the recent turn of events to neglect your favorite pastimes. Who was she now? Oh, never mind that, I don't want to know. I'm just happy you're back to your old self again. Please, go wash up before your mother notices."

Levi smiled faintly, feigning embarrassment for his father but really feeling rather glum. He didn't want his father to think him heartless, going out so carelessly after his blunder with BLACK. His smile faded quickly, however, as his father went back to his work and Levi caught sight of the newspaper at the corner of the desk. Below a rather bold and shameless headline, an article read:

LADY OPHELIA DIETRICH of the DIETRICH HOUSE was slain in an attack reminiscent of that three years ago in which the former EARL and LADY were murdered. The gang has been identified as a popular one, bearing masks and marked skill and monopolizing much good favor in certain crowds of New Londoners, but as of yet this gang is otherwise elusive and remains at large. The DIETRICH HOUSE promises to be getting to the bottom of it, and this present murder of the current EARL's aunt and former EARL's sister is only "FUELING THE FIRE," a DIETRICH source declares.

Levi smiled bitterly. He pointed at the paper. "They're catching on," he whispered. "Maybe BLACK should just *disband*."

Lord Ruslaniv sighed. There was no spark of frivolity in his eye.

Levi's smile lingered, awkwardly, before it faded altogether and he left his father to his paperwork. He had his own paperwork to attend to, anyway. He was bound and determined to draw up a rough draft of some agreement to sign with Cain. He'd worry about the rest of the confessions later.

SCENE THREE

IT WAS two days later that Lord Ruslaniv found Levi in his secret room in the library, the door opened by a very frightened Eliott. His father's face was redder than the appliqué on his collar.

Levi set his book down, eyes wide, feeling very much like a child again, wondering what he'd done wrong. But he didn't have time to greet anyone or seek out Eliott's eyes for explanation as his father's voice rattled the little room of books and privacy.

"Could you tell me, son, why the Honourable Bradley Dietrich has sent word that you, 'the Rook,' were found in bed with his nephew, the earl? Could you explain to me why you were in the Dietrich manor? Could you explain to me why you were in 'questionable positions' with their earl? Could you please repudiate these wretched allegations, or would you like to join Quinton to never step foot in New London again!"

A book fell off the table, not from his father's voice, but from the force with which he'd flung open the door. Levi was speechless, gawking up at his father. He could think of nothing to say. His father seethed. He fumed. He stormed out of the room and through the library, roaring something colorful and threatening. His voice faded away into echo as he raged away.

Eliott met Levi's eyes, his own bulging and his face white. His hair was up in one of those ridiculous ponytails again, his stare both doubtful and hoping for an explanation, should Levi find one necessary.

"I've really messed up," Levi whispered.

Eliott's brow knotted. "It's just like Finn and Rosalie all over again," he said as if afraid of the connotations. Levi nodded.

"You've added insult to injury," Levi's father said later, with his wife beside him and Levi sitting across the room. "I can't take any more, son. This game you're playing with the Dietrichs—it's over. It's over, because I'm sending you to Yekaterinburg. I am treating you like a child because you are acting like a child. You will not come back to

New London until I've forgiven you and can tolerate trusting you again, and I can't promise you that will be soon."

Levi understood that his father thought that his being *in a questionable position with the earl* was just another tactic at ruining the Dietrichs, and that pained him, that pained him so greatly. But he thought of the day his father had thrown the tea set and his gentle threats then. He didn't say anything to argue or agree. Nothing he could have said would have changed his father's mind.

Levi packed more books than clothes.

The Blond One gave him a tight hug. The One with Glasses smirked. William's frown tightened. The Witch hit him a good few times for being "such a damn good lay," then promptly left the room as emotion worked across her face. Eliott gave Levi a case of good Persian cigarettes and a tiny smile as if to say it was not the last time he'd be around.

His father watched him leave as soon as it was possible, and the driver of the coach could not be bribed enough to stop by the Dietrich manor on the way out of New London.

Straight to the barren Yekaterinburg it was.

SCENE FOUR

"The Earl, with a Ruslaniv gunslinger?"

"BLACK is a gang of nobility?"

"That's just unfair!"

Oh, Maggie knew who she'd found in the Earl's bed. She'd seen him in the hallway, after all, when Aunt Ophelia had been gunned down and Cain had assailed the man in question in a fit of cold panic. And if she hadn't known then, she had perfect access to information about the Ruslaniv family by listening to gossip in the marketplace, and if she knew now, that meant she'd told Uncle Bradley all she knew too.

"I never expected them to be part of the actual family!" Uncle Bradley exclaimed, laughing only because it was easier at the moment to laugh than to yell. The laughter itself was venomous and made Cain flinch. "Imagine that, an entire city fooled by pathetic *masks*. How about this? Fuck the authorities! This will be the justice they deserve: I'll send to Lord Ruslaniv and tell him exactly what's happened. He should know about his son's debauchery. Why, if that's how they want to play, perhaps Lord Ruslaniv can *join me for a drink* and we'll see how our desires fall? And if we can't settle this like *gentlemen*, well, *then* we'll whip out the guns!"

"Please stop," Cain hissed, in pure miserable remorse and stinging humiliation as he sat next to his uncle, who threw back scotch after scotch in the library. He already felt pathetic enough after admitting to his uncle that BLACK consisted of members of the Ruslaniv house. "Please, this is my mess, Uncle. Let me clean it up. I know exactly how to end it, and if you stick your nose in it, there will be no justice for anyone—not for Aunt Ophelia, not for my parents, not for our pride. Not for any of it—"

"You know"—Uncle Bradley looked at his nephew through the thick glass of his tumbler—"it's very hard to believe you after everything that's happened. Are you really man enough to lead this family, or have we been placing our trust in the wrong hands for so long, after all?"

Cain closed his eyes. His pride took the blow. He swallowed with a raw throat, fury churning within him.

"Again I say I'm sorry," he maintained, though it was torture to speak it. "But believe me when I tell you that *I know exactly how to end this*. I know how to take BLACK out, and I promise I will do so." A hard scowl came over his face as he sought out his uncle's eyes and fixed his stare. A log in the fire shifted and popped. Cain's voice cut through the silence, sharp and cold. "Why do you think I was seducing him, anyway? Lord Ruslaniv's son, I mean. I know exactly who killed my parents and exactly who killed Aunt Ophelia, and I'm going to take them all out. I was only doing these things with all the cunning of a *man*, dear Uncle Bradley, and you of all people should understand that sometimes in war you must sacrifice a pawn or two."

That lie was more than enough to give his uncle pause. Cain refused to give Bradley the list of names involved with BLACK. Uncle Bradley was in a fit about how Cain never told anyone anything and how were they supposed to make any kind of progress if the Earl didn't want his family supporting him?

Cain knew that his uncle referred to the time he'd been gone and his newly stoked fire of revenge upon his return. He still said not a word. He watched the fire blaze, wondering if it reflected in his eyes.

As if in reproof, Uncle Bradley brazenly sent the threatened letter to Lord Ruslaniv.

Suddenly all New London was alight with wildfires of gossip, and Cain found it easier to shut himself into the house than to go out and face it.

Lady Kelley was enraged. She arrived in a whirlwind of skirts and austerity, stomping right past the footman and closing herself into the library with Uncle Bradley and Mr. Renton to demand answers to all her questions. Cain listened outside the doors, shaking in anger, mouth bitten into a thin line as he glowered at the floor and felt the blood burning beneath his cheeks. Emily's family already hated him enough, after all.

"And the engagement with my daughter? I assume that's officially off now, what with our earl deciding to be *queer* all of a sudden?"

"He's just grieving. He's been through a lot. He's confused. Listen, Stella, he's a mystery to me too. He's depressed. He's a troubled, bereft soul, for Christ's sake! He's just lost his aunt, and his parents before that! He'll come around. He'll *come around.*"

Ah, so in the face of the public, Uncle Bradley stood up for him. Cain found no comfort in such duplicity.

Suddenly, being the earl held no sway in things.

The world knew, but it was not really his uncle's fault. People gossiped, and gossip was sold to writers for New London's paper, and gossip traveled faster than truth around cups of tea and full market baskets and corners where little boys sold copies of the *Daily Journal* for just a shilling.

Whispers.

"Really? The gang's all part of the Ruslaniv house? Do the authorities know that?"

"That seems like a grand scheme to me!"

"*If* they're of the Ruslaniv house—say, Randall, do you remember that night at Barry's with BLACK? We were in the presence of the Ruslaniv heir and didn't even know it!"

"It's not hard to believe. Lord Ruslaniv never let his children beyond that wall."

"Ooh, look, there's the street fairy now. I can't believe he's got the nerve to show his face after being found with Lord Ruslaniv's *son.*"

"Maybe he did it on purpose."

"He's asking for more trouble, rendezvousing with that rat. No wonder his aunt's dead now."

Cain wanted to throw himself down and cry like a child. This was so unfair. He wished Aunt Ophelia were there to council him, to shelter him, but he was responsible for this, and if anything, the memory of her haunted him in that sense.

Responsibilities.

He had responsibilities. He was the head of the Dietrich house, and he'd disgraced the name. His shameful inclinations had finally been outed, and of course it had to be when the heir of the Ruslaniv house was involved, the secret heir who was part of the same gang that had broken into the manor thrice now. What else was to be added to that? Was there more blood on Levi's hands than Aunt Ophelia's?

Would it be easiest to just pretend Levi had never mattered?

He didn't want to.

Cain tried to hold his head high, but his own household seemed afraid of him, and Dietrich supporters were deeply conflicted.

He stopped reading the *Daily Journal* after seeing on the second page that the son of Lord Ruslaniv had been sent out of New London. And what a flattering sketch the paper's artist had made of the heir, truly as beautiful in ink as he was in person.

A very long week passed, without the scent of cigarettes rising up from below his bedroom balcony.

When he woke in the morning, Cain could barely eat. It was a good day if he could keep his breakfast down or if he didn't rise from bed already sick to his stomach. He could hardly conduct business, too irritated by more and more messages from more and more aristocratic families who were suddenly declaring themselves unaffiliated in the world of Dietrichs versus Ruslanivs.

The Dietrich name was quickly becoming a joke, as the gang BLACK became something of celebrities.

How had this happened?

This was punishment for his sins, perhaps, all his wrongdoings, Cain guessed, but if that was the case, *who would punish those Ruslaniv dogs?*

Cain hurt.

With a black sense of despair thick in his chest, he went to his aunt's grave, and to his parents' tombs, surrounded by granite angels and deep green shrubbery, although Cain had no idea if his parents truly slept coffered there or not. The last he'd seen them, they'd been tossed to the grimy ground of Lovers' Lane.

He had to do something. He knew that with a shudder of cold clarity through his heart. He had to do something—for his blood, for his pride, for his family, for *himself.*

And, brushing dark hair from his eyes beneath a bruised sky on a soggy day in New London's High-hill Cemetery, Cain knew exactly what to do.

SCENE FIVE

"I'M REALLY sorry for leaving you at the Dietrichs' that one night," Eliott said for the umpteenth time, and also for the umpteenth time, William ignored him.

The marketplace was full of noise—dirty children playing in alleys and sweeping corners for a coin or two, babies crying as haggard mothers tried to placate them, the rapid, discordant racket of shopkeepers trying to convince passersby that their produce was fresh and should be bought in bulk. Voices, actions, commotion, the rattle of the infrequent coach through Blackchapel Street, which was where this particular market was and which coaches usually avoided for the mass of people clogging the pavement and cobbles.

William walked stiffly, his face drawn in a tight, disapproving frown of everything around him. It was especially disparaging of Eliott, but Eliott was accustomed to that. The raucous market probably didn't help.

"I miss Levi," Eliott complained, managing to sound offhanded about it, although just voicing such pained him in the pit of his chest. It honestly did.

William didn't reply. He didn't care if he was a satisfying companion or not.

They went to Carteret's, to pick up some ammunition orders under code names, per usual. Old Mr. Carteret was clueless as to the goings-on and drama of New London's politics, which was nice. Eliott had a pleasant conversation with him, while Will counted out banknotes rigidly and grew restive as Eliott wished Mr. Carteret a good day.

"Why are you so antsy?" Eliott mumbled, the cool January wind refreshing on his face.

They stopped for a Bavarian pastry, Will practically clinging to their packages.

"I'm not," William insisted. "I'm just sticking to orders instead of lollygagging like you so love to."

Eliott snorted around his midmorning snack, winking at the young lady who'd sold it to him. Her face was framed by curls of such a lovely shade of red. Eliott made sure to flip his own hair seductively as he strutted away with Will, and then he stopped short and forgot all about the lusty-eyed red-haired girl because he picked up on the word *BLACK* drifting in with the rest of the buzz of voices, and it came in clear enough. Like a dog heeding a signal, Eliott looked about, then promptly went to acting inconspicuous. He ignored Will's scornful murmurs as he listened to the gossip of two disheveled-looking men a few yards away at the mouth of an alley.

"No, I heard it for sure, from Ishmael Roscoe. He's always got the in."

"That's what he said, though? What does it even mean?"

"Yeah, just *listen*—if you listen enough, it's circling through New London anyway. The head of the Dietrichs is calling out BLACK, that Ruslaniv gang."

The men were obviously members of a petty gang. They wore no silver or blue, which meant they supported the Ruslaniv house. Their holsters were too obvious, so they were amateur or, at least, mediocre. Will hardly had time to sputter in distaste before Eliott was up and flouncing over, cornering them in the shadows of the narrow alley between streets.

"What's this about now?" Eliott purred, offering them his best smile.

It took a few threats, but they spilled information. William suggested it had nothing to do with threats, but all to do with the men's dawning realization that they were graced by the attention of members of the BLACK they'd spoken of.

They let the men go and stood together in the alley in a rather tense quiet as the gravity of the situation settled on their shoulders.

Earl Dietrich, calling out BLACK?

Well, the words the men had quoted were not exactly so sympathetic—the challenge went something along the lines of *spineless, paltry, filthy, rotten, diseased dogs*—but that was beside the point.

This was almost dire, and Levi was not in New London.

Who was designated team captain, now? Certainly none of them were as equipped as Levi—

"I guess there's your answer," William said suddenly, breaking the silence between them. He shifted with an icy clack of his weapons belt and glanced at Eliott curtly, and Eliott understood that he was referring to Eliott's earlier comments about missing Levi. He knew what Eliott would do now. It was only a day's drive to Yekaterinburg.

And Eliott didn't hesitate at all.

SCENE SIX

YEKATERINBURG WAS a desolate, disconsolate place. It was cold, and dark, and dreary, a ramshackle city that had once been a booming mining town. Now it was where the scarce fortunate lived in greedy palatial homes high in the hills and governed the poor with a less than diplomatic rule. Weathercocks rattled atop crooked buildings. The mountain range outside Muscov Bay loomed in the distance. Children's faces were always dirty, just like the storefront windows and the crumbling buildings, and the shrewd, tight-lipped people, and Levi wasn't sure if the emptiness he felt was meditation, or a mechanism of self-defense, or just what Yekaterinburg did to its inhabitants.

He woke to cold winter sunlight flooding his pathetic flat, which he shared with the occasional rat and a gruff old brute of an ex-bounty hunter, who didn't speak but didn't really bother Levi either. The ex-bounty hunter was now an aspiring poet and spent most of his time at his typewriter.

Levi woke stiff and mute on the tattered divan he called his bed.

He woke to nothingness—nothing planned, nothing felt, nothing waiting for him except perhaps his books, or the dishes piled in the basin and the dust on the floors under the rusty pipes and gray walls.

He felt like a ghost in a city of ghosts, with no direction and no meaning. Purpose gave way to pattern, and the pattern left him jaded and detached. There was too much room to think, so he embraced the emptiness. It had never been hard to embrace the emptiness, especially not when he was alone.

At first he'd been terrified of running into Quinton, somehow. Like he'd run into Red in the marketplace where the red-faced children hawked bruised apples and moldy pastries, and Red had looked weathered and bleached and wasted by banishment, and they'd just stared at each other in silent consideration of their sins.

"Good day, brother," Red had said, and disappeared again into the crowd, and by some merciful instinct, Levi understood that Quinton was not in Yekaterinburg. Good thing too, because Levi was sure that if he'd seen Quinton, brother or not, he would have shot him right there. No, maybe Quinton was up north past the mountains, probably the new ringleader of Father Kelvin's sick, relocated circus. Quinton had thought Father Kelvin's circus was one of the best secrets of New London back when it had been based under St. Mikael's.

Levi had the clinging intuition Quinton was dead.

All the people of Yekaterinburg looked at him like they knew he was Quinton's successor, and that was an intrusive and unsettling burden to bear. Whispering, whispering, nobody in Yekaterinburg seemed to talk beyond what was necessary, but it felt like they were all whispering about him as if he walked around with a target sign on his back, a declaration of his transgressions, a request to be crucified.

When Levi saw Eliott, he didn't quite know what to think. Was it a messenger from God, or a mirage in the desert?

But this was no desert. This was a clustered city with hard-packed earth beneath it, and Levi was smoking the last of his Persian cigarettes when Eliott, looking breathless and frenzied, came into the café below Levi's flat, where Levi sat for luncheon.

"I almost didn't go past the old militia camp," Eliott gasped as he sank down to sit before Levi at a dingy little table in the corner, where the sound of lazy dining activity was a mere echo. There was a wrinkle in his brow and a shadow in his eyes like nostalgia, speaking of the militia camp where they'd grown up together in a matter of weeks. "I thought maybe you'd be there, but… I'm glad I didn't turn back."

Levi flagged down the waitress with the small breasts and narrow eyes to order Eliott a drink. Eliott chewed his lower lip, seeming unsure of himself. He fidgeted, tying his hair back into a ponytail but doing so almost compulsively, which signaled to Levi that Eliott was very nervous about something.

"My father doesn't want me back yet, does he?" Levi asked slowly and surprisingly without bitterness.

"No." Eliott didn't hesitate, shaking his head with a deeply remorseful look on his face. "No, but you have to come back anyway."

Levi frowned, vexed. The waitress brought Eliott his drink. Levi leaned down across the table, lacing his fingers by his cold coffee and abandoned book.

"I cannot," he reminded gently, although Eliott's hurried insistence on his return sparked a chilling sort of excitement in him he hadn't expected to feel again so soon. Maybe refusing to tend to the pain in his chest kept a pit of feelings alive, blanketed and forgotten otherwise.

"You have to," Eliott said, eyes wide. He spoke low as if talk like this was really dangerous in a city of exile. "The Earl's calling out BLACK at St. Mikael's Church in four days. I think he means an end this time, Levi. For good, he means *an end*."

For a moment, Levi was apathetic.

Then an eerie shudder passed through him, which left him all mixed up and anxious inside, but he couldn't discern from which deadened emotion it stemmed.

He met Eliott's eyes, lighting his very last Persian cigarette.

"An end," Levi reiterated skeptically, but he understood. He understood Cain much more than Eliott ever would, and if Eliott was picking up the sense that this calling out meant *an end* to the feud, then there was seriously something dark and pivotal stirring. Dear Lord, at St. Mikael's too. The very monument to the heartbreak, shame, and trauma in Cain's soul.

This was the crux, he realized. This was the beginning of what one might call the *crescendo* of the entire saga.

"I saw him," Levi said, before he realized the words had even formed on his tongue, and then he frowned at himself for speaking without thought. Eliott didn't understand, though. Levi sighed, running a hand through his hair. He looked at Eliott grimly, his mouth bitten into a thin line. He had to say it. Like a man in the confessional with a priest, he had no other choice if he wanted peace inside. He had to say the words aloud. "Three years ago, when Quinton and the others ambushed the Dietrich house, I saw Cain, in Lovers' Lane. I'd wanted to do something to intervene, but I had no spine."

"Bullshit!" Eliott snapped.

A few old men reading the paper over luncheon glanced over from their table. Eliott waved an apologetic hand.

"I didn't," Levi insisted. "I had no mind of my own then. Quinton and BLACK told me about their plan, and from that moment I could have done something to stop it, but I didn't. I sat there, and they went out and killed so many people and then delivered an innocent to the devil's playground."

Eliott looked at him as if he couldn't grasp the gravity of it all. Levi didn't blame him. He licked his lips. "It was so bloody because of me," he husked, and although it ached so terribly to know this, and worse yet to admit it openly, it was almost too easy to wear a mask of nonchalance. It always was. Was that a bad thing?

"It'll be bloodier if you don't come back with me," Eliott urged, and the look on his face startled Levi. There was a dark sort of understanding there in his eyes, the faint appearance of pride and doom like a man on his way to war. It chilled Levi, and mildly comforted him at the same time.

Eliott shrugged idly, glancing out the window as if it were too hard to look in Levi's eyes anymore. He went on, quietly. "It's going to be far bloodier if you don't come back with me and try to dissuade the Earl. You're his *friend*, after all. At least that's what everyone's been saying."

There was a moment of silence between them in which Levi knew that Eliott understood the depth of his entanglement with the Earl Dietrich. And there was no condemnation, and no ignominy, and no judgment. Levi sighed. He didn't deserve somebody like Eliott. He'd never asked for his support and companionship, and he did nothing to reciprocate it anyway. He wished Eliott would stop handing it out so openly, because it would never be treated for its real worth.

"You didn't bring me more cigarettes?" Levi prompted, smirking faintly at Eliott's chagrin.

"No...." Eliott chuckled meekly, a tired and defeated laugh. "You have to come back to New London for them."

SCENE SEVEN

THE WHOLE city was talking about it, as they talked of everything, and they closed up their shutters that night because when the fray began, they needed to be inside or they'd be in danger.

Even petty gangs retreated, afraid to impose upon this rumored showdown. They didn't want to be involved—they were just innocent civilians, after all, and this was a fight between the Earl himself and the noble Ruslaniv gang. But they closed themselves up with a guilty curiosity because the air was volatile that night, and everybody knew why.

Within St. Mikael's, hardly a particle of dust stirred for the stillness.

St. Mikael's was a beautiful church. Its Elizabethan roots were clear to see. Gables and spires and smooth stone delivered a chilling beauty. As a winter rainstorm brewed overhead, as trite as nature could be at times, Cain wandered between the gleaming, wondrously rich woodwork and stalwart Flemish chairs in the sanctuary of St. Mikael's. There was the golden altar where the baptismal font sat, the forest of stumpy red candles, and the classical pediment and balconies up high where even a whispered breath echoed back down upon him.

Indelibly, intrinsically Eastern it was inside, almost gypsy with its iconostasis stacked neatly below the crucifix. The crucifix peered down at Cain sorrowfully. Was it wrong that he felt no regret and no apprehension, looking into the molded face of Christ painted with blood and a crown of thorns? Was it wrong that he felt strangely peaceful, strangely protected in this place, which smelled of old burnt-out tapers and melting wax as all the fat candles flickered? Incense and wine and the timeless, familiar scent of old parchment, choir books, dust, and age, and moisture in the rafters.

Below these beautiful wooden floors, he'd been a prisoner for almost a year. He'd been corrupted. He'd lost two kinds of innocence and gained all the self-possession in the world, and wasn't that something? It certainly was. It was a harrowing sort of analogy, wasn't it? Here, up above, the breathtakingly spiritual with all the saints' faces like guardian ghosts, and down below—not on ground level, no, but farther down, secreted below the streets of New London—had been a labyrinth of wicked chambers like the seven circles of hell.

That was something. That parallel to heaven and earth and hell that was this church, St. Mikael's.

In the silence, Cain imagined he could hear a choir. Stationed at all the most relevant corners of the sanctuary were the collection of gunslingers he'd brought with him to confront BLACK. Onyx, Devi, Warren, and Hans, their names were. They each possessed uniquely extensive criminal backgrounds. They were perfect to hire for the night. His family's security was unneeded.

"It's all a rumor," Cain had told his uncle earlier, curtly, unable to look at Bradley's face without becoming enraged. "Whatever you heard about me 'calling out' the Ruslanivs is all rumor. I didn't know we were operating by gossip now, Uncle. Why don't you have some more scotch?"

That had quieted him, and Cain's weapons belt and guns had chattered as he'd quietly made his way down over the edge of his balcony, cold fingers dirtied by the lattice and vines. Bundled up against the night, surely he looked as rugged as he ever had, and he met with the petty fighters he'd hired just outside the Dietrich estate so they could make their way to St. Mikael's, that wicked, wicked place.

Cain stood with hands clasped behind his back, squinting up at the Theotokos that sat among all the glittering candles in the dark of the church. The doors had been unlocked. They were always unlocked. And why not?

Cain studied the icon with an unswaying concentration just short of a trance, head tipped to one side. The flecks of gold in the sad religious painting glinted in the flickering light, and Cain was almost moved by it, except that he hated it for its evocative beauty and luster because it belonged to Ruslanivs.

There was a small sound from above, up in one of the galleries. It was a light scuffle—the sound of a gun being drawn, the scrape of movement.

Cain backed up to see the left balcony. His hand shot for his revolver, and he squinted though the dim light of the sleeping church, but when he felt the recognition click, he wasn't really shocked deeply. He'd only been hoping for as much as he found anyway.

The whites of Levi's eyes glinted in the darkness where he crouched, the perfect gunslinger, up in the gallery. Devi had caught him coming in through the painted-glass window there, thus the sounds of the gun. Cain smiled faintly. His heart fluttered, and a sense of relief did not seem strange to him, if only because it was warped and distorted by the madness of resolution. This was what he'd wanted. *Levi.*

Cain drew his revolver, leveling it with what he could see of Levi in the upper shadows of the sanctuary. Devi kept his pistol trained on Levi's lovely head. Levi looked like a ghost tonight, all loose linen shirt and no regalia. Just a broken man. God, his hair was even uncombed, a loose and wild blond mane breaking into curls at the tips. Rough-and-tumble looked delicious on him, as always.

"Are you alone?" Cain called up from the first floor, confident Levi would answer truthfully.

"Yes" came Levi's reply.

Ah, that cool, familiar timbre. Cain glanced over at Hans and Warren. One lingered near the confessional booths and the other near the side doors.

"Patrol the outside," Cain ordered quietly, gesturing with a brief tip of the chin. "All of you. Let me talk to this mutt myself, and whatever you do, *don't come inside*. It's fine."

The church fell still again. These men Cain had hired were professionals. They knew how to patrol a building, and they were, after all, receiving handsome remuneration.

Cain moved up the steps near the altar, standing there below the left gallery. He kept his Rapier aimed, out of practice, and he looked up at Levi imploringly where he danced through the shadows, mirroring Cain's movements. He was like a raven, flitting about in the dark. Or a spirit, a devil. His grace and elegance was unsettling at times, as it was then, his face a perfect mask of acceptance as he stared at Cain behind his own gun. Was this what a lovers' quarrel between trained fighters was like? There was something romantic about the tension, sensual in a very primal way.

With the fearlessness of an acrobat at a circus, Levi hoisted himself up and over the gallery balcony and leapt down to stand near the altar with Cain.

Cain's heart gave a sickening lurch. He wasn't afraid of Levi. He was afraid of himself. He was afraid of the way he lowered his gun—

the way he *trusted* this Ruslaniv in front of him—and he was afraid that the emotion that worked through him at seeing Levi again after his banishment would interfere with the steady, cold resolve about this night he'd had for the last few days.

Footsteps, and then Levi touched his face, and suddenly Cain wasn't ruthless anymore, he was a mess of pain and love that came together into one lovely ache. Maybe he uttered a tiny strangled sound of defeat. He lowered his gun and shrank forward, resting his head against Levi's chest. Again he thought he could hear the echo of a choir, ghost voices in the parish, but it was just a whispering memory of liturgies from his childhood.

Levi smelled like cigarettes and dirt, and the cold, sweet metal of his hidden weapons. He lifted a hand. Cain tensed, but Levi just put a palm to the back of his head, protectively, soothingly, and Cain stared at the Theotokos with his ear to Levi's shoulder. He could hear Levi's heartbeat and his breath.

"So is this an ambush, or is it just a battle?" Levi prompted.

He spoke so respectfully, so evenly, picking through Cain's strategies in a soft voice as if the church truly deserved his veneration. But it did, it did, the beauty of it did, not the corruption of it, and above all its depravity, it was still beautiful.

"I think you know what it is." Cain's fingers twitched on his gun. "Where were you hiding, Levi?"

"I wasn't hiding. You know very well I wasn't hiding. I was sent away."

"I faced it like a man, and you ran away, leaving me alone with it all!"

"That pride of yours will be your downfall."

"Levi, I knew you'd come if I did this."

"Again I beg, what are you planning this night?"

Cain tried to pull away. He didn't mean to sound cold and pitiless, but that was what he was. That was what he *felt*, at least. He shrugged idly beneath Levi's hands, and in the otherworldly silence of the St. Mikael's sanctuary, his voice was cool and composed as he explained. "I'm going to kill them all."

Levi's mouth crashed into his, and at first Cain backed away, startled, but then Levi chased his kiss again. He held him crushingly tight to his chest, there below the doleful face of the Christ, the tall crucifix above the altar whose molded face seemed to be full of pity now. The candles danced, and the echoes of gunmetal as Cain struggled in Levi's grip bounced off all the eaves and resounded back to them.

The kisses were rough, not out of lust but out of desperation. Cain didn't know what to do with his revolver. He couldn't put it away. He'd hear if the petty gang was apprehending somebody outside the little church, though. He was safe for now. So as they backed into one of the chairs near the altar and Levi sat down heavily, fingers curled in Cain's lapels to prevent interruption of the kiss, Cain laid his Rapier down on the communion table and climbed onto Levi's lap, reciprocating the affection with just as much violent fervor.

It hurt to kiss Levi. It hurt his lips, because the kisses were hard. It hurt his pride, because this wasn't what he'd intended for tonight. It hurt his heart in a grand way, because it was Levi, oh, it was Levi after so long. And it hurt his soul, because the face of the Christ on the crucifix above them stared down in disappointment, and the tristful face of the Virgin peered at them with that omniscient sorrow of hers, and Cain dreaded each passing second for fear a gunshot would sound to alert him of the presence of BLACK. They were coming, after all. It was inevitable. These pure moments were few.

Cain was a sinful, sinful, errant man, dirty and depraved and debauched and blasphemous. Levi yanked the Dietrich coat from his shoulders and tossed it aside, running his hands possessively up and down Cain's back as if he'd never before felt him in his life and would never again be able to.

There was a terrible ache in Cain's chest that felt like hope and despair commingling together, something wholly intimate and indescribable. It was a wretched feeling, one he didn't feel equipped to handle. It left him trembling as Levi's mouth trailed warm kisses down his neck and his hands spread across Cain's thighs covetously. Despite the rush, or perhaps because of it, Cain thought that if they kept on like this, if they had enough time, he would very well give himself to Levi right there below the mournful painted eyes of the statue of Christ and the other effigies.

It occurred to Cain suddenly, in one cold, clear current of thought, that this could perchance be a dire distraction.

It pained him to jump off Levi's lap, but that was what he did. It pained him to whip up his revolver again and look over the top of it at Levi, but he did. He knocked down a candle, thankfully unlit.

The gun trembled in his shaking hands. He was so torn between glaring and sinking to his knees. His face twisted with it. Did he look monstrous?

"Where are they?" he barked, scowling at Levi. His heart ached.

"Who?" Levi husked, innocently enough, but there was a sudden shadow on his face. His eyes hardened into a simple dark stare that expressed nothing but the reflection of dancing candlelight. His mouth drew in a tight line, and he sat far too casually there, arms propped on the chairs beside him and legs crossed.

"*BLACK*!" Cain hissed, gesturing with his gun.

Levi didn't seem all too worried with it pointed his way, except for a subtle spark in his eyes as they followed the revolver's every twitch. "I don't know where they are," he said slowly, carefully, as if speaking to an unpredictable child in the midst of a tantrum. "I came here alone."

"How did you hear of all this, then?"

"You'll never trust me, will you, Cain? Not all the love in the world could ever make you trust me."

"*How did you hear of it, Levi?*"

Levi regarded him coldly as if he was really going to refuse to answer, and then he licked his lips, stirred stiffly, and confessed, "Eliott came to Yekaterinburg and begged me to come reason with you."

"So this is all a ruse," Cain surmised, laughing loudly in disbelief.

Levi was immediately offended. He stood up, towering over Cain, unafraid of his weapon anymore. Cain quieted in an instant.

"I was hoping," Levi spat, looking nothing but resolve incarnate now, "that my disclosure of Eliott *begging* me to come back would convince you of BLACK's inability to contend against you. I'm sorry, not their *inability*, as we're all the best gunslingers you'll ever fight, but their *incapacity* to contend against you. They don't know the depth of your grudge as I do. They don't shoulder the guilt of it as I do. They're *ignorant* of it, don't you see? And Eliott risked his integrity, his *freedom*, to beg me to come back to *reason with you*. If that doesn't show you at least a glimmer of BLACK's true colors, *I don't know what will!*"

Levi's voice echoed in the church. A silence fell, thin and dangerous. Cain heard only his heart thundering in his ears, and the pop of a candlewick or two as the crucifix grimaced at him. His skin crawled. He shook. He felt as if he might explode in a vicious outburst that he couldn't control, and he felt so tiny and callow beneath the Christ's painted eyes, he lifted his Rapier and shot its effigy face.

Plaster rained down on all the little candles, and immediately after blowing the face of Christ to pieces, Cain understood he was damned.

He was broken inside, and demented, and unfixable, and he was irretrievably damned. He'd never imagined he'd feel such regret for shooting the face of a damn statue, but it was so beautiful, so placidly sad, and he was damned. They were all damned.

Levi looked a little panicked by Cain's sudden fire. He reached out. Cain didn't avoid his touch. He let Levi draw him close and press a kiss to his temple then whisper, "This hell needs to end."

There was no moment of resolution there. There was no moment of peace in the tumult that seemed to hold every one of them in its grip. There was love, of course, but it was part of that maelstrom.

As if in answer to the gunshot Cain had fired at the face of the crucifix, which now lay scattered about the altar, another round of gunshots came in response from outside St. Mikael's.

BLACK had finally arrived.

The petty men he'd hired knew they were to let BLACK into St. Mikael's, and that they did. Cain and Levi stood patiently in the flickering light beneath the ruined crucifix as if waiting to start a diabolical mass. They must have looked like evil angels to the Ruslaniv gang.

BLACK slipped in tentatively, weapons drawn. They drifted in and out of the shadows, slants of light skipping over them. They were wonderfully trained, but their attitudes were irreparable.

The light danced. Cain felt like he could recognize them all: the one with red hair like a lion's mane, whom Levi called *Eliott* in a faint whisper as he walked in; the lady, voluptuous and snarling; two with neatly clipped dark hair; one with a head of golden hair. They came bearing a rotten proud audacity. Seeing them brought Cain's vicious determination and loyalty to the forefront, that begrudging, smoldering hatred he'd stoked for so long under the guise of *revenge*.

"Good evening, BLACK," Cain said kindly enough, except he spit out the name of their gang like it was poison.

"Rook!" the lady cried suddenly, sounding surprised as she boldly approached the altar.

Cain's hand tightened on his gun. His body tensed. The girl only gestured with her chin, snarling at Levi.

"What are *you* doing here? I thought you'd been told to *flit away*!"

"Witch," Levi greeted, and Cain realized with a surge of disgust that they had code names for each other. *How cute.* "'Once upon a midnight dreary, while I pondered, weak and weary…' Well, you catch my drift."

The woman snorted. One of the men with glasses cocked his gun, ready to fight already. Everyone seemed to bristle when this one spoke, voice clear and concise. "I'm tearing up at this reunion, but can we just get to what you want, Earl? Don't waste our time."

"Excuse me," Levi hissed, hopping down the steps of the altar to stand between Cain and BLACK. "I think you're forgetting who is leader, Snake. Unless, of course, you've all decided I'm no longer sound enough, but *he* is?"

"That's not it," Eliott said. "He just feels freer to be an asshole in your absence."

"Shut up, Lion!" the Blond One hissed. He hardly looked older than Cain, a crazy vigor about his youthful face. Cain felt like he recognized him, a shivering but inhibited hunch. He knew him, and not from that night at Brackham's. No, before that. "Nobody cares what you think!"

Christ, they weren't in any condition to be a gang. They hated each other. Cain was in awe of this. He laughed incredulously and cut through their paltry disagreements, crying out, "Do you know what happened in the year after my parents were killed?"

They all quieted. The death of the former Earl and Lady Dietrich was a common enough history, especially to them. Levi looked absolutely terrified of what Cain might say next, and Cain was satisfied by that.

In the strange way of gangsters, it was time for wits and words to be exchanged without the fear of a gun going off, because that would err against the tacit, internal code of the gunman's honor. Cain paced beneath the altar, kicking some scattered plaster around. He stopped, momentarily stricken by the sight of Christ's mournful eye in a chunk on the floor. He picked it up and stared at it, then put it respectfully by the few glowing candles.

"My parents died," he announced. BLACK was listening to him with an eerie sense of respect—patient, or objective at the very least. Overhead, St. Mikael's bells should have tolled for the hour, but the rector and bellkeeper had been chased out earlier. Cain graced all the others in the sanctuary, scattered among the pews, with a cold gaze. He continued, "I found them in Lovers' Lane. And then your old friend Oberon took me and gave me to Father Kelvin, here below this very church."

The name *Oberon* seemed to stir some sort of emotion in nearly all of them. Cain didn't plan on giving a long heartfelt story about the tragedies these dogs had bestowed upon him, but he wanted to shake each member of BLACK to the core before he killed them. It was an outlet for the turmoil swirling so thick inside his chest, and it felt good to cut the words out effectively.

Cain shook his head, frowning in a travesty of disbelief and sadness. However forthright, whether they cared or not, he couldn't help but be coldly dramatic about it. It felt so good to be a few bullets away from revenge.

"I never told anyone about what happened to me at the hands of Kelvin. But you all know, don't you? You know about *all* the boys and girls, the little lambs brought to slaughter in that putrid hell. A *circus*! Ha! Leave it to you Ruslanivs to fail in the creation of sin too. But where did the kids go afterward? They certainly aren't below us now, are they? Oh, are they grown-up prostitutes now? Do they run their own businesses? No, I'm sure they were all sent away with Father Kelvin too. Weren't they?"

Cain uttered a resentful laugh. The mismatched members of BLACK stared at him. "No," he snarled in an icy tone, "I'll never alert the authorities of what happened here below St. Mikael's. Why further tarnish my pride that way? No, nobody ever asked me. And either way, I refuse to talk about it. All anyone needs to know—and all, indeed, anyone does know—is that from those long hellish months, I emerged even more determined to find my parents' murderers and *kill them*. And do you know where that led me, my friends?"

Levi stood with a grave sort of respect near the balustrade of the altar. BLACK showed looks of fury and impatience, of shock and fault on their faces, and Cain stood close to the altar where the crucifix hung, just in case he had to dodge from a spray of bullets.

He longed to enrage BLACK. He longed to hurt them before he slaughtered them.

"Somehow looking for the culprits led me to St. Mikael's again, and eventually to BLACK. Your Lord Ruslaniv is very good at covering mistakes. Do you know how long it took me to finally confirm that the BLACK who kidnapped me was the BLACK who killed my parents? Oh, I always *knew*, deep down, but I can't exact revenge on hunches, you see."

Eliott burst forward, lowering his weapon. He looked utterly distraught. Cain followed him with his Rapier out of reaction, but Eliott didn't look in the least dangerous.

"*Are you listening to yourself?*" Elliot cried, laughing for all the disbelief written across his face. "You just admitted that the BLACK you want isn't here!" He turned, beseeching Levi now. "Levi, I thought you were going to explain that to him!"

Levi was unyielding and inscrutably silent. Eliott looked panicked. The rest of BLACK appeared perplexed. Cain was confused and a little intrigued, but he didn't care. His heart pounded. He had BLACK before him.

He raised his voice, before anyone else could interrupt. "I'm giving you an option tonight, BLACK. *Kill me now* if you truly want to win this feud between our families, or accept conquest and kiss my feet before *I kill you* and *burn your bodies with St. Mikael's tonight*!"

His voice cracked and wavered. His words echoed.

They should have been shooting by now. Cain's defiance, his mad threats—he was brazen and careless with his words and certainly the BLACK Levi had trained with could have taken him out long ago. It was five against one, was it not?

Ah, but they were in disrepair.

BLACK had become their own downfall.

Or maybe it was that they still respected Levi's ultimate guidance beyond their own instincts or boiling pride. BLACK was not shooting at Cain, and Cain was not shooting at BLACK. It hit Cain then that whether or not BLACK sided with Levi, whether or not they understood what was really going on here, not a single soul—not even Cain himself—wanted to pull the trigger until *Levi* said it was all right. How painfully honorable.

And suddenly there was chaos in the sanctuary.

"Levi, you were supposed to tell him!"

"I didn't have a chance to say it again—"

"*Collusion*! There's *collusion* between the Rook and the Lion!"

"Shut the fuck up, *Spider*—"

"BLACK was involved with it? *BLACK did it?*"

So at least one of them hadn't known about Oberon and Quinton and the others. Cain laughed wickedly, tickled by this. He looked at the lady gunslinger, who seemed particularly distressed, and before he even realized he was capable of such spite, he said tenderly, "It's really a shame that Oberon is dead now. I could always tell he didn't like Father Kelvin or the whole plan, and he was so kind to me while I worked below this church. He was so very kind, and a surprisingly good fuck too."

The woman—had Levi called her *Witch*?—sprang forward, shrieking something in that harsh gypsy slang as she whipped out two ornate revolvers, which she aimed at Cain recklessly. Levi dived over and stopped her with an outstretched arm, but she was too hysterical to fire. She just continued to scream.

Suddenly they all spoke rapidly in that foreign tongue—Eliott, the Witch, Levi, the others—that familiarly coarse but beguiling clip, and Cain fought a cringe. He saw Father Kelvin's again, the gross Eastern decadence, the sound of everyone shouting in that ascetic language, the violent stutter of gunshots, and the way it felt to run away and leave those things as echoes. But here they were again, swirling about him, and for a moment Cain found it very difficult to breathe. The red-haired one's voice carried.

"Levi, *you were supposed to explain to him that it was Quinton and you couldn't stop him!*"

Cain cocked his gun and stormed to the edge of the altar, aiming at Eliott. His theatrics had blinded his judgment, and it came back to him, in one shuddering rush. "*You killed my aunt!*" he howled, through all the other strained voices. "You killed Aunt Ophelia!"

Eliott stared with wide eyes, but there was no terror in his face, just a gunslinger's critical thinking and apprehension. His eyes were bright and his face stony. He stood unmoving as if daring Cain to shoot. Cain couldn't.

The Blond One they'd called Spider hopped up on a pew, cutting through all the other voices with a manic laugh. "Wrong, Earl! I'm the one who shot those fatal bullets! I shot the Lady, and did you know that I remember her from when we were younger and I came to your manor to play?"

Cain uttered a helpless growl, feeling another sharp stab of betrayal in his chest. Yes. *That* was where he knew the Blond One. Petyr Byron. He was Petyr Byron!

Cain threw his fist against Levi where he stood with his arm tight around the Witch. "*You stole my friend*!" he screeched.

"*He* stole your friend!" The Blond One danced around on the pew, waving his guns.

"*You killed Aunt Ophelia*!" Cain spun on his heel, mayhem bursting inside him. The call to action pulsed through him, cold and fierce. He shot at Petyr—*Spider*—but he didn't hit him. Petyr dropped off the pew and crouched behind it, ready to fire back. Levi began speaking to him in that rapid foreign dialect again, and Petyr began to argue back. It seemed like a vicious disagreement.

Everyone was shouting again, an incomprehensible whirlwind of voices—screams, hisses, echoing, that invisible choir that warbled in the back of Cain's head.

Cain felt cold. There was chaos inside him and commotion in the sanctuary, but a single strand of desperate clarity pierced the confusion. A chill zipped through him. He didn't care, he didn't care, he wanted to see them *dead*. Dead like his parents, dead like Aunt Ophelia, dead like his soul.

He pointed his gun at the red-haired one, the one named Eliott, the one who'd told him he was attacking the wrong group—and then there came the familiar, chilling sound of a trigger being cocked, and it was very close to his ear.

Cain's eyes widened.

The muzzle of the ROOK was against his temple, and his heart gave a sickening thud. The entire sanctuary went quiet. All eyes fell upon them there at the front of the pews. Cain drew a wavering breath, looking up.

Levi stood with his gun to Cain's head. In the candlelight, Levi looked as young and tortured and sad as the face of the Christ before Cain had shot it.

Tears stung the backs of Cain's eyes, emotion thickening in his throat. His breath came in cold bursts, panicked and full of blind instinct.

"So this is how it will end, then?" Cain whispered. He looked up at Levi, brow knotting as his vision doubled, and then trebled. Beautiful Levi, his handsome face and his dark depthless eyes that expressed nothing but love sometimes, and how was that even possible? How was it possible for a trained killer to be so full of unquestioning love?

Funny how he thought about that now, with Levi's gun to his head a second time.

SCENE EIGHT

Levi knew his men and comrades.

He could tell by the looks in his comrades' eyes, shining bright and ruthless.

His comrades…. His family, and his friends. He was certain—he would bet money—that outside St. Mikael's, as the night deepened and the brumal winds swirled, the petty shooters Cain had hired were dead, unconscious, or struggling in the ice and snow, choking on lead. No, this night never had a chance to end well. From the start it had been a death wish, and a death wish alone.

Within the warmth of St. Mikael's, as the candles flickered, the words on his gun looked so tragic next to Cain's beautiful face, that dark hair and those pale gray eyes.

"As the head of BLACK, I should kill you." Levi spoke slowly and evenly, words carefully measured, although his heart was pounding at such a clip he thought it might burst. He was surprised his hands didn't quake. Ah, the cold emotionlessness ingrained in him paid off at times, didn't it? "I've said it before—it *is* very much like you to want to die by the hands of your only real friend."

Cain looked in complete shock. Levi could sympathize. He wondered what was running through the minds of his team. What did BLACK think, truly, now that so many revelations had been unearthed? What did they think of Levi's merits as a leader, seeing him with his gun to Cain's head? What did they think of his secret involvement with the former BLACK? About his involvement with the Earl Dietrich? Did they think he'd shoot Cain here, now, closing the grueling chapter of irony that his brother had slain the former earl, and tonight BLACK might again watch the son of Lord Ruslaniv murder the head of the Dietrichs? Was that what they were thinking?

Surely, by the look in the Blond One's mad eyes, the cold impatience on Claude's face, the tragic uneasiness of Eliott and Will, the panting confusion of the Witch as she shifted to and fro and looked utterly torn between crying and screaming with everything that had been said. She had been so close to Oberon. Her heart must have been ripped to pieces discovering his hand in the catastrophe of two years ago and his deplorable actions with Father Kelvin.

"Tempt not a desperate man...," Cain whispered, breathlessly, and Levi bristled. The moment in which Cain met his eyes again with such tenderness felt like eternities of raw beauty, but it was short-lived. There was but a brief rustle of linen as Cain shifted his aim and fired once in the Blond One's direction.

It just barely missed Petyr, biting slivers of wood from the pew above the stiff velvet upholstery. Levi had fought with Petyr enough times to know exactly what would happen next, and as if in a waltz with death itself, Levi hooked an arm around Cain's neck and spun him along, evading the bullets as Petyr's gun went off.

Levi fired back, removing ROOK from Cain's temple. He shot to scare the Blond One, but the Blond One just scowled at him from between the pews, like a wild animal.

Those gunshots were a crux. The discordant staccatos and deafening pops meant the beginning of the end, and Levi thought, *Indeed, tempt not a desperate man....*

The real showdown started then.

Light reflected off the barrel of his gun as Cain aimed for the Witch. She shrank into the shadows, firing a round toward the altar. With his arm around Cain's neck, Levi staggered back and sank down into the corner that cradled the Theotokos and its prayer candles, and the little alcove provided a bit of protection as they wriggled into the dark. Minds fell to deeper instincts, and the tension snapped.

It was a conversation in bullets, simple enough. They ricocheted. They chipped the beautiful ceiling and woodwork, the Doric columns, and organ case. Candles went tumbling. The organ played eerie notes as if possessed, as somebody shot into it by accident and hit the strings inside. All the old sixteenth-century fixtures of the parish were going to be destroyed, and the lingering smell of altar incense mixed with the stench of gunpowder.

Below the prayer candles and icon, Cain whispered, "Why, Levi, if I didn't know better, I'd think you were protecting me."

"You're mad!" Levi seethed in his ear. "You're absolutely mad! There's a window in the eastern gallery we can escape through, and we can try this again."

"I am not signing a pact with you."

"Cain, for the love of God—"

"*I need release from this hatred, Levi!*"

Levi didn't shoot. His body was stiff and cold with urgency, but he hardly thought of it. There was a brief pause in fire. BLACK knew he had Cain in his grasp, and they weren't going to shoot for fear of harming their leader. Ah, how deeply loyalty ran, even when they thought him an unfit commander. But really, what was going to happen now? Were they going to waste all their ammunition in scare tactics or would the night end in blood? BLACK had not expected to see Levi tonight. It had completely thwarted their plans to kill. Perhaps the same went for Cain. If that wasn't the case, surely someone would have been dead by now.

Levi looked up at the painting of the Virgin Mary and the baby Christ, and he thought about Cain shooting the face of the crucifix as a bullet grazed the surface of the Theotokos, all the candles flickering as it zoomed by. All right, so they weren't going to shoot *at* them for fear of hitting him, but that shot had been fired as if to say "Come on, then, out with the Earl."

Cain moved against his leg. Perhaps it was because Levi was accustomed to the smell of gunpowder and the ringing in his ears, the almost merry jingle of ammunition as revolvers and pistols were reloaded, but he thought that the warmth and twitch of Cain's body was very tempting, and here, below the painting and the candles, he could take Cain again and again right on the velvet prayer stools. What a creature he had become, what a monster of a man, to think something like that during a gunfight! Cold metal and murderous intent had become normal to him, then.

Levi looked at Cain again, the brutal and terrifying shadows of his icy gray eyes. There was no meticulous Earl here, just a man imprisoned by his own dark, cold desperation, shooting a gun with exquisite aim. He looked innocent and savage all at once—no elegance, only lethal intent. Levi wanted to smile.

Yes, there was a parallel here, wasn't there? This gunfight between them was like the conflict of their souls, the internal war between right and wrong and death and salvation. Because Levi loved the monstrous, homicidal look on Cain's face and the way his body twitched with the gunshots. He loved it. He desired it in a desperate, carnal, primal way. He was hungry for it. Ravenous. *Sex.*

The Blond One was laughing again, a maniacal laugh. It echoed around the ruined sanctuary. Levi wanted to hit him for it. He tried to look around, to gauge where everyone was. How was this fray supposed to end? Were they going to run out of bullets and come to an impasse, where nobody knew what to do next? Would BLACK not be satisfied until Levi did something drastic and regrettable?

Two loud shots shattered the eerie silence between firing. One hit the icon of the Theotokos again, scraping across the gold leaf of the Virgin's face. The second didn't seem to hit anything, but Cain went tumbling into the Flemish stand with all the prayer candles, and the most frightening part of it was that he didn't make a sound.

Cain.

What happened next was something of a blur. Levi sprang to his feet, acting wholly on impulse, and by the time he blinked to clear his vision and understood that he had done something, his ears rang and he watched in the upper gallery as Claude fell over the balustrade and hit the sanctuary floor, his face and neck a simple smear of dark crimson red.

And Levi still had his gun aimed, and he'd fired the bullet that had blazed right through Claude's throat and its gushing arteries, because Claude had climbed above like a sniper.

The Blond One's cries of distress sounded to Levi as if they came from underwater, muffled and far away. The Blond One—no, he deserved to be known by name. Spider. *Petyr….*

Levi watched, in a state of dumb confusion, while the world moved a little too fast for him to keep up. Petyr stumbled up the altar steps, dropping his gun and falling to his knees near Claude, whose glasses had bent in his fall from the balcony. His hands were still twitching, and Petyr held one tightly, bawling so hard his scrawny body shook, and it was hard to think of him as a gunslinger, for at that moment he seemed just a broken soul.

Tempt not a desperate man.

Suddenly Levi's cousin William was there next to Petyr and Claude, his mouth moving, but Levi didn't hear a word. Will checked Claude's pulse. Petyr rocked to and fro, the very image of agony. And wasn't there a long-running joke between them all, that Petyr and Claude were lovers? How terrible, then! Oh, well. That was life. And Claude had shot Cain, after all.

Nobody was shooting anymore. The tension in the air had soured. The gunfight was over. Levi had shot Claude in the face, or the throat—somewhere in that fatal vicinity. Blood had probably spattered in the gallery like it pooled on the altar floor.

Tempt not a desperate man.

In one sudden dizzying rush of clarity that left his ears ringing again, everything swung back into focus, and Levi turned to Cain and the prayer corner.

Cain's hair was tousled and his face drawn tight. He leaned against the candle stand with his hair falling in his face and his arms limp in his lap, breathing with great labor. He seemed to sense Levi's eyes and lifted his hands slowly, pale fingers shaking. Levi had to gather willpower to wrench his gaze from the awful blooming *red* across Cain's left shoulder and throat.

Cain had dropped his revolver. Levi kicked it aside, hearing BLACK as they became panicked with Claude's gory demise. Petyr screamed and screamed. Levi heard him kick something over as they tried to calm him. Levi crouched on his haunches and grabbed Cain's hands, pressing them to his face to let Cain know he was there. Cain's eyes flashed, so alive and bright still. Oh God, he was going to suffer—

"You *cannot*," Levi blurted stupidly, grabbing Cain's face.

Cain uttered a gentle moan at the sudden movement. Levi guessed that the bullet was still somewhere inside him, and that it had entered at the curve of his neck and shoulder, the warm place that Levi so loved to kiss. That meant it was lodged somewhere dangerous, oh, somewhere very, very dangerous.

"I cannot what?" Cain croaked, and it was terribly weak and choked.

He sounded as though he couldn't breathe well, and Levi wondered if the bullet had gone through his lungs or his windpipe.

"You cannot *go*," Levi mumbled. He could feel himself breaking. He was a grown man, for Christ's sake, he could not break—he could not let the emotion clench like that around his heart, he could not let the tears spring up in his eyes—panic, oh panic. "Cain, you cannot go! We have a pact to make, we have a feud to end, Cain. *Everyone I've ever loved has left me, and you cannot, you cannot!*"

Levi broke under the weight of it all like an overwhelmed little boy because Cain smiled the most soft, angelic smile then.

"Kill me," he whispered, very flat and faint.

And that was Cain Dietrich, wasn't it? Shaken and scarred, a beautiful, dark thing, giving nothing and taking it all. Why wouldn't he smile so beautifully as he asked for death? Because that was what he wanted. Release from the hell of his own soul.

Love had not been enough.

"Tempt not a desperate man!" Levi cried, using Cain's very words. And *damn* the obsession, *damn* the tragedy, *damn the entire world and its demons of hatred and spite*! Where was the justice here? He was not a fighter, damn it, he was a romantic, but the world didn't seem to be fond of romantics.

Eliott was there suddenly. He grabbed him. Levi shook him off. He wrapped his arms around Cain, carefully, and cradled him close below the ruined painting of the Virgin Mary and baby Christ.

"Levi!" Eliott hissed, and he didn't have to say anything else.

Levi understood. They were leaving him. They were done with this. Claude was dead. It was probably better if they left. The Blond One—*Petyr*—was unpredictable and full of grief.

"Go," Levi husked.

"Levi, bring him with you, for Christ's sake!" Eliott was near hysterical. Petyr's shrieks were echoes from outside the sanctuary now, like the howl of the wind. "Bring him with you," Eliott urged, pulling on Levi's shoulders. "Please. Good Lord, Levi, they've got Claude's body outside, but we can figure this out—"

Eliott must have realized it was futile. He fell suddenly still and silent, and Levi didn't look at him because it was about time Eliott realized Levi was doomed, anyway.

His father hated him. His household and gang hated him. There would be no peace, no justice, no relief for him if he left the church with BLACK, even bringing Cain. He wasn't even supposed to be back in New London, and now he'd killed Claude. He was utterly and wholly doomed, and he suspected he had been from the day he'd been born.

Eliott lingered a few more heartbreaking moments, and then his rapid footsteps echoed as he fled the sanctuary.

BLACK left.

There was just the silence in St. Mikael's.

The flicker of candles reflected in the dark puddle on the altar floor and the commingling scents of gunpowder, melting wax, timeless secrets, holiness, and spilled blood.

"Poor Romeo," Cain cooed.

He looked dizzy. He had to rest his head on Levi's shoulder. Levi didn't mind. Cain was dying. What did it feel like when a soul left from your arms like this?

"How are you joking with me even now?" Levi gritted out. The emotion was so much, it came in waves—overwhelming, painful, and then nothing, only to wash back through him in crushing currents.

Cain smiled faintly, eyes hooded. In the candlelight it was brutally gorgeous. "Because," he gasped, "you're my friend."

Levi laughed, although it sounded something like a sob. His eyes stung. He felt like a boy again, so alive with the most tragic of emotions. "Oh, please tell me I'm more than that!"

Cain peered up at him as if dazed. He looked comfortable against Levi's shoulder, at least, his clothes stained dark red. Levi reached down to brush hair out of his pale eyes.

"You are, you are," Cain managed. "I promise you that." He paused as if he'd lost his breath. "I love you, somehow," he said next, and it was Levi's turn to go breathless.

"You tell me this now!" he cried, hating that Cain waited for such a moment to be honest. He'd probably seen it as weakness until then. Levi was sure of it. But no, he didn't hate Cain for it. He hated *love*. Damn the obsession. Damn the indiscriminate need, the force to end all forces. Damn it all!

"I don't want to leave, Levi," Cain mumbled hoarsely, frowning. It was stubborn.

Levi shook his head. Cain reached up with quivering fingers, pushing hair out of Levi's eyes. Levi let him. "I don't want you to leave either," he insisted.

"Not like that." Cain made a face of silent laughter. "I don't want to leave the church, I mean."

"What do you mean, *malysh*?" Levi's voice had hardly left his lips before he regretted using the pet name, but nothing changed on Cain's face. His gaze was dark, and his hand sank back down to his lap. He took a slow breath, shaking a little against Levi's chest. Levi held him tighter for it, like a frightened child clinging to company. The shadows danced in the sanctuary.

"Levi, I don't want to leave, because it's so peaceful here." Cain looked up at him in almost sarcastic awe. "I shot Christ's face," he whispered, in wonderment of himself.

"Yes, you did," Levi said, chuckling even as the tears broke free.

"But I still feel Christ here." The words were raspy, almost inaudible.

Cain's gaze had fixed on the ceiling of the sanctuary, like he was thinking about something distant and deep. His brow furrowed. He drew another tremulous breath. Levi could hear the death in it already, the wheeze and the shiver and the slightly wet sound of blood somewhere in Cain's chest.

And what a terribly daunting moment, this instant where Cain spoke of Christ. He, the bloodstained earl of the turbulent kingdom of revenge and violence and sin. He looked absolutely spiritual suddenly. Surely, staring up at the ceiling, he seemed torn between the dark forgotten world of his soul and the beauty of life bursting around him in the rafters and corners of the church, and Levi choked up. He tried not to let Cain see it, but he felt too cold—too full of a desperate, irreparable ache that was half love and half horror. Certainly this pain was what those who suffered in Hell would experience for eternity, and it was excruciating.

"Levi," Cain murmured, meeting his eyes again. It was undeniable. Cain saw the nascent terror in Levi's face, and Levi clenched his teeth against it, brow knotting. Cain shrugged with one shoulder, peering up at him comfortably. "I like this," he said. "I like the peace here. It's beautiful. It's so comfortable against your chest, and I love you, I love you—"

There were the tears Levi didn't realize he'd been waiting to see. They bubbled up in Cain's thick lashes and rolled down his cheeks. Levi thumbed some away, shaking his head. Yes, Cain loved him for who he was, and Levi loved him too.

"Don't cry, Cain. You won't be able to breathe," he whispered.

It didn't matter. Cain couldn't breathe anyway. His body was jerking with each sharp breath as he spoke, urgently.

"We're all doomed, Levi," he said. His eyes widened suddenly. His hands were cold when they touched Levi's face, forcing eye contact. With the tears and the terrible look on his face, he looked mad, and Levi didn't like it. "There is no salvation. Just please let me feel this peace a little longer before—"

Levi shook his head. This was taking far too long. It was torturous. He pushed Cain's hands from his face. "No, not doomed. You're not doomed."

The sound when Cain's body rattled with a deep cough was unsettling. It deepened Levi's despair. The cough became a wet choke, something just short of a retch, and it stained Cain's hands with blood, thick and dark in his hand, on the end of his sleeve. Levi tightened his arms around him, eyes widening. Surely the anguish could choke him to death, crush him, one emotion at a time.

Cain tried to say something more, the perfect image of humiliation and hopelessness. He looked up at Levi with such an expression of fear that Levi groaned. He was dying. "I just wanted them to pay for what they did to my family," he whimpered.

"Don't you leave me alone, Cain," Levi gasped. "Don't you say those things. They don't matter now."

"You'll come to my funeral?" Cain whispered, suddenly calm, staring with such indignation that Levi utterly broke. He sobbed like a child, shaking his head against Cain's. He didn't care. He didn't care about revenge or their families' nonsensical feud. He didn't care about BLACK or what had happened two years ago, or contracts or murders or even that wretched gun his father had given him.

"I refuse to see you in a coffin! Death may want you, jealous thing it is, but I *refuse*," he sputtered. That dark sadness was not the last expression Levi wanted to see. It was not Cain. The indomitable spark of pride was him, but not that sad, sad frown.

"You're so sweet, love." Cain's words were thick with blood.

"*Miserere mei, Deus*," Levi whispered, voice quavering on his lips and skin cold with terror as he went on with the Orthodox rites, hoping it would soothe Cain. There was blood at the corner of his mouth. His lashes fluttered; his head rolled on Levi's shoulder. He felt it when Cain fell unconscious. He wasn't dead—perhaps not yet—but he couldn't breathe. He'd been laboring with it for minutes now, and he'd fainted. It was a strange, unsettling sensation to feel a body go limp in his arms, and Levi did not like it.

Suddenly the church was too silent.

Levi stared at the faceless crucifix for a moment, feeling rather empty and numb. The sobbing left him with a single breath; how, he wasn't sure. That familiar and unforgiving emptiness swallowed him in one gulp.

His eyes moved to the icon, the Virgin Mary above the flickering candles. He saw Cain's gun, off to the side. His own was back in its holster. Levi didn't even remember putting it there.

Our Father who art in Heaven, hallowed be Thy name.

Rejoice, O Virgin Theotokos, Mary full of grace, the Lord is with thee.

Have mercy on me, O God.

How had this happened?

Cain looked peaceful.

Levi couldn't stare at him anymore. He laid Cain down gently on the altar floor and walked around the sanctuary, humming the Cherubic Hymn to himself as he remembered being in St. Mikael's years and years ago, as a child, meeting the clergyman Kelvin when he'd first entered as Father.

There was nothing left anymore, really.

Fate was cruel, and everyone was doomed.

Levi lit a prayer candle for Cain's soul. He figured he might as well light one for himself too. And then, one by one, he picked up the candles and threw them around the church until the tapestries were catching fire and the woodwork was smoking. There was a sense of finality, really, as the flames popped. It was heavy and comfortable on Levi's shoulders.

His eyes looked their last.

The sanctuary began to fill with smoke. The flames ate up the dust and wood, and Levi thought that, even bloody and on the horizon of death, Cain was so beautiful.

Levi sat down beside him, unconscious on the altar floor. He ran his hands through his hair and smiled faintly as he kissed both his closed eyes. Cain's mouth was limp and pliant when he kissed it next, just a dust of the lips. He did not wipe at his own mouth, if Cain's blood had stained it. He licked it away if it was there. He tried to position Cain in a proper way, a regal way, a way that Cain would have wanted to be lying. He looked like he was sleeping, serene, a bloodstained angel with fingers laced as Levi had arranged them.

The smoke stung Levi's eyes and the flames leapt closer to the crucifix. He could hear shouts, outside, on the wind, unless he just imagined them. But surely by now someone had noticed the church going up in flames and had notified the city.

There was no other solution that was clear to him. There was no reason for him to be alive anymore. His reason to live was dying, and so should he.

He and Cain were so very alike, and he knew Cain would have been pleased by that.

LEVI AND Cain both might have thought it such a shame that when Levi lay down on the altar floor beside Cain, with the pool of Claude's blood mere yards away, and shot himself in the head with the ROOK, his blood dirtied Cain on the side Claude's shot hadn't. But perhaps, in a dark way, one of them might have found it romantic. Intimate, even.

What a pity, then, that the painting of the Virgin, the shattered face of Christ, and the other effigies of saints and angels were the only witnesses to the curtain closing on the tragedy: the death of the gunslinging romantic and the last, unconscious breath of the bloodstained earl.

EPILOGUE

WHEN THE rector arrived with the constabulary, signing cross after cross upon his chest, his stomach was heavy with dread and his nerves electric with fright. He'd expected bodies. He'd expected bloodshed. But he hadn't expected after frantic neighbors pounded on his door to get up in the dark and cold of the wee hours of a winter morning to find St. Mikael's was on fire.

The rector stood with his neighbors and other brave civilians as the flames licked the dark sky. Authorities rushed to the scene, but it mattered not.

St. Mikael's was ablaze. Parish members cried and wailed at such a sight, tragic and jarring of faith. Others stood frozen in unease. The sight of a burning chapel was not a comforting one.

They found the remains just after daybreak, when they'd finally put out the flames.

Religious icons and artifacts were gone, irreparably charred or nonexistent as the last embers popped and sizzled. It was like the aftermath of holy warfare, a glimpse of hell—items of faith and sanctity, destroyed and defeated by fire.

Some of the most faithful were hoping for miracles, but what was discovered were not bleeding statues or shining paintings that had somehow survived the flames, but a blackened faceless crucifix, scorched woodwork, bullet casings, and the burned bodies of two of the most pivotal faces in New London.

Bradley Dietrich was named temporary Earl. The aristocrat Reginald Williams's son proposed to Emily Kelley, and Lady Kelley accepted for her.

Lord Ruslaniv suffered an apoplexy. He did not awake from it.

Lady Ruslaniv donned black immediately. Newspaper clippings speaking of her youngest son's death joined the clippings speaking of Quinton Ruslaniv's admission to the sanitarium in Yekaterinburg, all kept tied together in the rosewood box with the angels carved on it. Her sons' first pairs of shoes were there too, and a poem Levi had written her when he was very small, and a daguerreotype of Quinton in Ruslaniv regalia.

Gloom settled over New London.

Not even the Queen's visit on the day of the interments, coach rattling through on the cobbles as New London civilians gathered in their best fashion, could lift the sense of calamity that had fallen like the funereal shrouds over Ruslaniv and Dietrich faces.

The Earl Cain Dietrich and the Honourable Lawrence Levi Ruslaniv were laid to rest on the same day, at opposite ends of the same cemetery, a fenced-in place of elaborate gothic tombs, draped urns, and weeping angels.

"Peace?" the undertaker cackled as he rattled his way through Lovers' Lane, slushy and quiet as most of New London gathered in High-hill Cemetery for the joint funeral, which was rather lavish for an event of such morbid circumstances—ah, the graces of nobility.

The undertaker cocked his head back. His ratty muffler fell from his shoulders and into a murky puddle.

"There is no peace!" he howled, so tickled he could hardly stand it. "There is no peace for anyone, and I told him so! I told him not to misunderstand the value of each and every soul!"

He paused, hoisting the stiff body of an orphan up off the broken cobblestones of Lovers' Lane and into the back of his cart. He hummed to himself, crouching down and grinning at the orphan in his cart. He brushed hair from the dead child's eyes and sang to her, whether she heard his off-key lilts as they echoed off the walls of Lovers' Lane and sprayed spittle on her limp, dirty hands or not.

Overhead, rooks scattered from their roost above Lovers' Lane.

Eliott watched them, the way their dark wings rustled and flapped against the mother-of-pearl sky. Beneath his funeral black, he felt light without his guns. He'd left them at home, on his bed, in the Ruslaniv manor. But there was a weight on his chest that made it hard to breathe.

He stood on the rooftop at the north end of Lovers' Lane, eyes following the undertaker as he made his way out with his ghastly little cart. None of this seemed real. Running from St. Mikael's that night, the fire, too many funerals. BLACK was no more. At least, for now. Its leader was gone; so was the head of its house.

Down below, in Lovers' Lane, two children huddled under a crooked fire escape, watching the undertaker rattle away and around the corner. The children were dirty, scraped up, and scowling with the wide-eyed caution of every street urchin. The dead girl in the undertaker's cart must have been a friend of theirs, maybe a sister.

Eliott smiled faintly, brow knotting. He remembered being that age—twelve, thirteen. Full of hope for growing up and having the whole wide world to wrestle with. Responsibilities and misfortune had been part of the allure; having those things meant finally being more than a child.

"Hey," Eliott called down to the children. They looked up, distrustful. He shrugged, digging through his pockets. "Don't be sad. 'We learn little from victory, but much from defeat.'"

"What's that supposed to mean?" the braver of the orphans snapped from the alley.

Eliott's smile deepened nostalgically. A knot jumped to his throat, but it was all right. He was getting used to it. He'd rather ache for his friends and loved ones forever than feel nothing at all. He drew a few coins from his pocket and flipped them down at the children, who caught them deftly, without hesitation.

"I don't know," Eliott sighed, tossing hair out of his eyes. "A friend of mine read that to me from a book when we were about your age. I can't say I remember who said it first."

The children frowned up at him, lingering there in the shadows of Lovers' Lane, though they had every right to leave without listening, coin in hand.

Eliott nodded curtly, waving a hand to bid them adieu as he turned away. "What it means, though… well, the curtain's closed on this particular saga."

Yes, the curtain had closed. But a new one would rise tomorrow, and the next day, and the next.

As Eliott made his way down from the rooftops over Lovers' Lane, he heard the undertaker from just up the block, the creak of his cart, and the chortle in his voice.

"Go hence! Have more talk of these sad things! Some will be pardoned and some will be punished, but never was there a story so tragic as this, the terrible, terrible death of Cain Dietrich and the heir of Ruslaniv!"

CURTAIN CLOSED

J.I. RADKE goes by a variety of handles and pseudonyms, most commonly "themissinglenk" and/or "white silver and mercury."

Once upon a time he wanted to be a marine biologist because of sharks. That lasted a year or so. A Seattlite at heart, Radke is currently studying English/history, Classics, and Russian studies at USF in Tampa.

Radke writes ghost stories, romance novels, transgressive fiction, and fanfic that's sometimes all of that in one. He loves passionate speeches and tangent-studded discussions, strong coffee, rainy days, swimming in coves with bioluminescent algae, sushi and pad thai, and pizza. He specializes in Victorian-era English and Russian history, and loves folklore, classical music, parapsychology, Greek mythology, and true crime/forensics shows—to keep things brief.

E-mail: radkejisaac@yahoo.com

http://www.dsppublications.com

http://www.dsppublications.com

DSP PUBLICATIONS

visit us online.
WWW.DSPPUBLICATIONS.COM